PUFFIN BOOKS

MIGHTY FIZZ CHILLA

Philip Ridley was born in the East End of London, where he still lives and works. He studied painting at St Martin's School of Art and by the time he graduated had exhibited widely throughout Europe and had written his first novel. As well as three books for adults, and the screenplay for the award-winning feature film *The Krays*, he has written five successful adult stage plays: *The Pitchfork Disney*, *The Fastest Clock in the Universe*, *Ghost from a Perfect Place*, *Vincent River* and *Mercury Fur*, and five for young people: *Karazamoo*, *Fairytaleheart*, *Sparkleshark*, *Moonfleece* and *Brokenville*. He has also directed two films from his own screenplays: *The Reflecting Skin* – winner of eleven international awards – and *The Passion of Darkly Noon*. Philip Ridley has written eleven other books for children: *Mercedes Ice*, *Dakota of the White Flats*, *Krindlekrax* (winner of the Smarties Prize and the W. H. Smith Mind-Boggling Books Award), *Meteorite Spoon*, *Kasper in the Glitter* (nominated for the 1995 Whitbread Children's Book Award), *Dreamboat Zing*, *The Hooligan's Shampoo*, *Scribbleboy* (which was shortlisted for the Carnegie Medal and received a commendation at the NASEN Special Educational Needs Children's Book Awards 1997), *ZinderZunder*, *Vinegar Street* and *Zip's Apollo*.

Stephen Lee was born in Ilford, Essex, in 1957. He studied Art and Graphics at Walthamstow College, but went on to become involved in social work, particularly with children. Several years later he became a freelance illustrator, and made a reputation for himself producing political illustrations. Stephen then moved into the general publishing market and his work can often be seen on books, magazines and illustrations. His interests inclu

MIGHTY FIZZ CHILLA

Illustrated by Stephen Lee

PHILIP RIDLEY

PUFFIN

PUFFIN BOOKS

Published by the Penguin Group
Penguin Books Ltd, 80 Strand, London WC2R 0RL, England
Penguin Group (USA) Inc., 375 Hudson Street, New York, New York 10014, USA
Penguin Group (Canada), 90 Eglinton Avenue East, Suite 700, Toronto, Ontario, Canada M4P 2Y3
(a division of Pearson Penguin Canada Inc.)
Penguin Ireland, 25 St Stephen's Green, Dublin 2, Ireland (a division of Penguin Books Ltd)
Penguin Group (Australia), 250 Camberwell Road, Camberwell, Victoria 3124, Australia
(a division of Pearson Australia Group Pty Ltd)
Penguin Books India Pvt Ltd, 11 Community Centre, Panchsheel Park, New Delhi – 110 017, India
Penguin Group (NZ), cnr Airborne and Rosedale Roads, Albany, Auckland 1310, New Zealand
(a division of Pearson New Zealand Ltd)
Penguin Books (South Africa) (Pty) Ltd, 24 Sturdee Avenue, Rosebank, Johannesburg 2196, South Africa

Penguin Books Ltd, Registered Offices: 80 Strand, London WC2R 0RL, England

www.penguin.com

First published 2002
9

Text copyright © Philip Ridley, 2002
Illustrations copyright © Stephen Lee, 2002
All rights reserved

The moral right of the author and illustrator has been asserted

Set in Palatino
Made and printed in England by Clays Ltd, St Ives plc

British Library Cataloguing in Publication Data
A CIP catalogue record for this book is available from the British Library

ISBN-13: 978-0-140-38510-6
ISBN-10: 0-140-38510-X

**For all the Milos
of the world**

'We are all
somehow
dreadfully
cracked about
the head
and sadly
in need
of mending'

– Herman Melville

First Day

— One —

Ocean, innit!
  Me – in middle.
  Not big, wet stuff full of fishes.
  It's where I live, innit.
  Ocean Estate, innit!
  Big concrete stuff full of people.
  But now ... no people.
  Scary, innit!
  Heart – it's punching in me chest.
  Sweat – it's trickling down me face.
  Me – screaming, 'WHERE IS EVERYBODY? WHERE IS –

... EVERYBODY?'
  'Wake up, Milo Kick!'
  'Wh-whaa?'
  'You were dreaming.'
  'Humpff ... so whaa?'
  'So your moaning was distracting me. Driving a vehicle like this requires concentration. And *do* sit up straight. You'll do untold damage to your spine, slouching like that.'
  'Comfy, innit.'
  'What's comfortable, Milo Kick, rarely does us any good.'

III

Milo snorts an extra loud, 'Humpff', then starts picking cracked leather from his seat.

Like peeling boiled eggs, innit! he thinks. *And look outside! Cars on the motorway zooming past! Why ain't this car zooming?*

IV

'We there yet, eh?'

'Halfway, Milo Kick.'

'Been driving hours, innit.'

'Four and a half, to be precise.'

'So … another four and a half to go?'

'That's what being halfway would imply, yes.'

'This car ain't nothing but a pile of old junk, innit!'

'Well, according to the dictionary,' responds Dee, glancing at Milo beside her, 'the only "junk" to be used as a means of transportation is a flat-bottomed boat used in China. So, no, this is *not* a pile of old junk. It's a pile of old truck. And, at the moment, it's doing a perfectly adequate job transporting us from London's East End to England's Land's End. Now, if you don't mind, this tedious conversation has occupied my brain cells long enough – And do stop picking your seat!'

'Humpff!'

V

Milo is thirteen years old and has full, sensitive lips (*Like they've been stung by a bee, innit*) and sparkling, green eyes (*Just like me mum, innit*) beneath hooded eyebrows (*Dunno where I get those from, innit*). He has a stocky build, extremely large fists, and he's wearing jeans, trainers, T-shirt and silver puffa jacket.

VI

'Like a sauna in here, innit.'

'Well, according to the dictionary a sauna is a –'

'Hot! All I'm saying, ya Robot-Woman! Hot!'

'Open your window then.'

'Can't! Blows me hood off!'

'It's summer, Milo Kick! Hardly the weather for a hooded jacket!' Dee notices a red light flashing on the dashboard. 'Aha! Fuel.'

'Whaa …?'

'Petrol, Milo Kick.' Dee peers at the motorway signs. 'I'm sure there's a garage … along this stretch … Aha! There!' She shoots Milo a look. 'Does *your* tank need re-filling?'

'Whaa? Petrol?'

'*Food*, Milo Kick! *Food!*' Dee swerves into the garage and parks in front of some petrol pumps. 'Do you require nourishment?'

Milo thinks, *Yeah*.

Milo says, 'Nah.'

'As you wish,' snaps Dee, jumping out of the truck. 'Robot-Woman doesn't ask twice.'

VII

Dee Dee Six (to give 'Robot-Woman' her full name) is sixty-five years old, tall, thin, and wearing pinstripe trousers (*Bloke's stuff, innit*), lace-up shoes (*Bloke's stuff, innit*) and a black polo-neck jumper (*Blokes stuff, innit*). Her hair is grey and cut in a straight line (*Like a bowl on her head, innit*). Her face is covered with countless tiny wrinkles (*Like a shattered windscreen, innit*), and has small, beady eyes, round-rimmed spectacles, pencil-line eyebrows and a tiny, lipless mouth.

VIII

Beep-beep!

Milo takes a mobile from his pocket and mumbles, 'Whaa ... ?'

'It's me, sweetie! Mum!'

'Don't call me sweetie!'

'But you are my sweet –'

'Don't gimme aggro, Mum!'

IX

'Oh, I *do* wish you wouldn't raise your voice at Mummy.'

'Stop telling me how to talk!'

'I'm not telling you –'

'Are! Always do! It does me head in!'

'Keep your voice down –'

'Ya doing it again! I can feel the Fizzy Wasps coming on, Mum! All buzzing in me head! They'll make me say nasty things if ya don't quit telling me what to do.'

X

'Don't blame your vile temper on Fizzy Wasps. It's you! YOU! It's a typical male reaction –'

Fizzzy Waspzzz

'– to shout when he can't get his own way. I thought I bought you up more –'

Fizzzzzy Waspzzzz

'– intelligent than that. You always *used* to be. You used to be –'

Fizzzzzzy Waspzzzzzz

'– Mummy's little angel. But now you're Mummy's little –'

BZZZZZZZZZZZZZZZZZZZZZ

'– monster!'

'SHUT IT, MUM! I'M GOING AWAY FOR A WEEK! THAT'S WHAT YA WANTED! TO GET RID OF ME!'

He turns the mobile off and retreats further into his hood.

XI

Dee gets back in the truck and plonks a Coke and bag of crisps in Milo's lap. 'Just in case,' she says.

Milo thinks, *Thanks*.

Milo says, 'Humpff.'

'Let's hope we finish our journey before dark,' Dee sighs, turning the engine on. 'We've got a long way to go.'

— Two —

I

'We're here, Milo Kick.'

'Whaa …?'

'Oh, not dozing again, surely?' Dee jumps out of the truck, walks round and opens Milo's door. 'You'll need this.' She thrusts something in his hand.

'Whaa …?'

'It's a torch, Milo Kick. No street lights here, you know. When the night sky's cloudy – as it now is – you can't see your hand in front of your face.'

'Humpff.' Milo grabs a sports bag from between his feet ('I've packed seven pairs of underpants,' his mum had told him. 'Make sure you wear fresh every day.') and clambers out of the truck.

II

Dark, innit!

Like pulling the hood right over me head. And that smell! It's like … like the fish counter in the supermarket. And what's that noise? Sounds big and empty like the lift-shaft in flats –

Oh, can't turn torch on!

Can't turn torch –

III

'Press here,' instructs Dee, pressing. 'Now, follow me. And be careful! We're on top of a cliff.'

'Cliff!'

'Surely your mum told you!'
'Just said … by beach or something.'
'Exactly. By beach. On cliff.'
The sea, innit! That's the fishy counter smell and the lift-shaft noise –
'Don't dawdle, Milo Kick.'

IV

'Is it a big cliff?'

'You mean, is it a *high* cliff? Well, yes, it is. Very. And the house we're going to is perilously close to the edge. Which is why you must be careful where you tread. It's the only house for miles and miles so, if anything happened to you, help would be a long while coming – Oh, aim the torch at the ground in front of you, Milo Kick! Not me! Please use your brain cells now and again otherwise they'll jump out of your ears in boredom – Stop! STOP!'

V

'Whaa …? Is it the edge of cliff?'

'No. It's the edge of the moat.'

'Whaa …?'

'A ditch full of water that, usually, surrounds a castle.'

'Castle!'

'See for yourself!'

Milo shines his torch ahead and sees …

VI

Walls made of big stones and …

He shines the torch up, up …

… turrets!

'A castle, innit!'

'Well, not quite. The moat and turrets have been added to the house to make it *resemble* a castle, that's all.' She starts turning a handle. 'Ooo, this needs oiling.'

'What ya up to?'

'I'm lowering the drawbridge.'

'Whaa …?'

'Oh, just look, Milo Kick! Look and learn!'

VII

A wooden door coming down until it becomes –

'A bridge, innit!'

'You see how rewarding a little patient observation can be? Now, come on. Cross over.'

'Why's the house so dark?' asks Milo, stepping on to the rickety wood. 'Ain't nobody home?'

'Of course somebody's home,' snaps Dee, taking a bunch of keys from her pocket and inserting one into the solid-oak door. 'Now, be patient. This lock is stiff so it sometimes takes a little time to unlock …' She tries to turn the key but it won't budge. 'It needs a firm twist …' Again and again she tries, but still nothing happens. 'Goodness!'

'Out the way,' says Milo, pushing her aside. 'We'll be here all night at this rate.'

'Well, if *I* can't do it I'm sure *you* won't –'

Clunk!

'I do weight training, innit!'

VIII

'I'm ... I'm impressed, Milo Kick,' comments Dee, stepping into the house and turning the light on. 'Well, stop looking so smug and enter!'

Milo steps inside and sees ...

IX

Biggest light shade I've ever clapped eyes on! All made of sparkly glass. Tinkling like ice-cubes in a fizzy drink and ... Look! The carpet! All thick and green. Like I'm walking on grass. And lots of wood everywhere. The colour of tea without enough milk. And doorknobs shining like gold. And shelves full of tiny glass animals. All sparkling and twinkling and –

X

Beside the stairway Milo sees a small reception desk. It has a large book on it and a row of keys (from 1 to 7) on the wall behind.

XI

'A hotel, innit!'

'It's a guest-house,' clarifies Dee, turning on some more lights. 'There's lots of them along the coast. This one's called called "Avalon Rise". Oh, your mum *must've* explained this to you.'

'Humpff ... didn't hear if she did.'

'Didn't *listen* more like.' Dee looks round impatiently. 'Oh, where is that Cressida Bell female of the species?' She slams the flat of her hand on the counter-bell.

Tinnnnnngggg!

'WE'RE HERE!' yells Dee. 'CRESSIDA BELL! CRESSID –! Aha! Here she is!'

— Three —

I

There, innit! At the top of the stairs. Like a Polaroid developing. Only coming out of black stuff not white. Hair all whirling round like ice cream in a cone. And curly on her forehead like … like fish hooks. And it's a strange colour. Sort of pinky-blue … And she's wearing a tiny crown thing. All seashells and sparkly. Seashell earrings too. And a face like the crinkly skin of cold custard. And her dress is long and green as moss on concrete. Shines like it's wet too. Sounds like crunchy crisp bags. She's wearing sunglasses and holding –

A stick!

White stick!

That means she's –

II

'Blind, innit.'

'Is that his voice?' gulps Cressida. 'Is it? Is it?'

'Well, it's certainly not mine, Cressida Bell.'

'Oh, it *is*!' She tap-taps her way down the stairs, moving with surprising agility considering –

'She's fat, innit.'

'Oh, yes! Yes, I am,' chuckles Cressida, swooping down the last few steps. 'I weigh more than a whale after banqueting on seven octopuses.' She glides up to Milo, every inch of her quivering and trembling. 'Oh … let me touch you, Beloved.'

III

She's wearing posh green gloves up to her elbows. She smells like flowery air freshener. There's make-up in her wrinkles. And I don't want her to touch me –

IV

'Back off!' snarls Milo.

'But … oh, I *need* to feel your face, Beloved. It's how I know what you look like.'

'Nah! Nah!'

Fizzzy Waspzzz

Milo stares into her dark glasses. He can see his own face glaring back. Two spiteful eyes in a dark hood. Lips curled back revealing teeth. For a moment he wonders who this vicious boy is.

V

'Don't smother him, Cressida Bell,' says Dee, going behind the reception desk. 'The boy's been travelling for nine hours. He's in need of nourishment and personal hygiene. I'm sure I wouldn't want my face mauled by a perfect stranger.'

'But I'm *not* a stranger, Dee!'

'Friend of his mum's you might be, but Milo Kick doesn't know you from Adam. Now, get a grip and act like a sensible human being and not a melodramatic wedding cake.'

VI

'I … I'm sorry, Beloved,' Cressida says in the calmest voice she can muster. 'I tend to get carried away. You … must want to get to your room.' She taps her stick on the desk. 'Don't forget, Dee! He's in room No. 1.'

'I don't forget anything, Cressida Bell,' responds Dee frostily. 'Milo Kick, sign the book.'

VII

'Whaa …?'

'The guest book. Here! Sign!'

'Oh, really, Dee,' trills Cressida. 'I'm sure we can skip formalities. After all, he's our *only* guest and –'

'Guests sign the guest book,' insists Dee. 'Not to do so is a severe breach of protocol.' She thrusts a large feather at Milo. 'Take this!'

'Whaa …?'

'It's a quill pen,' explains Dee. 'Dip the nib in the inkpot there. Go on!'

Milo stabs the quill into the pot, then scrawls:

VIII

'I bet my Beloved has beautiful handwriting,' breathes Cressida, clutching her bosom.

'Oh, do put a sock in it, Cressida Bell.' Dee takes a key from the wall. 'All your sweetness is making my teeth rot.'

'Didn't know false teeth *could* rot!'

'Cressida Bell!' gasps Dee. 'I'd be grateful if you didn't discuss my dental circumstances in front of strangers.'

'But he's *not* a stranger,' quivers Cressida. 'He's my Beloved.'

'Ain't no one's Beloved, innit!'

IX

'Pay no attention, Milo Kick. She's been sipping the sherry and is, quite clearly, drunk as a skunk.'

'Lies!' exclaims Cressida. 'How dare you slander my good name!'

'Here's the key to your room.' Dee hands it to Milo. 'Now, Cressida Bell, will you kindly show him where it is.' She switches the stair light on. 'That's if you're not too sozzled.'

Cressida sniffs indignantly. 'Follow me, Beloved.'

'No chance of losing sight of her,' whispers Dee in Milo's ear. 'Not with buttocks that size, eh?'

'I heard that!' snaps Cressida.

X

'I've had your mum on the phone, Beloved,' says Cressida, making her way up the stairs. 'Have you turned your mobile telephone device thing off?'

'So whaa?'

'Well, your mum's been trying to get through.' Cressida turns into a corridor. 'She's very, very worried. Ring her before you go to bed. You can use the phone on the counter downstairs – Aha! Your room! Unlock it, Beloved.'

Milo pushes the key into the lock. He turns it left, then right, but nothing happens.

'Keep trying, Beloved. All the locks are a tad troublesome ... but with patience and care they –'

Clunk!

'Bravo! Now enter ...'

— Four —

I

Wallpaper with all sorts of sea stuff, innit.

Ships! Whales! Dolphins!

And look! Lots of tiny glass ornaments. Animals again! Same as downstairs. And a huge bed with a wooden frame thing –

II

'You've got a four-poster bed, Beloved,' Cressida informs him with a sigh. 'So utterly, utterly romantic! And there's a writing desk for you. See? And through this door' Tap-tap '... your very own bathroom and toilet. You know what that's called?'

'Whaa ...?'

'*En suite!* It's a special luxury for a special guest.' She points her stick at a painting above the bed. 'And what do you think of *that*?'

III

'Humpff.'

'Oh, a little more enthusiasm, if you please! It may not be the *Mona Lisa* ... but it's all my own work. Did it years ago. Before I became this blind old hippopotamus. And please don't think it's my idea to hang it in such a prominent position. Oh no! Dee got it into her head to put it there. She assures me it complements the room. The painting's called *Merlin and the Boy King*. It's from the legend of King Arthur. You know that story?'

'Naahh.'

'Oh, it's utterly, utterly magical!' She taps her stick on the painting. 'You see the old man … On the left … Here? That's Merlin in his cave. And over on the right -' Tap, tap – 'this boy's the future King of –'

'Boring, innit!'

'Boring! How can you find such a story bor –'

'*All* stories are boring! Just like you!'

IV

Cressida gasps and staggers back. 'Well … I … I'm very sorry you think that, Beloved. I … I certainly didn't mean to be bor –'

'Well, ya are! Where's the telly?'

'We … we haven't got a television.'

'Boring! Where's the computer?'

'We haven't –'

'CD?'

'Afraid not.'

'DVD?'

'No.'

'Boring! BORING! BORING!'

Cressida clutches her white stick like a shipwrecked person clutching a lifebelt. 'Well … perhaps you won't find it so boring once you settle in.' She regains her composure a little and continues, 'Now, let me help you unpack.'

'Nah!' growls Milo. 'Don't! Back off! BACK OFF!'

Fizzzy Waspzzz

'Oh … Beloved. I seem to be constantly annoying you. And I really don't mean to. Why are you so angry with me?'

V

'Don't have to tell you anything! Leave me alone!'

'Leave you? But your dinner's downstairs and –'

'Gonna stay in me room!'

'But … oh, I've been looking forward to chatting –'

'NOT GONNA TO CHAT TO YA!' yells Milo. 'NOT GONNA CHAT TO ANYONE!'

Dee strides into room, holding a tray. 'What's all the shouting about, Milo Kick? The whole of Cornwall can hear you!'

VI

'You're boring too, innit!'

'Goodness, what a temper, Milo Kick.'

'Just as his mum told us, Dee –'

'Mum! You been talking behind me back? Don't! DON'T!

'There's no need to yell, Milo Kick.'

'Don't tell me what to do, Robot-Woman.'

'Beloved!'

Fizzzzzy Waspzzzzz

VII

'Ain't your Beloved! Ain't never seen ya fat, ugly mush before. I'm only here cos Mum phoned up and said, "Take that kid off my hands for a week! He's changed into something I don't like!"'

'Not true, Beloved!'

'Incorrect, Milo Kick.'

Fizzzzzy Waspzzzzzzzzz

VIII

'*Is* true! *Is* correct! Don't lie to me, ya silly old wrinklies! Mum's sent me here so … so ya can try and – what? Sort me out?'

'Not true, Beloved!'
'Incorrect, Milo Kick!'
FIZZZZZZZZYY WASSSSSSPPPPPZZZZZ

IX

'Stop lying to me! Mum thinks I'll tell ya why I changed, don't she? She ... she thinks I'll spill the beans about what happened five months ago. Well, I ain't spilling nothing!'
BZZZZZZZZZZZZ
'I'm not Mum's little angel any more. I'm a –'
BZZZZZZZZZZZZZZZZZZZZZZ
'– MONSTER!'
And, with that, Milo pulls his hood down.

X

'Interesting, Milo Kick!'
'Uh ... what's happened, Dee? What? What?'
'His haircut, Cressida Bell. It's been shaved at the sides. Just a black ridge of hair now. Like a horse's mane.'
'A Mohican, innit!'
'Oh, Beloved, your mum told me you'd done something silly to your hair, but I never thought you'd become half-boy, half-stallion –'

XI

'Out! OUT! OUT!'
BZZZZZZZ
Can't control it now!
Fizzy Wasps making me pick things up and –
Smash!

XII

'No, Beloved! Not the glass animals! They belonged to my dear Papa –'
'OUT!'

BZZZZZZZ
Smash!
Smash!
'All right, Beloved! We're going!'
'We're leaving, Milo Kick!'
Milo shuts door after them –
SLAM!
And locks it.
CLUNK!

XIII

'AND STAY OUT!' he screams through the wood. 'I
DON'T WANNA SEE YA! DON'T NEED YA! YOU FAT
AND THIN PILES OF OLD BONES WITH TOTALLY
NAFF HAIRCUTS! JUST LEAVE ME ALONE! DON'T
NEED ANYONE!'

— Five —

I

Can hear 'em in corridor, innit!
  Both saying nasty things about me, I bet.
  Calling me 'trouble' and 'wild'. Just like everyone else.
  Bzzzzzzzzz …
  They're … yeah, they're moving away.
  Bzzzzzzzzzzzz …
  They're going downstairs.
  Bzzz …
  Gone!
  Bz …

II

No more Fizzy Wasps.

III

For a while Milo leans against the door, his heart
pounding so hard it shakes his chest, blood gushing as fast
as water down a plughole.

Gradually, the pounding and gushing loses strength
and speed.

There's the tray on the desk, innit!

Milo goes over and sees a plate of casserole, a bread
roll, butter, slice of apple pie and a can of Coke.

IV

Dee guessed! Even before I blew me top. She guessed I didn't wanna to eat downstairs. Hang on! What's this –?

V

Propped against the can is a small card with a view of the ocean – white surf crashing against rocky cliffs, seagulls, a blazing sunset.

Milo picks it up and, on the back, reads:

Dearest Beloved,

We are both so happy to have you with us. I hope you have a wonderful time exploring this part of the world

Love

Cressida

xxxx

Dee Dee Six

VI

Milo notices the remnants of the glass ornaments he'd thrown: half a dolphin, an eagle's head, a dragon's tail, all shattered and cracked, yet still sparkling in the amber lamplight.

And, suddenly, he hurls himself on the bed and punches the pillow.

VII

Don't wanna be like this!
   Don't wanna be controlled by the Fizzy Wasps.
   Don't wanna smash and kick and say nasty things!
   Wanna be how I was before!
   Wanna get rid of the monster inside!
   Someone help me!
   Please!
   Anyone!
   Oh, help me!
   Help me!
   HELP!

Second Day

— Six —

I

Knock! Knock!

'Milo Kick?'

Knock! Knock! Knock!

'Wake up, Milo Kick!'

'Whaa …?'

'You've locked your door and I can't get in.'

'Stay out then!'

'It's eight o'clock, Milo Kick. Didn't you hear the gong?
Come down to the dining room at once.'

'Whaa for?'

'Breakfast! Haven't you read the Avalon Rise
Information Sheet?'

'Nah.'

'Well, it's on your bedside cabinet. I suggest you study
it carefully, then join us for some early morning nutrition.'

Avalon Rise Information Sheet

1. Breakfast is served at 8.00 a.m daily in the dining room.

2. Lunch is served at 1.00 p.m. daily in the dining room.

3. Dinner is served at 7.30 p.m. daily in the dining room.

4. Eating in rooms is not permitted.

5. A pay phone for patrons is located by reception desk.

6. The drawbridge is lowered at sunset and raised at sunrise.

7. No pets allowed.

III

Ain't going down, innit!
> *Don't care what stupid bit of paper says!*

Milo steps carefully over the broken glass and dinner tray (he'd eaten half the casserole and all the dessert during the night) and gazes out of the window.

IV

All smoky white outside, innit!
> *Can't see ... anything ...*
> *Can hear stuff though ...*
> *Distant whooshing of sea, innit.*
> *And ... what's that noise?*
> *Like squeaky bike brakes.*
> *Cwaaa ...*
> *Cwaaa ...*
> *Cwaaa ...*
> *Seagulls!*

V

'Beloved?'

Rap-rap.

'Whaa …?'

'Your breakfast is getting cold.'

Milo thinks, *I'm starving!*

Milo says, 'Not hungry.'

'Well … I'll leave it here. Outside your door, Beloved. If you get a little peckish, just take it in your room and nibble in privacy. By the way, Dee tells me it's misty outside, but when the mist lifts … oh, you'll have a breathtaking view of the ocean and –'

'JUST LEAVE ME ALONE!'

VI

Not gonna eat any breakfast! Don't care how hungry I get. Ain't ever gonna open the door. It's a trap, innit. They're probably waiting outside. Gonna jump on me when I grab the tray …

Can't hear them though.

Corridor sounds quiet.

I'll open the door and see what the breakfast looks like …

VII

Bacon. Fried eggs. Baked Beans. Sausage. Toast.

Looks tasty, innit. Perhaps I'll have a little nibble.

'… needs help …'

'… won't accept it …'

Whispering downstairs, innit!

'… give it time, Dee –'

'… silly idea anyway, Cressida Bell …'

They're talking about me, I bet!

Milo creeps to the top of the banisters and –

VIII

'… got to try …'
    Rattling pots.
    '… another way …?'
    Clunking cutlery.
    Can't hear properly, innit! Ain't never heard two people make so much noise doing the washing-up.

IX

Milo takes a step downstairs.
    '… it *will* work …'
    '… what if it doesn't …'
    He takes another step as –

X

Shadows!
    They're coming out the kitchen!

XI

Milo runs back up the stairs.
    Into room! Quick!
    Drags tray inside.
    Lock door!
    Clunk!

XII

Milo thinks, What are they saying about me?
    What?
    What?

— Seven —

I

Milo sits at the desk, eating breakfast and looking out of the window. It's still very misty so all he can see is –

Horror-film smoke, innit!

– and hear –

Cwaaa!

Cwaaa!

Noisy gulls, innit!

He looks at the painting above the bed. The boy kneeling at the feet of the old Wizard. Firelight glimmers in their eyes and makes the dank rock of the cave sparkle. The walls of the cave are covered with paintings of strange animals – mermaids, unicorns, a serpent – and, in the background, sand and shells have been shaped into a dolphin.

I'm so bored, innit!

II

Thirty minutes later.

Milo, his belly full of fried eggs, bacon and baked beans, lays on the unmade bed and stares at his mobile phone. He wonders if his mum has left a message on it.

Don't care if she has or ain't! Don't bother me!

Who wants to hear her telling me what trouble I am anyway? If she's left a message, I bet that's all it is ...

Oh, let's check ...

III

'Milo, it's me, Mum. Oh, how could you just hang up on me like that? A typical male reaction! When there's a problem, just bury your head in the sand and make out nothing's happening. But we've got to talk about this –'
   No we ain't!

IV

'– otherwise we'll just … well, I'm not having you turn into some monstrous brute like … like most of the men I've known. Of course, you know who I blame, don't you –?'
   Don't say it, Mum!

V

'Mojo Fluke! That horrible boy! I told you not to go near him, didn't I? That boy is nothing but –'
   Fizzzy Waspzzz

VI

'– trouble! Big, big trouble! But would you listen to me? Oh no! You made friends with him against my wishes and look what happened –'
   BZZZZZZZ

VII

Milo turns his mobile off and –
   Don't wanna hear her whinge any more!
   – he throws the phone out of window and –
   Splash!
   – into the moat!

VIII

*Mum don't know what happened. She just thinks five months
ago I became mates with Mojo and then ... I turned into a
monster!*

Well, it ain't that easy, Mum!

IX

*Oh, yeah, sure, it's a bit of the truth. But it ain't the whole story.
Not by a long stretch.*

And I ain't ever gonna tell the whole story.

Not to you.

Not to anyone.

Not ... ever!

X

*I JUST WANT
THE WHOLE
WORLD TO
LEAVE ME
ALONE!*

— Eight —

I

One hour later.

Milo sits on the edge of the mattress and looks out of the window.

The sun is high and warm, patches of blue appearing in the sky and the mist is –

II

Pulling back like a sheet off a bed, innit!
Can see more and more!
Rocks!
A tree!
Look how twisted its branches are! Like skeletons' hands. All its leaves have been blown off too. And look! There's the old truck we came in last night –

III

Gonnnggggg –
Must be lunch, innit!

IV

Knock! Knock!
'Milo Kick!'
'Whaa …?'
'Surely you heard the gong this time.'
'So whaa …?'
'So it's lunch, that's so what.' Dee rattles the handle

impatiently. 'Oh, *do* unlock this door, Milo Kick. We've got no secrets here.'

Milo thinks, *ME – I have!*

Milo says, 'Clear off, Robot-Woman!'

V

As the morning wears on, and the summer heat intensifies, Milo's room becomes a cauldron of different pongs, none of them pleasant.

Casserole gravy stinks like unwashed socks! And me unwashed socks stink like … oh, I can't even describe! Makes me eyes water! Me armpits are so gungy I could scoop the sweat off with a spoon.

VI

Rap-rap.

'Beloved?'

'Whaa …?'

'I'll leave your lunch on a tray outside your room. It's a refreshing salmon salad. Do you like salmon?'

Love it!

'Humpff.'

'Well, it's here if you feel like another private nibble. And, Beloved, please leave your trays outside the door. Things begin to smell so quickly in this weather. Especially fish. And don't forget the lovely view! Dee tells me the mist has risen –'

'YOU'RE BORING ME AGAIN!'

VII

Milo drags the tray into his room.

The fish is succulent and tinged with lemon. The lettuce is as fresh and crunchy as green ice. There's a can of Coke to drink and a bowl of strawberries for dessert. Milo eats and drinks everything, then watches flies settle on the fish bones.

VIII

Stink bad, innit!
Milo sits by open window.
Don't help much. No breeze or anything. Bet this is a plan!
Cressida 'n' Dee trying to stink me out of the room and –
Wait!
Look!
Who's that?

IX

On the edge of the cliff, thrashing his arms and punching the air, is a man. He's tall and, although in his mid-sixties, still very muscular. His grey, almost white, hair is long and whiplashing in the sea breeze. He has a short beard and a face so ravaged and wrinkled it appears to be hacked from stone. He's wearing a white singlet (revealing tattoo-covered arms and hairy chest) and a kilt (revealing muscular and hairy legs). There's a black patch over his left eye and a large gold earring in his right ear. And as this man punches the air wildly and thrashes his arms he's –

X

Yelling at the ocean, innit!
Milo leans out of the window –
Gotta hear what he's saying –

XI

'… curse ye …'
Curse who?
'… curse ye …'
Curse what?
And, then, the man freezes. The grey hairs on his shoulders bristle like a cat's whiskers. With a feral growl, he spins round and glares in Milo's direction, like a hunted

animal sensing danger –
Hide behind curtain! Quick!
The old man's eyes are like bloodshot, ping-pong balls.
Hope he can't see me.

Saliva drips from the man's lips. Sweat runs in rivulets through his wrinkles. Long hair lashes like snakes. His growling continues, as if something wild and savage is clawing its way out of his chest.

XII

Knock! Knock!

Mustn't move! Don't want man to see me.

'Milo Kick?'

Rattling at the door!

'Milo Kick? You all right?'

Milo looks towards the door and manages a faint, 'Whaa …?'

'I need to collect your trays, Milo Kick. You've been hoarding them in there like a squirrel hoards nuts.'

Milo peeks back through the curtains and –

XIII

The man's gone!

XIV

'Who … is he?' Milo calls through the door.

'Can't hear you, Milo Kick.'

'I just … copped sight of a bloke on the cliff and –'

'Can't hear a word you're saying through this door, Milo Kick. It's solid oak. Now I'm perfectly prepared to answer your questions – an inquisitive mind is a wonderful thing – but I've got to be able to *hear* them first.'

Slowly, Milo reaches for the key.

Don't wanna let her in but –

'Well, Milo Kick?'

Wanna know who that bloke is!

'Come in,' says Milo, turning the key.

— Nine —

I

'What an unpleasant odour, Milo Kick! I'd've brought a gas mask if I'd known. And –' sniff, sniff – 'your trainers! What a pong! In the event of war, we should just hurl your footwear at the enemy.' Dee opens the bathroom door. 'I'm going to run you a bath this instant and –'

'The man! The man!'

'What man?'

'Shouting at the ocean, innit?'

'Oh … *him*! I'm afraid we don't talk about *him* in this house.'

'Ya said you'd answer my questions. Ya said! YA SAID!'

Fizzzzy Waspppzzz

II

'All right, all right, calm down.' Dee takes a deep breath. 'I'll make you a deal, Milo Kick. I'll tell you what I know about … that disgraceful male of the species. But only if you let me clean this room. And you – yes, you, young man – take a bath. Have we got a deal?'

'Yeah!'

III

Bath water is steaming and stinks like … apples, innit!

The door's ajar and Milo sees –

Dee's dusting the wardrobe!

'Tell me, then, Dee!'

'Are you in that bath, Milo Kick?'

'Yeah, yeah!' He splashes water to prove it. 'The bloke! Who is he?'

'That man is the wildest male of the species I've ever had the misfortune to meet,' Dee informs him, vigorously polishing the bedside cabinet. 'He can be seen most days, knee deep in the waves, clutching his harpoon and crying "Curse ye!" As if he's trying to halt the tide itself. I told him, "It's pointless you doing that. The tide, as anyone with a brain can tell you, is controlled by the moon. And, no matter how loud you yell, or how hard you strike, you are not stronger than lunar forces."'

'What he say?'

'He implied I was something for carrying shopping.'

'Ya mean ... a bag?'

'Just wash behind your ears, Milo Kick.'

Milo suppresses a chuckle, then asks, 'Where does he live?'

'Oh ... near by.'

'But I thought ya said this is the only house for miles.'

'That statement is correct, Milo Kick.'

'So how can the man live near by?'

'Because that particular male of the species does not live in a house,' explains Dee. 'He lives in a cave.'

IV

'Cave!' Milo jumps out of the bath, apple-soapy bubbles sliding down his legs, wraps a towel round him (covered in dolphins and ships) and dashes into the bedroom. 'What d'ya mean he lives in a –'

'Careful, Milo Kick! There might still be shards of glass stuck in the carpet. Sit on the bed while I hoover! Quick, quick!'

'Where is it, Dee?'

'The bed's right in front of you.'

'Nah, nah! The *cave*!'

'Oh ... down the shore a little way.'

'What direction?'

Dee gives Milo a severe look. 'Now, Milo Kick, you are *not* to go anywhere near that totally scandalous male of the species. You hear me?'

'Mmm ... yeah, yeah.'

'I'm *serious*, Milo Kick. That male of the species is out of bounds! If you see him, close your eyes. If you hear him, put your fingers in your ears. If you find yourself dreaming about him, wake up instantly and recite Einstein's theory of relativity.'

'Dunno Einstein's – whatever ya said!'

'The seven-times-table will do! Just don't think of that wild and lawless male of the species. Not now! Not tomorrow! Not ever!'

V

'But I wanna to know more!'

'My lips are sealed,' declares Dee, stamping her foot. 'If you do want to know anything more ... well, you'll have to ask Cressida Bell. Let it be *her* responsibility. After all, *she's* your mum's friend, not me. Besides, Cressida Bell was always more fascinated by the Captain than me.'

'Captain!' gasps Milo.

'Oh, didn't I tell you?' murmurs Dee, picking up the hoover and striding out of the room. 'His name's Captain Jellicoe.'

— Ten —

I

Me – looking out of window!
The sky's getting all orange. Clouds like yellow feathers. Shadows getting longer and –
Oh, where's Cressida?
Been waiting for her to come up!
Want her to spill the beans about Captain Jellicoe!
Can hear her downstairs chatting –

II

Gonnnggg!
Dinner!

III

Cressida's sure to come up now. She'll bring me a tray of food! Then I can ask her about Captain Jellicoe. Where did he come from? Why's he cursing at the sea? Why's he living in a cave ...

IV

Oh, where's Cressida?
Why ain't she bringing me dinner?

V

She's still not here!
Can hear them rattling knives and forks.
Don't wanna go downstairs but ...

Oh, I've gotta find out more about Captain Jellicoe.
I must! I must!

VI

Slowly, Milo opens the door.

As warily as walking a tightrope over shark-infested water he makes his way down the corridor and –

VII

Me – on stairs!
Me – walking downstairs!
Me – in hallway!
Me – standing by the dining-room door…

VIII

Cressida and Dee sit at a round table. A candelabrum bathes them in flickering light. Both women are nattering and eating as –

'Humpff!'

'Is … is that my Beloved?'

'Well, unless Milo Kick has a twin he didn't tell us about, I assume it must be, Cressida Bell.'

'Er … hello, innit.'

'Oh, what joy to have you join us, Beloved. Dee's cooked cod in parsley sauce, peas and boiled potatoes.' She indicates a chair and a plate of food. 'Your place, Beloved. You see? Come and join us.'

Milo hovers in doorway. 'Don't wanna eat.'

'Really? Then … why are you here, Beloved?'

'Want ya to … tell me.'

'About what?'

'Him!'

'Who?'

'The Captain!'

IX

'The Captain!' splutters Cressida, choking on a pea. 'How did you …?'

'Milo Kick saw the Captain this morning,' Dee explains, thumping her friend on the back with such force that Cressida's dark glasses nearly fly off. 'That lawless male of the species was on the cliff acting like a hysterical haddock again. Correction: haddock have more sense!'

'Oh, really, Dee! You're too hard on that man,' insists Cressida, dabbing her mouth with a napkin. 'True, he does have his … wild side, but there's a certain charm as well.'

'Ha!' spits Dee. 'He's about as charming as an elephant poo! Correction: elephant poo is better company!'

X

Cressida shakes her head. 'I'm afraid, Beloved,' she sighs, 'Dee is not a fan of the Captain. She's disliked him from the moment he set foot in Avalon Rise.'

'Set foot?' gasps Milo. 'You mean … he's been in here?'

'He stayed for a week, Milo Kick.'

'When?'

'Last month.'

'And … then what?'

'And he went to live in a cave, Beloved! Oh, how utterly, utterly romantic!'

XI

'But where did … I mean, how …?' Milo's mind is racing with so many questions he hardly knows where to begin. 'Why did –?'

'The male of the species is a disgrace!' snaps Dee. 'That's the answer to every question, Milo Kick.'

'He is most definitely *not*!' Cressida thumps her hand on the table. 'He's … he's suffering, that man. He's in pain.'

— 44 —

'A pain in the neck, you mean!'

'STOP BICKERING, YOU TWO!' shouts Milo. Then adds, in a softer voice, 'Just … just tell me about him. Please, Cressida! Tell me!'

XII

'Do you mind if I tell him, Dee?' asks Cressida. 'Please! Pretty pleeaasse!'

'You're a big girl now,' replies Dee frostily. 'In fact you're a *huge* girl. Gigantic! Do what you want. That's what you usually do anyway.'

— Eleven —

I

'Imagine this!' begins Cressida, her dark glasses glinting in the candlelight. 'I'm on the top of the cliff! Wind all around me! Clothes billowing. Hair flapping. Above me – clouds! Churning! Swirling! My stick – oh, it's blown from my hands! And then –' she points up in terror – 'thunder! The skies are exploding! Rain! I'm lost, Beloved! Who will help me? Who will save me from this tempest?'

II

'Oh, stop frothing, Cressida Bell.' Dee winces with disgust. 'Why must you turn everything into such ridiculous melodrama?'

'It's what happened, Dee.'

'It's your frothy *idea* of what happened,' sneers Dee. 'But froth, may I remind you, is not fact. And the boy wants facts.' Dee looks at Milo. 'These are the facts ... It is 29 July of this year. Three o'clock in the afternoon. Cressida Bell decides to go for her usual afternoon stroll. It's perfectly safe for her so long as she sticks to the route she knows. This afternoon, however, she's had one sherry too many –'

'Lies!'

'Facts, Cressida! Facts!'

'All right, all right, you horrible newscaster of a woman!' concedes Cressida. 'But let *me* tell the story! You make it sound as interesting as the telephone directory.'

'At least the telephone directory is honest!' retorts Dee.

— 46 —

Then relaxes a little and adds, 'Oh, very well. Tell your story. If it gets too much I'll stick some fish in my ears.'

III

'Imagine this!' continues Cressida, her arms windmilling. 'The tempest ... oh, it gets stronger and stronger! Almost lifts me off my feet – Oh no! No!'

'What's happened?' asks Milo, stepping forward.

'I'm being blown along – Ahhhh!' She clutches the tablecloth in front of her. 'I'm hanging off the edge of the cliff! Hanging on by my fingernails! Legs dangling! I'm too young to die –'

IV

'Enough!' cries Dee, throwing her knife and fork on to her plate. 'There's more froth in this story than a tumble dryer full of shandy!' She looks at Milo. 'These are the facts: Cressida is walking – or should I say, drunkenly staggering – along the cliff. She comes to the steps that lead down to the beach. Again, usually, perfectly safe. She knows them very well. And there's a rope to hold. Except this time, being sozzled out of her skull, she slips on –'

'An enchanting seashell!'

'Seagull poo!'

'Lie!'

'Fact!'

'She twists her ankle. Falls to the ground moaning and groaning –'

'In a tempest, don't forget, Beloved.'

'In a gentle drizzle, Milo Kick.'

V

Cressida sniffs angrily and resumes eating dinner. 'I'm not saying another word,' she mumbles. 'Not. One. Single. Word.'

'Oh, *please*, Cressida.' Milo takes another step forward.

'Not with *her* in the room, Beloved!' She rattles her necklace in Dee's direction. 'How can I create poetic truth with a ... *critic* in the room?'

'Don't mind me.' Dee gets to her feet. 'I'll start clearing the table. That's all I'm here for anyway. A skivvy!' She clanks some plates together in discontent, then glances at Milo. 'Why don't you try some food, Milo Kick? Fuel! Remember?' She takes the dirty plates to the kitchen, elbowing the door shut behind her.

Thud!

Milo pops a potato in his mouth. 'Robot-Woman's gone, Cressida,' he says. 'Tell the story your way.'

VI

'Imagine this!' erupts Cressida, really letting rip now. 'An old blind woman – though looking twenty years younger and as glamorous as any opera singer – clutching the edge of the cliff in the middle of the worst tempest known to mankind! My heart is ... oh, it's pounding in my chest. Rain lashes my face – thank goodness my make-up remains intact! And then – a hand!'

'A hand!'

'It grasps me by the wrist, Beloved! The firmest, most manly grip I've ever felt. And then ... oh, Beloved! I'm being lifted! Lifted higher and higher –'

'Must have had a forklift truck with him,' sneers Dee, striding back into the room. 'Try some cod, Milo Kick!' And she strides out, taking more dirty cutlery with her.

'That withered stick insect of a woman,' murmers Cressida. 'She's has no sense of ... theatre!'

'Just ... tell me.' Milo tastes some fish.

VII

'Imagine this: I'm lying on top of the cliff! Saved, Beloved! Saved! And, as I lie there, the tempest fades. I ... I begin to feel sunlight on my face. Birds start singing. I smell flowers. And the most masculine voice I've ever heard asks, "Are ye all right, most pretty lady?"'

'Blind too, was he?' Dee returns to collect the remains of the crockery.

'Ignore her, Beloved.'

'Ignore the facts, you mean.' Dee indicates Milo's plate. 'Try some peas. Fuel! Fuel!' She brushes crumbs from the table, nudging Cressida with her elbow! 'What happens next, eh? I suppose a sea-serpent appears and blows you a kiss! Ha!'

'You're jealous, that's all!'

'Jealous! Why?'

'Because the Captain kissed *my* cheek and wouldn't touch you with an octopus tentacle.'

'He said I had the sharpest mind he'd ever encountered.'

'And the sharpest elbows!'

Dee snorts and returns to the kitchen.

Thud!

'Go on, Cressida,' pleads Milo, cramming a potato and the remains of the cod into his mouth. 'Froth all ya want.'

VIII

'Imagine this: I'm being carried. Carried by my saviour. "Who are you?" I ask. And that deepest of most masculine voice replies, "Why, I be Captain Jellicoe, most pretty lady, and a stranger to these shores."'

'A stranger to these shores!' echoes Milo, thrillingly.

'And ... oh, he's so strong, Beloved. I can feel muscles hard as rock through his shirt. The hair on his huge chest tickles my nose. I tell him the location of Avalon Rise. He carries me all the way home. The drawbridge is up but, oh, he leaps across! The strength and agility of a stallion. He carries me into the house and lays me on the sofa! Over there! That sofa! You see?'

'Yeah, yeah!'

'I ask him, "Where are you living, Captain?" And he replies, "I only arrived this morning, most pretty lady, and have nowhere to rest my weary bones at present, thank ye for asking." I tell him, "You must be my guest here. After all, you did save my life. You must have my special room: No. 1 – "'

IX

'No. 1!' Milo splutters on a spud. 'The Captain – he stayed
… in *my* room!'

'He did, Beloved. And, oh, he adored it there. After

having a bath, he went straight to bed. I took him a cup of cocoa and some digestive biscuits. Oh, Beloved, he was so tired. I could hear it in his voice. If he'd told me he'd just walked three times round the world, I would've believed him. "Sleep, brave Captain," I said. "Rest your weary bones in the safety of Avalon Rise."

'But, that night, I hear a sccrreeeeeeeeeaaaammm!'

X

'Who is it?' asks Milo.

'The Captain! I rush to his room. Knock on the door. "Captain!" I cry. "Are you all right?" Still the scream persists. Oh, it's like the howl of a soul in eternal torment. I open the door and rush to his bed and – he's … oh, I can imagine it now!'

'What? What?'

'The way he was thrashing about. The sheets wet with sweat. He was in the midst of a terrible nightmare. And he was shrieking, "Curse ye! Curse ye! Curs –"'

'Can you blame him?' sneers Dee, putting a bowl of rice pudding on the table. 'Seeing your ugly mush in his room in the middle of the night must've scared him witless!'

XI

'That's it!' cries Cressida, standing so abruptly she knocks her chair over. 'I can take no more! I'm retiring to my boudoir. I refuse to be insulted by this … Robot-Woman!'

'What about your rice pudding, Cressida Bell?'

'Put it on your head.' Cressida strides towards the door. 'It was *your* fault he left, Dee Dee Six! Don't forget that!' She tap-taps her way upstairs, her voice fading. 'It was *your* fault … *your* fault … *your* fault …'

— Twelve —

I

'Have you finished your fish, Milo Kick?'

'Whaa …? Oh, yeah.'

'Some rice pudding then?'

'I want … facts. Not pudding.'

'Then you've come to the right person.' Dee spoons some rice pudding in a bowl for herself. 'What particular facts-not-pudding do you require?'

'Why was it *your* fault the Captain left?'

II

'Very well,' says Dee, after a few thoughtful moments. 'I *will* tell you. Even though, if you remember correctly, I vowed not to talk about that vulgar male of the species again. But … well, I won't have you thinking I did anything wrong.' She sits very straight and takes a deep breath. 'Fact one: Nightmares every night, screams and torn sheets. Fact two: Wading out into the sea, then stomping back in here with his muddy boots. Fact three: Getting angry for no reason and shouting and breaking things. Fact four: Scrawling meaningless things on the wall above his bed, ruining the wallpaper and plaster beneath.' She leans towards Milo, her usually cold eyes blazing. 'And who do you think cleaned up all his mess, eh? Who d'you think mended all those torn sheets, scrubbed mud from carpets, glued together shattered vases, tried to cover up the damaged wall? Me! Little Miss

Skivvy.' Her lipless mouth is trembling. 'Chaos!' she blurts out. 'That's what that man brought to this house! Chaos! CHAOS!'

III

'And so … ya told him to clear off?'

'That is factually accurate, yes.'

'What did Cressida say?'

'Oh, there were tears and tantrums. That woman's always been soft when it comes to males of the species. Especially males of the species with thighs like tugboats and hairy shoulders. But I said, "Either *he* goes or *I* go. Who's it to be?"'

'And she chose the Captain?'

'Eventually … yes.' Dee eats some rice pudding. 'Now, if you don't mind, I'd rather not discuss the subject any further.'

'But I wanna know –'

'No, Milo Kick! I've divulged all the facts I intend to. Cressida, no doubt, will tell you more. Personally, I'd prefer it if you never mentioned that male of the species ever again.' She chews thoughtfully for a moment, then adds, 'This rice pudding is full of nourishment. Have some before it gets cold.'

'I'll take it upstairs.' Milo puts some in a bowl, then heads for door. 'Ya know,' he says, looking over his shoulder at Dee, 'Cressida tells stories better than you. Just the facts are boring without a bit of froth.'

— Thirteen —

I

Captain Jellicoe in this room – just like me!
   Captain Jellicoe sat on the edge of bed – just like me!
   Captain Jellicoe walked on this carpet – just like me!
   Captain Jellicoe looked out of this window – just like me!
   Breaking things – just like me!
   Scrawling things on wall –

II

The wall!
   That's what Dee said, innit!
   The wall above the bed!
   But above the bed is –
   That painting!
   Cressida said Dee put it there!
   Of course!
   The painting is covering where Captain Jellicoe scratched into the –

III

Milo jumps on to bed …
   Gotta get painting off!
   He tries to lift, fingers clutching golden frame …
   Oh, it's heavy, innit!
   Tight grip, arms trembling, gasping …
   That's it! It's off!
   Put it on the bed, innit!

Now! Let's look at wall —

IV

Scratched, as if clawed by a savage animal, are three letters …

V

What's it mean?
  Must mean something.
  But … what?
  What?

VI

Milo goes to window.

What secrets ya got, Captain Jellicoe?

He leans forward, breath misting glass.

Why ya cursing, Captain Jellicoe? Why ya angry, Captain Jellicoe? Why ya shouting at the sea, Captain Jellicoe? Why ya stabbing at waves, Captain Jellicoe? And why … oh why'd ya write MFC, Captain Jellicoe?

  Why?
  Why?
  Why?

Third Day

— Fourteen —

I

Gonnngg –
Breakfast, innit!

II

'Well … good morning, Milo Kick.'

'Er … wotchya, yeah.'

'To what do we owe this change of heart?'

Milo thinks, *Wanna ask Cressida about Captain Jellicoe.*

Milo says, 'Just … bit peckish, innit!'

'Well, sit down then. Do you want your eggs scrambled or fried?'

'Er … fried. Just like yesterday.'

'Well, I don't know if I can fry them *just* like yesterday,' comments Dee, heading for the kitchen. 'But I'll certainly do them in a *similar* fashion.'

III

Milo sits at the table and looks out of the window.

Everything looks so … big!

Big sky.

Big cliffs.

Big sea.

It's all so bright and … well, clean.

Like everything's been polished, innit.

'Fuel!' announces Dee, putting a plate of breakfast in front of him. 'Fill your engine, Milo Kick.'

IV

Full up now!

Belly's gonna burst!

But where's Cressida got to?

'Don't Cressida want any grub?'

'Oh, *now* I understand,' sneers Dee. 'You're just here to see *her*!'

'Nah! It's not like that. Just wondered where she –'

'Drink your orange juice, Milo Kick.'

'Don't like that stuff, innit.'

'It's full of vitamin C.' insists Dee. 'And as for the Queen of Sheba – she's still in her room. Sulking. Refuses to come down after that … nonsense last night. Oh, what a big, hysterical hovercraft she is.' Dee indicates a breakfast tray she's been preparing. 'I'm about to take this up to Her Majesty now.'

'Me – I'll take it!'

'You're still eating your breakfast.'

'Finished! Look!'

'Your orange juice remains untouched!'

'If … if I drink me juice can I take the tray up?'

'Oh … very well.'

Gulp!

V

Knock! Knock!

'Who … who is it?'

'Me!'

'Beloved! Enter!'

Milo opens the door and – clutching the breakfast tray as firmly as possible – goes into –

VI

She's in a bed like mine! Oh, what's it called …? Four-poster! Only hers is bigger. And got curtains round. And Cressida –

*she's propped up against a mountain of pillows. And she's
wearing a big, frilly nightgown. She's still wearing her dark
glasses. And smiling wide … yeah, smiling really wide at me.*

'How wonderful of you to visit, Beloved.'

'Gotchya breakfast, innit.'

'How thoughtful!' She taps the blanket in front of her.
'Lay the tray here, Beloved! That's it! Perfect! Bless you!
Oh … where's my napkin?'

'Here!'

'Bless!' She lays it across her chest, then starts to butter
a slice of toast. 'Will you do one more thing for me,
Beloved?'

'Whaa …?'

'Wait and chat with me while I eat. Mainly, of course,
because I'd be utterly, utterly thrilled by your company.
But, also, I'd like you to take the tray down afterwards. I
certainly don't want that talking clock of a woman coming
up here. She'll be as welcome as the North Pole after a
bout of flu.' She gives Milo a flicker of a smile. Then asks,
'Will you do that for me, Beloved? Pretty pleeaasse.'

Milo thinks, *Exactly what I want!*

Milo says, 'Yeah, if you like.'

VII

'Feel free to browse round my boudoir, Beloved,'
announces Cressida, munching a rasher of bacon.
'There're so many little knick-knacks to enjoy. The glass
animal collection was started by my dear, dear Papa when
he was a boy. And I'm sure you'll find many other things
to interest you.'

VIII

*Look at all this stuff! Like a museum or something. Here! On the
window ledge. Shells! Lots! Didn't know they came this big.
This one's like a crash helmet … And here! Ships in bottles.*

How'd they get big ships in tiny bottles like that? Hang on! No time for all this! Gotta ask about the Captain –

'Cressida … will ya tell me more about –?'

'Are you looking at the Phoenix, Beloved?'

'The … whaa?'

'Sounds to me like you're standing right in front of it. On the window ledge. The wooden phoenix. See it?'

'Mmmm … Oh, yeah.'

'Just look at the workmanship in that, Beloved. Such glorious carving. Every feather on the Phoenix's wings is perfectly formed – oh, you do know what a phoenix is, don't you, Beloved?'

'Er … nah.'

IX

'A phoenix,' explains Cressida, 'is a mythical bird that – after living for five or six centuries – burns itself on a funeral pyre and … oh, it rises from the ashes! Renewed youth! Imagine, Beloved! Renewed youth!'

'Yeah … very interesting. But I really wanna know about the Captain –'

'It's got a secret compartment in its chest. You see? You can unlock the Phoenix and keep something utterly, utterly special inside. That's how the object gets its full name: the Phoenix of Secrets. It was given to me as a gift, you know. Can you guess by who?'

'The Captain?'

'Oh no, no, Beloved. By someone far more special than that.' Cressida clutches her bosom, her lips trembling with emotion. 'The Phoenix of Secrets,' she tells Milo, 'was a gift from … your mum.'

— Fifteen —

I

'Mum!' gasps Milo. 'But ... when?'

'Oh, many years ago. She was about your age at the time.'

'My age!'

'Oh, I know what you're thinking,' chuckles Cressida. 'Mums can't be young! Mums just exist to be ... mums!'

'Well ... yeah!'

'Well ... *wrong*! Your mum once was a beautiful fourteen-year-old girl. With luscious red hair and – oh, look in that drawer, Beloved.' Cressida points at her bedside cabinet. 'There's a photo album! Get it! Pretty pleeaasse!'

II

Milo opens the drawer and sees a large leather-bound book with 'Memories' embossed in gold leaf across the cover. He puts it in Cressida's lap.

Cressida counts through the pages, feeling each one until she finds what she's after. 'Here, Beloved! Take a look!'

Milo sees a photo of a girl wearing a dress covered with mermaids. The girl's red hair is decorated with two seashell clips. She is standing on the drawbridge and smiling.

'Your mum!' declares Cressida triumphantly.

III

This is ... weird! Ain't never seen Mum wearing anything except ... well, Mum's baggy jeans 'n' T-shirt. Ain't never seen her anywhere except the flats. Ain't never seen her body look ... so slim. Face so ... unwrinkled. Ain't never seen her smiling like this. Yeah! That's it! Never seen Mum look so –

IV

'She's happy, innit.'

'Oh, she was!' Cressida agrees. 'When she was with me she didn't stop smiling. It's only when *he* appeared her mood changed.'

'He?'

Cressida turns a page. 'Him!' she spits, indicating a photo. 'See him? Standing behind your mum! Oh, I would've got rid of the photo long ago were it not for your mum being in it. I have so few of her, you see. And, yes, I know I can't actually see them any more, but ... oh, they have such memories, Beloved. Such wonderful, wonderful memories.'

'Who's the bloke in the photo?'

'Well ... surely you *know*, Beloved. Look at the clothes he's wearing – oh, *surely* your mum must've mentioned him.'

'Nah.'

'Not once? Not ever?'

'Nah. Nah. Who is he?'

'Why, Beloved, he's your mum's dad. Your –'

V

'Grandad, innit!'

The photo shows a large, bald, chubby-cheeked man with a thin moustache and bulbous red nose. He is wearing a suit covered in black and white squares, a shirt with ruffles up the front and a bow tie.

'He looks … funny, innit.'

'He *was* funny! At least … *he* thought so. He was a comedian, Beloved. Being funny was his job. The first thing he ever said to me was, "You're a fat one, ain't ya, luv? If I had to carry you across that drawbridge it'd take me two trips!"'

VI

'Ha!'

'Don't, Beloved!' pleads Cressida. 'That's not funny! It's cruel! It's vulgar! Just like the man himself. A vulgarian of the highest – or should I say *lowest* – order. Ugh!' She shudders so violently the whole bed shakes. 'I remember when I saw him for the first time –'

'You … you *saw!*'

'Of course, Beloved! I wasn't always this monumental mole.'

'Then how did ya … get blind?'

'It … it was an accident, Beloved.'

'What sort of accident?'

'I fell and struck my silly head. The sudden jolt … did something to the lenses in my eyes. Or the optical nerve. I never fully understood the medical explanation. All I knew was, after I hit my head, I couldn't see any more.' She slaps the mattress with impatience. 'Now, this is *quite* enough about my silly problems. Do you want to hear about when I first met your grandad or not?'

'Yeah! Tell me!'

VII

'Well, all of this was … oh, sixteen years ago. Can it be so long? Well, yes it *must* be … Sixteen summers ago.' She slips into a trance of memory for a moment, then asks, 'Beloved, are you *sure* your mum hasn't told you just an insy-winsy bit about her dad or … *anyone* she knew before

you were born?'

'Well … she told me she knew you. And she told me she used to stay here when she was a kid. Well, my age. And then she moved away and had me.'

'And … that's it?'

'Yeah.'

VIII

'But … haven't you asked her questions?'

'I used to.'

'And what did she reply?'

'Ask me no questions and I'll tell you no lies.'

'Goodness! I never thought things were … well, this bad. She should've told you *something*. It might've helped …' Her voice trails off for a moment. Then, suddenly, she sits up and declares, 'Right! It's up to me! I'll tell you. But ... oh, where to start?'

Milo taps the photo. 'Where were ya when ya first met him? When he made that terrible joke about you and the drawbridge. Start there!'

'Oh ... I was downstairs! At the reception desk. It was late in the evening. I was just about to lower the drawbridge. And that's when I came face to face with Checker Kick.'

'Checker!' gasps Milo. 'My grandad was called Checker! Go on!'

IX

'Checker Kick says, "You got a room, mrs?"

'I reply, "I have. And it's *miss*."

'"Miss!" he gasps. "You mean an old bird like you ain't hitched yet?"

'"It's my choice to stay single,"' I inform him.

'"Not surprised, luv," he says. "Last time I saw a face like yours, Tarzan was feeding it peanuts. Now, let me explain me situation: I went to the posh hotel in town and they're far too pricey. Some toff there told me your rooms are cheap."

'"Cheap!" I gasp. "Well, we charge lower rates because we're not near the centre of town. But, I do assure you, Mr ..."

'"Kick!" he tells me.

'"I assure you, Mr Kick! My rooms are most tasteful and –"

'"Stop the hype and give us one, miss," he interrupts. Oh, his manners were appalling, Beloved. Utterly, utterly deplorable! "All I want is a place to kip 'n' poo," he says. "Won't be here much, you see. I'm working the pier." Do you know what a pier is, Beloved?'

X

'Er … nah!'

'Then you must *ask*. Any word you don't understand. Always ask, ask. A pier is a structure that goes out into the sea. It's used as a promenade! That's something for people to walk along. Oh, the pier was so splendid. It had shops and a small theatre at the end. All gone now! Just like the town you heard me mention. Gone, gone, gone.'

'Gone … where?'

XI

'Washed away. The cliffs, you see, are being constantly battered by sea and wind. When my dear Papa built Avalon Rise – for it was that inspired visionary who transformed a humble house into the castle we now inhabit – this entire area was a popular holiday resort. Why, when I was a girl, and Avalon Rise was new, every room here would be occupied from early April to late October. But then … *erosion*, Beloved!' She butters another slice of toast. 'I suppose it had always been going on, but none of us had really noticed. Then, one summer, in the middle of the night – Craaashhh!'

'What's going on?'

'A section of the cliff crumbled into the sea, Beloved! The very earth shook like an earthquake! The glass ornaments vibrated and tinkled. Poor Papa. He never got over the shock. He took to his bed and left me to run things. Within seven years he was … dead.' For a moment she becomes very still, her bottom lip quivering. Then, suddenly, she bursts into life and says, 'Where's the marmalade?'

XII

'Here,' says Milo, putting the jar in her hands. 'Or … do ya want me to put it on the toast for ya?'

'Oh, how gallant of you, Beloved. I do adore being

waited on. Especially by a dashing gentleman like yourself – spread it on nice and thick.'

'Keep telling me about Mum!' urges Milo, sticking a knife into the marmalade. 'What happened after you first saw … Checker Kick?'

'You see what stories are like!' exclaims Cressida. 'Like a Russian doll sometimes – You know what a Russian doll is, Beloved?'

'Er … nah!'

XIII

'Then what must you do, Beloved?'

'Ask?'

'Bravo! Ask! It's the only way to learn.' She taps Milo's knee. 'A Russian doll is lots of dolls. One inside the other. You start with a big one. Open that up and inside, a smaller one. Open that up and inside –'

'A smaller one!'

'Bravo, Beloved! And that's stories all over. Inside every story is another story – Ooo, is that my toast?'

'Yeah … Enough marmalade for ya?'

Cressida takes a bite and moans in ecstasy. 'Mmmm … The best marmalade on toast I've ever tasted!'

'The story! Tell me more … Pretty pleeaasse!'

'Aha! Pretty pleeaasse, is it? Who can resist that, eh?' She munches thoughtfully for a few moments. Then, suddenly, cries out, 'Suitcases!'

— Sixteen —

I

'Suitcases?' Milo frowns. 'What d'ya mean?'

'Imagine this!' gasps Cressida. 'I'm at the reception desk. Checker Kick is standing in front of me. I'm so insulted by his vulgar nature I'm about to refuse him a room when – There!'

'Wh-what?'

'A girl!'

'Mum!'

'She's got red hair – in need of a good brushing I hasten to add – and she's wearing scruffy jeans, and a man's button-up shirt and men's shoes! And not just any man. By the size of them, I'd say they were her dad's cast-offs. Worse still, she's struggling with – can you guess, Beloved?'

'Suitcases!'

'Bravo!' cries Cressida, nodding enthusiastically. 'Your mum's hands are covered in blisters. She's whimpering with pain. "Shut up, you!" growls Mr Kick. Then looks at me and winks, "Kids, eh? More trouble than a fart in a spacesuit. Now, let's have the key to me room. Me feet pong and need a soak."'

II

Milo asks, 'Did ya give him a room?'

'What else could I do, Beloved? That poor girl needed somewhere to stay. After he'd signed the book, I said, "I'll help you up with your bags, Mr Kick."

'"The kid can manage 'em," he booms. "Don't stick ya hooter in me business and I won't stick me hooter in yours!"'

III

'Poor Mum,' sighs Milo.

'Oh, it gets worse, Beloved,' Cressida informs him, shaking her head. 'Later, as I raised the drawbridge, I could hear him in his room. Giving orders like a sergeant major. "Clean me boots, kid!" "Iron me shirt, kid!" "Wash me pants, kid!" Oh, it was horrible. Truly. Night came and still his booming voice bossed that poor girl around. "Pour me a drink, kid!" "Open the window, kid!" "Massage me feet, kid!" Finally, I could stand it no longer. I went up to his room to give him a piece of my mind.'

'Yeah! Go for it!'

IV

'I knocked on his door. Your mum opened it. Oh, how sad and scared she looked. And then – there he is! Checker! Fast asleep on a bed. Or, I should say, on the *two* beds! For that selfish vulgarian had pulled the two single beds together and made one big bed. Just for him!'

'So … where did me mum kip?'

'Exactly what I asked! Your mum pointed into the bathroom! And then I saw – blankets! He was making his own daughter sleep in the bathtub while he … oh, that horrible, horrible man!'

V

'Poor Mum,' Milo says again.

'There was the stench of whiskey everywhere. Quite revolting. Then I realized … Checker wasn't just asleep! He was *unconscious*! Knocked out by the booze. An empty bottle was on the mattress beside him. I said to the girl, "You must be hungry."

'She said, "I am."

'"Come down with me," I told her. "I'll make you a nice sandwich and a glass of milk." She did so. We nattered late into the night. Your mum tells me all about her life with her vulgar father. They live out of suitcases. Travelling from theatre to theatre –'

'Because Checker's a comic!'

'Exactly, Beloved! Well remembered! Mr Kick goes all over the place performing his routine and treats his poor daughter like a ... a servant!'

'You've gotta help her!'

'Oh, I do, Beloved! Believe me, I *do*.'

VI

'How?'

'Next day I make Mr Kick an offer. I say to him, "Mr Kick, you can stay here for nothing! You won't have to pay me a single penny. But on one condition: your daughter helps me with the chores here at Avalon Rise!"' Cressida giggles with excitement. 'Of course, I had no intention of making your mum work at all. But ... well, I knew a skinflint like Mr Kick couldn't refuse! Money meant everything to him.'

'So ... he agreed?'

'Of course! Every day Mr Kick went off to the theatre on the pier and I ... oh, I was left with the wonderful Fliss.'

VII

'Fliss!' gasps Milo.

'That *is* your mum's name, Beloved.'

'Yeah! I know! It's just ... well, sounds odd, innit.'

'I know, I know. As far as you're concerned she's just called "Mum". She doesn't have a real name. I bet you think she never had a childhood either. As far as you're concerned she didn't exist until you were born. Well, let me tell you, your mum's name is Fliss and once she was a girl and when she and I first met ... oh, it was one of the happiest times of my life. She made me blossom like a rose in sunlight.' She swallows the final piece of toast. 'I felt blessed! Truly! Blessed!'

'What ... what sort of stuff ya both get up to then?' asks Milo.

VIII

'Everything, Beloved! We walked along the beach collecting seashells. We read poetry. We listened to music. Read to each other. We went landscape painting together – oh, how your mum *loved* painting.'

'She did?'

'I bought her an easel. And her own set of watercolours. We'd sit on the cliff top and paint the ocean and the ships and gulls ... Oh, we were so utterly, utterly happy. Deliriously happy. I let her grow her hair longer. Brushed it for her every morning and before she went to bed. Made her a dress – that one in the photo! I gave her those seashell hairclips too. Fliss was ... well, she was the daughter I never had. I loved her – why, I *still* love her – more than all the sunlight and starlight that have ever twinkled and shone. My sweet, adorable Fliss.' For a moment Cressida drifts off in a haze of memory. Then, suddenly, in a surprisingly harder voice, she says, 'But summer had to end!'

— Seventeen —

I

'You mean … Fliss – Mum! – she … left ya?'

'Checker Kick *made* her, Beloved,' replies Cressida. 'Your mum didn't want to go. But the summer season was finished. The pier closed. And that vulgar man was moving off to another theatre. Oh, how I cried the day your mum departed. To see her struggling with those suitcases once again. To hear her being bossed around. "Get a move on, kid! We've got to be in Manchester by evening, kid!"'

'Ya should've thumped him one, innit.'

'I wanted to, believe me. But, instead, I hugged Fliss as hard and long as I could. We were both on the drawbridge. I could feel her tears against my cheek. Taste them salty on my lips. "Write to me, Fliss," I told her. "Avalon Rise is your home now." And do you know what she replied, Beloved?'

'Whaa?'

'She said, "You are the mum I never had." And with that … oh, my Fliss left.'

II

'Poor Mum! Mum!'

'I know, Beloved,' says Cressida, reaching out and squeezing Milo's knee. 'It breaks your heart, doesn't it? I was inconsolable for weeks. Utterly, utterly desolate. And then a parcel came through the post. It was a present!'

'The Phoenix of Secrets!'

'Just so! How clever of you, Beloved. Fliss had seen it in a shop and she thought I'd like it. She wrote me such a lovely letter too – Oh, where is that letter? I'd love you to read it, Beloved. Have a look in the drawer! It's in a lavender envelope –'

'Same colour as your hair!' sneers Dee, striding into the room. 'Why can't you just go grey all over like any sensible old female of the species.'

III

'Because I am *not* grey all over!' cries Cressida. 'I'm just grey *at the roots*! And I'm only old in the number of years I've been alive. Apart from that I'm young! Young! Now – *out*! I'm having a private conversation with my Beloved.'

'Well, you can stop jabbering and start eating. I want your breakfast things and I'm not coming up again!'

'You don't have to!' Cressida tells her. 'Beloved's taking the tray down for me! And knock next time! Storming into my world unannounced! It's an outrage!'

'You liked it when Captain Jellicoe stormed in!'

'*He* was thrilling!'

'Thrilling! Ha! That man was nothing but a … weirdy-beardy!'

'Weirdy-beardy!' gasps Cressida. 'Why, you vicious old bag of bones. The Captain was here because … because he *loved* me!' She sticks her fingers in her ears. 'I refuse to listen to any more of your spiteful slander. Tra-la-de-da.'

'You're a fool, Cressida Bell.'

'TRA-LA-DE-DA-DAH –'

'Worse! You're a *romantic* fool! AND ROMANCE NEVER GOT ANYONE ANYTHING EXCEPT A BROKEN HEART!'

And, with that, Dee storms out of the room, slamming the door behind her –

THUD!

IV

Cressida removes her fingers from her ears and slumps back into the pillows. 'Oh … that Gorgon! You see what I have to put up with, Beloved? I'd have an easier life juggling electric eels.'

Milo can't help chuckling.

'Oh, you can laugh,' says Cressida, smiling despite

herself. 'But you haven't got to live with her.' She fluffs up the frills on her dressing gown. 'Fancy calling the Captain a "weirdy-beardy". What nonsense! Admittedly, his behaviour was ... well, erratic. But, my goodness, he was exciting, Beloved. The house was *alive* with him in it. *I* was alive!'

V

'Is the Captain ... a *sea* captain.'

'What? Oh, yes, I suppose he must be.'

'Then ... has he got a ship?'

'To be honest, Beloved, I never found out anything about the Captain's private life. Of course, I tried. Asked question after question. But the Captain's lips were super-glued on the subject. Honestly, he had more secrets than a roomful of sphinxes playing poker.'

'So ... didn't ya find out *anything* about him?'

'One thing only,' replies Cressida, leaning forward and indicating Milo should lean forward also. 'The Captain was hunting!' she whispers in his ear.

'Hunting what?'

'A monster!'

— Eighteen —

I

'Monster!' cries Milo.

'Shhhh! I don't want that ice-hearted harpy to hear.' Cressida holds Milo's hand and pulls him closer. 'That poor man had been hurt in some way. Hurt by a terrible creature and now … oh, he's in search of it. Travelling the world with his harpoon. His heart aching and full of some nameless sorrow. Oh, the romance of it makes me swoon – Oh!' She sits bolt upright and gasps, 'Food parcel!'

'Wh … what?'

'Oh, Beloved! I need your help. The Captain – *he* needs you … Oh, I only hope I'm not too late.'

'Too late for what?'

'This must be our secret, Beloved. Do you promise me that? Before I say another word. Do you swear?'

'Swear!'

II

Cressida leans even closer and says in a voice so low that Milo can barely hear. 'Ever since the Captain was banished by that dried-out fig of a female downstairs, I've been leaving food for him.'

'Wh … where?'

'On the dining-room window sill. I leave it after breakfast. Not much. Some toast, fruit, rolls, rashers of bacon. It's my gesture of love and solidarity. Of course, Dee will make my life hell if she finds out. But … oh, that man needs help!' She wraps the remains of her breakfast in a napkin. 'Food parcel!' she exclaims, placing it in Milo's hands. 'Now, Beloved, will you be the bravest thing ever to grace Avalon Rise? Will you sneak down and put it on the window sill for the Captain? Will you do that? Will you?'

'Yeah!' Milo declares, rushing for the door.

'You are my Knight in Shining Armour!' Cressida calls after him. 'Bravo! Bravo!'

— Nineteen —

I

Me – standing in the dining room.

Me – looking at open window.

Me – watching Dee walking in and out, clearing up breakfast things.

Me – still holding parcel.

Me – trying to look innocent.

Me – watching Dee walk up and stare at me –

II

'What *are* you up to, Milo Kick?'

'Whaa ...? Oh, just watching.'

'Watching *what* exactly? Me working my fingers to the bone while that Jurassic jellyfish upstairs leads a life of leisure?'

'Just ... watching the sea. Through the window. It's very ...'

'What?'

'... romantic!'

'Romantic!' splutters Dee, as if she's just swallowed sour milk and vinegar. 'I think you've been talking to Cressida Bell too much!' She strides into hallway and starts dusting the counter, murmuring, 'It's just water! That's all the ocean is. Lots and lots of H_2O.' She turns her back to dust the clock and –

III

Me – rushing to window.
  Me – putting food parcel on sill.
  Me – rushing back to where I was standing.
  Me – trying to look innocent.

IV

'May I clean your room, Milo Kick?'

'Whaa …'

'Goodness, am I speaking ancient Aztec? May I go upstairs and transform your room from a pigsty into a place fit for male of the species habitation?'

'Yeah! Go on! Go on!'

'Well, there's no need to sound *quite* so enthusiastic,' murmurs Dee. 'Anyone'd think you were glad to get rid of me!'

V

I am!
  I'm gonna hide behind this chair.
  I'm gonna wait for the Captain.

VI

Ten minutes later.

Milo is peering from behind the chair at the open window. The curtains billow gently on either side, revealing a drama of sweeping seagulls, blue skies and a calm sea.

But, so far, no Captain Jellicoe …

VII

Me – been here for twenty minutes.
  Me – got pins and needles in me leg.
  Me – afraid Dee's gonna come back in any second and –

VIII

Wait!
> *There!*
> *A figure approaching!*
> *It's him!*
> *It's Captain Jellicoe!*

IX

Captain Jellicoe sneaks up to the edge of the moat, looks round warily then – with one almighty leap – jumps across the moat, his kilt flapping, his grey hair thrashing, and lands, with a gentle thud, and an explosion of breath, outside the window, grabs the food parcel, tucks it under his arm, turns around and – leap, flap, thrash – lands on the other side and runs away.

X

Follow him, innit!
> *Don't wanna lose him.*
> *Quick!*
> *Out into hall and –*

XI

'And where d'you think you're going, Milo Kick?' Dee is at the top of the stairs, bottle of bleach in one hand, dirty towels in the other. 'Answer! Now!'

'I … er … a walk, innit.'

'A *walk*, indeed! To see what? Your romantic ocean?'

'Why not? It'll be … educational.'

'Aha! Well, *educational* is much better concept!'

'See ya!' says Milo, heading for the drawbridge.

'Wait! Be careful out there, Milo Kick!' Dee calls, rushing after him.

'Yeah, yeah!'

'You're a city boy, don't forget! The coast has surprises

and dangers. Remember these facts. Wait! Listen to me, Milo Kick. WAIT!'

Milo comes to a halt and looks over his shoulder as Dee arrives on the drawbridge.

XII

'Fact one: do not go near the edge of the cliff. Two: if you want to go to the beach, only use the steps provided. Three: don't touch any unusual items on the beach. Four: don't go into the sea. Five: be back for lunch! Deal?'

'Deal!'

'And one more thing!' Dee dashes back inside, gets a straw hat from behind the counter and pops it on Milo's head. 'Wear this!'

'Nah!' Milo cries, taking it off.

'Yes!' insists Dee. 'It's hot out there! Do you want a long lecture on the ozone layer and the dangers of too much sunlight?'

'Er … nah!'

'Then hat on!'

'All right, all right.' Milo puts the hat back on.

'And another thing! Don't go anywhere near Captain Jellicoe. Deal?'

'Deal!'

'Off you go then! Get educated.'

— Twenty —

I

Me – running!
   Across the top of the cliffs …
   Oh, where's the Captain gone?
   Wind in me face, fish-finger smell …
   Seagulls swooping and making squeaky bike break noises and –
   Oh, where's the Captain?
   Where –?
   There!
   He's walking down those steps to the beach, innit!

II

Milo tucks himself behind a rock, watching the Captain. He can hear the old man muttering to himself, and see him wave a fist in the direction of the ocean. As soon as the Captain reaches the beach –

III

Me – I'm following again.
   Me – I'm going down steps.
   Me – holding on to rope.
   Me – treading carefully.
   Me – one eye on Captain.
   Me – other eye on steps.

IV

Milo reaches the beach, his feet crunching into sand and shingle. The sound of gulls gets louder. Wind in his face gets stronger. Smell of fish and salty sea tingles his nose and –

V

Me – following the Captain.
  Me – hearing gulls.
  Cwaaa …
  Cwaaa …
  Cwaaa …

VI

Me feet are going –
  Crunch!
  Crunch!
  Crunch!

VII

Occasionally, the Captain – like a pursued animal – senses something and snaps his head around, glaring and snarling –

VIII

Hide!

IX

Milo jumps behind a moss-covered rock!
  Then, with a spit and a growl, the Captain moves off.
  Crunch!
  Crunch!

Follow …
  Follow …
  Cwaaa!
  Cwaaa!
  Cwaaa!
  What's the Captain up to now?

Captain Jellicoe has picked up a piece of driftwood. He studies it for a moment, then gives a snort of approval. He clutches the wood under his arm and strides forward –
  Crunch!
  Crunch!
  He walks right into –

A cliff, innit!
  The Captain – he's walked straight into cliff and –
  Look!
  A hole in the cliff!
  Like a big black mouth – the size of a car – and it's swallowed the Captain and eaten him in one gulp.
  Walk closer …

Crunch …
  Crunch …
  Crunch …

A cave!
  The Captain's gone in a cave!
  I'm staring into the gloomy mouth but … nah! Can't see a thing.
  Cwaaa!

Cwaaa!
Cwaaa!

XV

Me – creeping up to cave.
  Crunch …
  Crunch …

XVI

Hang on!
  What's that –?

XVII

A sign has been stuck into the sand. It's written in the same frantic, clawed scrawl Milo remembered from above his bed:

KEEP OUT EVERYONE!!

— Twenty-one —

I

Heart – punching in me chest.
   Sweat – trickling down me back.
   Blood – faster than water down plughole.
   But I gotta go in …
   I gotta …

II

Slowly, Milo negotiates his way over the pebbles and sand
and – slowly, oh, so slowly – goes into the cave –

III

So dark!
   Crunch!

IV

Everything sounds odd – like sticking me head under water –
   Crunch!
   Crunch!

V

Eyes getting used to dark now!
   Crunch!

VI

Beginning to see …
   Crunch!

VII

Crunch … Step…
   Crunch … Step…
   Then –

VIII

HIM!

IX

Captain Jellicoe strikes a match.
   He lights a tiny oil lamp.
   He places the lamp on a large rock and the flickering light reveals –

X

Rock, innit!
   Rock everywhere.
   Rock covered in green slimy stuff.
   Look! Pointed rocks hanging from the ceiling.
   And pointed rocks standing up from the ground.
   And – in the far corner – piles of driftwood.
   And – in the middle of the cave –

XI

'A boat!' gasps Milo, before he has a chance to stop himself. He slams his hand over his mouth to stop further blurtings, but it's already too late –

XII

'WHO BE THERE?' roars Captain Jellicoe.
   Milo tucks himself among the shadows. He presses himself so tightly against the rock that he can taste the salty greenness of the slime.
   'IF SOMEONE'S THERE, YE BETTER ANNOUNCE YERSELF!' continues Captain Jellicoe. 'OTHERWISE

THERE'LL BE HELLFIRE AND BRIMSTONE TO PAY, I
WARN YE OF THAT!'

XIII

Me – heart pounding!
   Me – sweat trickling!
   Me – blood whooshing!

XIV

Slowly – and muttering, 'Hearing things I be … Aye, that
be it … Getting senile in me old age, aye, aye, aye …' – the
Captain picks up a length of driftwood and takes it to the
boat, sits at a rock and opens the food parcel …

XV

The boat – it's all made of driftwood.
   All shapes and sizes.
   All nailed and glued together.
   Ain't finished yet though.
   Still got lots of big holes in it.

XVI

'Curse ye!'
   His deep voice echoes round the cave.
   'Curse ye … ye … ye … ye … ye …'

XVII

Boat ain't very big, innit.
   Size of a sofa.
   And – oh, look!
   The Captain's taking off his vest and –

XVIII

The Captain's whole back is a whirling, swirling tattooed
sea of mermaids, whales, dolphins, anchors, turtles,

waves, whirlpools –

Milo can't help gasping out loud.

'YE SCALLYWAG, YE!'

XIX

Suddenly, faster than a cat pouncing, the Captain spins round, rushes at Milo and grabs him by the scruff of the neck –

'HOW DARE YE!'

'Heeeeelllllppp!'

'NO ONE CAN HELP YE HERE! YOU'RE ALONE! YOU HEAR ME? ALONE! ALONE!'

— Twenty-two —

I

He's lifting me up.
Up … up …

II

'D-don't hurt me!'

'HURT YE! HURT YE! WHY, I'M NOT GOING TO HURT YE! JUST … TELL ME WHAT YE BE DOING HERE?'

'I … I … I was curious –'

'CURIOUS! WELL, DON'T BE CURIOUS! NOT ABOUT ME! IT'S DANGEROUS TO BE CURIOUS ABOUT ME! NOW … GET OUT! YE HEAR? GET OUT AND NEVER RETURN FOR AS LONG AS YE LIVE!'

III

Captain Jellicoe lets go of Milo's torn shirt and –

Thump!

– Milo hits the ground.

'GET OUT!'

IV

The Captain – he's picking up a piece of driftwood.
The Captain – he's picking up a hammer.
The Captain – he's picking up nails.
The Captain – he's going to the boat.
The Captain – he nails driftwood over the holes in the boat.

The Captain – he's got his back to me.

V

I should go! I know! Should! He don't want me here and … this is his cave. Not mine.

And he just scared me so much I nearly pooed me pants …

And yet …

VI

There are too many things Milo wants to know. His head is swimming with questions about the Captain: What's he hunting? What did it do to him? Does it live in the sea? Is that why he's building a boat?

Milo knows that, if he leaves, these questions will never be answered.

And so –

VII

'C-C-C-Captain …?'

'Shiver me timbers, ye still here? Ye be not wanted … Go!'

'But I … I wanna ask ya –'

'Don't anger me again, laddy. I've got a wicked temper. I can't control it any more than a wave can stop from splashing.'

VIII

Oh … what can I say?

Gotta make him change his mind, innit!

I've got it!

Might be dangerous but …

Oh, here goes …

IX

'MFC.'

— Twenty-three —

I

Captain Jellicoe drops his tools.

Nails scatter at his feet.

He turns to face Milo.

His face is pale, mouth open, lips quivering.

'M ... F ... C ...' Milo says again, his voice echoing round the cave.

'Ye ... Ye *know* about the terrible creature?' asks the Captain, stepping forward.

II

Slowly, Captain Jellicoe approaches Milo. 'Oh, laddy, what do ye know? Do you know where it be? Do ye know where I can find it? I'm an old man and I haven't got much time. You hear me, laddy? I refuse to die till I've slain that accursed monster! Tell me where to find it, I beg of ye!'

III

'D-dunno, Captain.'

'But ye just said –'

'I ... I just saw them letters. Written above me bed –'

'AHHH!' Captain Jellicoe clutches his skull, his scream echoing and re-echoing. 'How much longer can I be tormented like this? How much can my ancient bones bear? I get lifeboats of hope, only to have them spring a leak on the rocks of disillusion. I am in despair. DESPAAIIRRRHHHH!!!!!!!!!'

Look at him!
Tears streaming down his face.
Veins throbbing in his neck.
Dunno what to do except say –

'S-sorry.'

The Captain wipes tears from his face. 'Its not your fault, laddy! Ye don't know the whole story. The agonies I've suffered! And all because of that accursed ...' He shakes his head sadly and walks back to the driftwood boat. 'Just go, laddy! I be not fit for human company. Go back to ... why, if ye saw my harpoon-marks on the wall ye must be in Avalon Rise. Why, it must've been ye watching me yesterday. I could feel eyes burning into my skin. It *was* ye, wasn't it?'

'Er ... yeah.'

'Well ... just go. Go back there! Go on! It embarrasses me to weep in front of ye.'

'But ... but I wanna to know?'

'Know what?'

'About MFC. The creature!'

'The story is too horrible ...!' The old man shudders with fear and disgust. 'Nay, nay, I don't want to pollute ye innocent ears.'

'I ain't innocent.'

'Ye look it to me, laddy.'

'I ain't,' insists Milo, taking his straw hat off. 'See!'

The Captain's eyes grow wide.
Wider.

His mouth opens wide.
Wider.
'It … can't be!' he gasps 'Nay! Nay! It … can't … be … possible!'

VIII

Didn't think me Mohican was that bad!
Look at him!
He's falling to his knees now!
Kneeling in front of me.
Hands clasped tightly.
A whimpering sound at the back of his throat –

IX

'Is it ye, laddy? After all this time? Have I found ye at last?' He grabs Milo's hand and squeezes tight. 'Are ye the promised one? Are ye? Are ye?'

— Twenty-four —

I

'Don't … think so, innit.'

'But … ye hat! Aye! Aye! All that fits! And … ye hair! Aye! That too! Tell me ye age, laddy.'

'Th-thirteen!'

'Aye!' cries the old man. 'That could be it too! Five and eight makes thirteen! And ye hair! Aye! That surprised me. And this place … oh, laddy! Aye! All the signs point to it! Ye are the fulfilment of the ancient prophecy.'

'I … I dunno what ya jabbering about.'

'I'll show ye, laddy!'

II

The Captain's rushing to a chest – like a pirate treasure chest – and he's … he's taking out a small black box …

Oh, what's going on?

What's my hair got to do with anything?

Or my age?

Or this place?

Perhaps he is a weirdy-beardy after all.

The Captain – he's taken a piece of paper out of the black box.

The Captain – he's handing it to me.

'Read this, laddy!'

III

Where land doth end
and Sea doth rage
is one wHose age
be Five and eigHT.
WiTh a hat disguiSing
a HeAd surprisiNg
This PRomised One
wiLL the Heart LocaTe.

IV

'The writing ain't much cop,' remarks Milo. 'Looks like a monkey did it.'

'Ignore the *style*, laddy,' the Captain tells him. 'Look at the *content*! For it's why I'm here in this neck of the woods. Or should that be ... neck of the shore.'

'What d'ya mean?'

'That prophecy is part of my search for the accursed creature and – look! The first line!' He points at the piece of paper. 'It tells me to go "where land doth end".' And what's this place called, laddy?'

'Cornwall, innit.'

'What *part* of Cornwall?'

'Land's End.'

'Aye!' cries the Captain in triumph. 'Land's End! And read on – ye see? Here! I'll meet someone whose age is five and eight. And how old be ye, laddy?'

'Thirteen, innit!'

'Aye! Ye see? Five plus eight is thirteen! So ... oh, it must be ye – aye, *ye*, laddy – who will locate the

— 98 —

Legendary Floating Island of Heart! Oh, I know what some say: the Floating Island of Heart is a myth. Like Atlantis or the Loch Ness Monster. But it's not!' The Captain grasps Milo's arm and squeezes tight, his good eye blazing. 'It's real, laddy! For the Floating Island of Heart be the home of my monster!' He squeezes tighter, spitting as he talks. 'So tell me, laddy, I *beg* of ye! HOW CAN I LOCATE THE HEART?'

— Twenty-five —

I

'I ... I dunno!'

'Ye *must*, laddy!'

'Nah! Dunno anything! Ain't never heard of this ... Floating Island of Whatever! Ain't heard of anything! Honest!'

The Captain stares at Milo for a while, lips twitching, eye glaring, then says, slowly and thoughtfully, 'Listen very carefully, laddy. What I'm saying to ye might sound a little weird at first but, well, it may be possible ye *know* things without ... well, *knowing* ye know.'

'Wh-what d'ya mean?'

II

'Well, a Promised One don't always know they're the Promised One. It be like the Legend of King Arthur –'

'The painting in my room!'

'Aye, laddy! The very same! Ye see, King Arthur didn't *know* he was destined to be the King of England. He thought he was just a little boy like every other little boy. So you could –'

'I could know how to find the Floating Island without ... well, knowing I knew it.'

'Aye, laddy!'

III

Milo couldn't help tingling with excitement. Perhaps he *did* have some information, some clue, locked inside him and all he needed was to find the right key and everything would come tumbling out.

'What ... what I gotta do, innit?'

IV

'Don't rightly know, laddy,' sighs the Captain, twiddling with his beard thoughtfully. 'All I know is that ... in here –' he raps his knuckles on Milo's skull – 'could be the precious knowledge I be needing. It could be something ye have seen. Or heard.' Twiddling his beard again. 'Oh ... how to get it out!' He sits on a rock and bites into a bread roll. 'That's the problem, laddy! How ...? How ...? Oh, how ...?'

'I could ... tell ya things, innit.'

V

'About what, laddy?'

'About ... me.'

'What things about ye!'

'Dunno ... anything!'

'Anything? Nay, laddy, it'd be like searching for a tadpole in the Atlantic Ocean.' The Captain takes another bite of bread roll and munches. 'And, to be honest, I've neither the patience nor the inclination to listen to ye talk about a life that – compared to mine – will be as boring as counting shingle.'

'Boring!' gasps Milo. 'Don't ya call *my* life boring!'

'All right, laddy, all right! Don't get ye pants in twist!'

'And besides ... well, what choice we got? Eh? It's the only way. If I knew something without knowing ... well, I've gotta just talk about me, innit.'

'Ah, well ...' Munch, sigh, munch. 'If ye must ... Talk ye! Talk!'

VI

'Me – I'm Milo Kick!' begins Milo, speaking very fast and pacing round the cave. 'I was born on 24 March.'

'I be bored already,' murmurs the Captain. 'But … well, carry ye on! If there be no other way … carry on.'

'Mum's name is Felicity,' continues Milo, pacing faster and faster. 'Or Fliss! Yeah, Fliss! We've … we've lived in lots of places. First place in Dalston somewhere. That's in the East End of London. I was too young to remember that. Then we lived in this flat in Hackney. That's in the East End of London too.'

'Do ye remember that place, laddy?'

'Yeah! Two rooms. Walls had big cracks in. Played indoors most of the time cos Mum said the streets were too rough.'

VII

'Too … rough?'

'Yeah. Mum don't like me mixing with all the rough kids, ya see. One day, at school, this kid … well, he swore at me. A real naughty word. When I got back home I said it in front of Mum. Didn't mean to. Didn't even know what it meant. Mum went ballistic. She said, "Listen to you! A typical male. This place is turning you wild. We're moving!"'

VIII

'And did ye?'

'Yeah! Next few years we lived in this flat in Whitechapel. East London again. Mum liked it at first. But, one day, I fell over and came home with my clothes all scuffed up. Mum said, "Look at you! A typical male. This place is turning you wild. We're moving."'

IX

'I take it, laddy, ye mum don't care for typical males much.'

'Too right! Mum says, "Men are nasty pieces of work." She never likes me doing anything too ... oh, what's the word?' Milo scratches his shaven head in concentration. 'Macho! That's it! She won't even let me eat pizza with me fingers.'

'She won't *what*?'

'I have to use a knife and fork. If I pick a slice of pizza up with me fingers, Mum says, "Stop eating like a wild thing! Typical male! Macho!"'

'But, laddy, that's just ... well, it's unreasonable, laddy. Lots of people eat pizza with their fingers. It's not typically male or macho. *Girls* eat pizza with their fingers. *Old ladies* eat pizza with their fingers. *Everyone* eats –'

'I know, I know! But try telling Mum that. She just gets these ideas in her head and ... Oh, it does me head in.'

X

'But, laddy, have ye any idea what made ye mum so ... well, like this?'

'I've ... I've got an idea, yeah.'

'And what be it?'

'I think it's got something to do with me dad.'

'And what makes ye think that, laddy?'

'Well ... Mum never talks about him, innit. And if I even hint that I'm wondering about him she says, "He was a nasty piece of work. Typical male if ever there was one. Wipe him from your mind. Tippex him from history." And that's it. Nothing else. Except ...'

'Aye, laddy?'

XI

'Well, it's just that sometimes her eyes fill up with tears, innit. So I guess ... well, he must've hurt Mum in some way. And I don't wanna hurt Mum any more. So ... well, I don't tell her she's doing me head in or say, "Everyone eats pizza with their fingers!" I just pick up my knife and fork and eat.' Milo sighs and looks very thoughtful for a moment, then murmers, 'I never did anything to upset Mum until ... until ...'

'Until?'

'Well, last year we moved to the Oasis.'

'The Oasis?'

XII

'It's what the flat where we live now is called,' explains Milo. 'Well, it's two flats knocked into one really. A hostel sort of place. For women who ... well, who want to get away from men who treat 'em bad. It's on an estate called Ocean. It's in Bethnal Green.'

'That in the East End of London too?'

'Yeah.'

'So ... how many of you be living at this Oasis, laddy?'

'Me, Mum, two other mums. And three daughters. All the daughters belong to the other mums. The daughters call my mum "Mum" and I call their mums "Mum". And all the mums call each other "Mum". It's a house of Mums and Daughters, innit?'

XIII

'And you ... be the only boy?'

'Yeah ... Any clues yet, Captain?'

XIV

'Nay, not yet. But I tell ye this much ... it's beginning to get a little bit less boring. And, I beg ye, sit down. Ye be making me dizzy with all ye walking about … That's better! Now, tell me about ye life in this … Oasis. There might be some clue to be found there.'

XV

'Well …' Milo takes a deep breath, then continues, 'I used to help Mum get breakfast ready. I used to like Cocoa Pops. You tried them? It's spectacular the way the milk turns brown. Mum eats that muesli stuff – Any clues yet?'

'Nay, laddy. Carry on.'

XVI

'Sarah and Jackie – they're the two younger girls that live with us. They're eight years old. They like peanut butter and jam on toast for breakfast. Ugh – Any clues yet?'

'Nay, laddy. Carry on.'

XVII

'Well … I go to Oaklands School. So does Trixie. My favourite subjects are sport and –'

'Wait, laddy! Who's this Trixie?'

'She's the other girl who lives with us. She's two years older than me. And, if ya want my opinion, she's a total waste of space.'

'Why, laddy?'

XVIII

'Trixie's got all this curly hair and she … she's always flicking it and giggling and – oh, let's forget about her.'

'But surely, laddy, just because a lassy flicks her hair and giggles, that's no reason to –'

'I don't wanna talk about it!'

Fizzzy Waspzzz

'Ye sure ye are not being a bit unfair –'

Fizzzzzy Waspzzzzz

'– to the lassy?'

XIX

'SHUT IT, CAPTAIN! I DON'T WANNA TALK ABOUT TRIXIE! YA HEAR? I DON'T WANNA HEAR HER STUPID NAME MENTIONED EVER AGAIN!'

— Twenty-six —

I

'Why, laddy,' says the Captain after a moment's silence, 'that be a mighty ferocious temper ye have there.'

'I ... I ... yeah, I know.'

'Ye know I didn't mean to annoy –'

'I know, I know. I'm ... I'm sorry, Captain.'

Milo takes a few deep breaths –

Calm

Calm

Bzz

Calm

II

'I'm OK now, Captain.'

'Then ... do ye feel ready enough to continue telling me things about ye?'

'Yeah.'

'I be all ears, laddy.'

III

'Well ... I used to help Mum with washing. Ya know? Clothes 'n' stuff. We used to put it all in a big pram and take it down the Big Launderette. There's two, ya see. The Small and the Big. We need the Big. We have lots of dirty clothes. Most of it's girls' stuff, of course – Any clues yet!'

'Nay, laddy. Carry on.'

IV

'Well ... I used to play indoors most of the time. With the girls. Sarah and Jackie, that is. They've got lots of toys. Sarah used to practise haidressing on me. That's when I used to have more hair – Any clues yet?'

'Nay, laddy. But ye keep saying "used to"! Things be different now, eh?'

V

'Well ... yeah. I ... I changed.'

VI

'*Changed*, laddy? How do ye mean?'

Milo scuffs his feet over the sand and pebbles 'Mum – she always said I was her little angel, ya see.'

'Well, ye were by the sounds of it, laddy. Helping ye mum getting the breakfast ready. Going to the Big Launderette with ye mum. Letting Sarah practise hairdressing on ye. Why, if that be not pure angelic, I don't know what it is.'

'Well ... I didn't wanna upset Mum, did I?'

'Obviously not, laddy.'

'But ... one day ...'

'Mmm, laddy?'

'One day people on Ocean Estate started talking about someone. All you'd hear was, "He's back! He's back!"'

VII

'Who, laddy?'

'I didn't know at first. But whoever he was ... well, he was causing a lot of excitement. I asked around. It was somebody who'd been in a sort of prison for a while.'

'A ... *sort* of prison?'

'Not a prison for grown-ups. A prison for kids. He was fifteen years old. He'd been causing trouble – fighting and stuff. And so they'd put him … in a secure unit! That's it! Secure unit! But now … he was out. And his name was …'

'Aye, laddy?'

'Mojo.'

VIII

'Go on, laddy.'

'Well … one day I looked out of me bedroom window and I saw this spectacular bloke. He was wearing this sleeveless T-shirt. There were tatoos all over his arms. And his hair was cut short and had shaven lines going through it. And he had a ring going through his eyebrow. Ya know? A pierced thing. And … HE WAS EATING PIZZA WITH HIS FINGERS!'

IX

'Go on, laddy.'

'Well … Mum saw me looking at him and said, "That Mojo is a nasty piece of work. Stay away! Stay away!"'

'But … ye didn't, eh?'

'Well …'

'What happened, laddy?'

'It don't matter.'

'It does, laddy.'

Fizzzy Waspzzzzzz

X

'Don't wanna talk about it, Captain.'

Fizzzzzzyyy Waspzzzzzz

'But it might hold a clue, laddy.'

'It won't!'

'It might!'

Fizzzzzzzzzzzzzyyyy Waspzzzzzz

'NAH!'

'AYE!'

BZZZZZZZZZZZZZZZZZZZZZZZZZZZ –

XI

'DON'T PUSH ME, CAPTAIN! I DON'T WANNA TALK ABOUT MOJO! YA HEAR?' Milo kicks a piece of driftwood. 'DON'T CARE IF YOU NEVER FIND YOUR SILLY FLOATING ISLAND! I'M NOT SAYING ANOTHER WORD. HEAR ME! NOT ONE MORE WORD!'

— Twenty-seven —

I

The Captain twiddles his beard in silence for a while.
Milo clenches his fists in silence for a while.
'Temper, temper,' says the Captain.
'Yeah, yeah,' says Milo.
Calm!
Calm!

II

'Perhaps … I can help things along,' says the Captain gently,
sitting opposite Milo. 'Ye see, there be three ways it's
possible to find the Floating Island of Heart. If I mention
them to ye, laddy, it might strike a chord somewhere in ye.
Do ye mind if I attempt this, laddy?'
'… Humpff!' Milo turns his back to the Captain.

III

'Thank ye, laddy.' The Captain takes a deep breath and
begins. 'One: a dog with peacock feathers for a tail and the
tongue of a lizard will be able to sniff the island out
anywhere in the world if you feed it seven peppermints and
whisper in its left ear, "Take me to the Heart, ye old sea
dog."' He leans forward and taps Milo's knee. 'Have ye ever
seen such a dog, laddy?'
'… Nah,' Milo glances over his shoulder at the Captain.

IV

'Two: a plant with leaves the colour of bread-crust and flowers the shape of seagull heads turns in the direction of the Floating Island of Heart, thus acting like a botanical compass.' Again he taps Milo's knee. 'Have you ever seen such a plant, laddy?'

'Nah.' Milo turns to face the Captain.

V

'Three!' continues the Captain. 'And, I fear, this is the least likely of all, laddy. Many years ago a man stumbled on the Floating Island by accident. While he was on the island he chopped down a tree. Now, this man was a carpenter, laddy, and he made five objects out of the tree's wood. If any of these objects can be found it will be possible to locate the island.'

'But … how?' Milo leans forward, captivated.

VI

'Because if any of these objects are burnt, laddy, the smoke will always travel in the direction of the Floating Island of Heart. Thus becoming a … well, a smoke compass. Now, tell me, have you seen any of these Floating Island of Heart wood objects: a walking stick shaped like a crocodile that squeals "Shiver me timbers!" every time it touches the floor. Ye seen that, laddy?'

'Nah! Go on though! What're the others?'

VII

'A chair with eight legs, shaped like an octopus, and that sings "Ave Maria" whenever you eat haddock while sitting in it.'

'Nah, Captain.'

VIII

'A clock shaped like an ostrich egg with no numbers on its face and that chimes thirteen times once every seven years?'
    'Nah, Captain.'

IX

'A doll with the head of an eagle and the legs of a frog and which cries "Dadda!" whenever you turn it upside down?'
    'Nah, Captain.'

X

'A phoenix that has a secret chamber in –'
    'In its chest!' gasps Milo, jumping to his feet. The Phoenix of Secrets! I've seen it! Cap … I've *touched* it!
    'Where, laddy? Where?'
    'In Cressida's room!'

XI

'Laddy!' cries the Captain, jumping to his feet also. 'Ye be my Promised One! Oh, I'm really too excited to … oh, I can't breathe! Can't think! To think I was in that magnificent woman's bedroom and never noticed the Phoenix, but … oh, nay, I wouldn't've done. Only the Promised One would notice it! The Promised One has to fulfil the prophecy, ye see, no matter what I try to say or do. And now … oh, the end of my journey is nigh! You, Promised One!' And, with that, he points at Milo. 'Get me that Phoenix!'

XII

'I will, Captain! The Phoenix … well, it was a present from my mum to Cressie so she –'
    'A present! Oh, laddy! Cressida will never give it to ye! Not for me to burn!'
    'She will, Captain! Cressida – she really likes ya, innit.'
    'Ye … think so, laddy.'

'I *know* so, Captain. She told me thinking of ya made her swoon.'

'Swoon!' gasps the Captain. 'Well, it surely warms the cockles of my heart to hear that. She be a mighty fine beast of a woman and no mistake. Aye, she can bring my kettle to the boil any time.' For a moment his eye glazes with kettle-boiling thoughts. Then, abruptly, he snaps out of it and exclaims, 'Get ye gone, laddy! I need that Phoenix. Now!'

'I will …!' Milo grabs hold of the Captain's arm. 'On one condition.'

'Oh? And what might that be?'

'Tell me the story of MFC.'

XIII

'Nay, laddy.' The Captain shakes his head. 'The story is far too … strange.'

'Then … see ya!' Milo goes to leave the cave.

'Wait, laddy! Wait!'

'No story! No Phoenix!'

'But, laddy, I'm refusing to tell ye for ye own good. The story is so bizarre – the adventure of it so unpredictable – that it might make ye question the very ground ye walk on. Why, braver men than ye have had their hair turn white and their teeth curl at the sheer horrific nastiness of it all.'

'See ya!'

XIV

'Wait, laddy! Wait! WAIT!' The Captain scratches his head in frantic thought. Then he sighs deeply and says, 'So be it, laddy. Bring me the Phoenix and I … I will turn ye hair white and curl ye teeth.'

'Is it a deal?' Milo holds his hands out.

'Aye, laddy,' says the Captain, shaking his hand. 'It be a deal!'

— Twenty-eight —

I

'Just in time, Milo Kick.'

'Wha ... what?'

'It's one o'clock.' Dee indicates the clock behind the counter. 'I was just about to strike the gong. Like this –'

Gonnnngggg!

II

'Lunch, innit!'

'Yours is on the table. A nourishing bowl of chowder. Do you know what chowder is?'

'Er ... nah.'

'The dictionary definition is "a stew or soup of fresh fish or clams with bacon and onions. Well, I've replaced the bacon with peas, but it's a chowder nonetheless. There's some wholemeal bread and –'

'This must be Cressida's tray!' says Milo, picking it up. 'I'll take it up.'

Gotta explain things to Cressida and get the Phoenix and take it to the Captain so he can tell me all about MFC –

III

'Milo Kick!' cries Dee, stamping her foot. 'Is my company so offensive? Do you dislike me so much you can't even face eating chowder with me? Don't you think you're being a bit ... unfeeling? Or perhaps you think *I've* got no feelings? Is that it? I'm just ... Robot-Woman!'

IV

I … I've been out of order, innit!
So eager to get the Phoenix I didn't think about …
Oh, I just didn't think …
Thoughtless, that's me!

V

'I'm … I'm sorry, Dee!' Milo puts the tray on the table. 'Let's have lunch! It smells spectacular!'

'Well … if that means "nourishing" then I assure you it is.'

Milo sits down and puts a spoonful of chowder in his mouth. 'Mmmm … spectacular – yum!' Another mouthful. 'What did you get up to this morning, Dee? Tell me.'

Slowly, Dee takes her place at the table. 'Oh … housework! Then cooking! Then … well, I had to keep watch at the window.'

'Why?'

'That weirdy-beardy of a Captain, of course. With the drawbridge down, this place is vulnerable.' She dips some bread into the creamy fish-dish. 'That particular male of the species is devious through and through.' She shoots Milo a frosty look. 'You didn't see any sign of him on the beach, did you?'

'Er … nah.'

'So what *did* you see? You were down there all morning.'

'I saw … stones hanging from ceiling. Like icicles made out of rock.'

VI

'Stalactites!' exclaims Dee with delight. 'Oh, yes, they are most fascinating. And it's interesting you describe them as icicles because that's exactly what they are. Made from the deposits of calcite in dripping water – Do you know what calcite is, Milo Kick?'

'Er … nah.'

'Then you must *ask*. Always ask! Otherwise you'll never learn.' She coughs to clear her throat. Then explains, 'Calcite is crystallized calcium carbonate. The longest stalactite is six point two metres – that's twenty point four feet – and it's to be found in County Clare.'

'Where's that?'

'Ireland, Milo Kick,' she replies. Then adds with a sparkle in her eye, 'Good boy for asking.'

'I saw rock growing up from the ground too!'

VII

'Stalagmites!' exclaims Dee. 'Again, most interesting. They're made drip by drip as water falls from the roof and hits the ground. Like stalactites, it can take several thousand years for one to grow. The tallest stalagmite is thirty-two metres – that's one hundred and five feet – high and can be found in a cave in the Czech Republic. A cave!' She stops suddenly and glares at Milo. 'Cave!' she says again, slowly and deliberately. 'Were you in a cave, Milo Kick? Did you go to Captain Jellicoe's cave? Despite all my warnings? Did you? Answer me!'

'Er … as if I'd do that, eh?'

'Is that froth or fact?'

'Er … yeah.' Milo gets to his feet, still avoiding a straight answer. 'I've finished now, Dee,' he says, picking up Cressida's tray. 'Can I take this?'

Dee stares at him suspiciously.

'Well? Can I?' he asks again.

'As you wish,' she replies curtly.

Milo dashes to door, then hesitates. He turns and, smiling, says, 'I enjoyed having lunch with you, Dee. Honest. I learnt lots of facts.'

'Milo Kick!' Dee blushes with pleasure. 'That's the most gratifying thing you could ever say to me.'

VIII

Don't like misleading Dee like that!
  But ... oh, what can I do?
  She'll stop me seeing Captain Jellicoe.
  And I can't stop seeing him.
  There's too many things I have to ask –
  Ahh! Cressida's room.
Knock!
Knock!

IX

'Who is it?'
  'Me, innit.'
  'Oh, Beloved! Enter, enter!'

X

'Brought your lunch, innit!'
  'What joy!' Sniff, sniff. 'Chowder! Quite divine! Although I bet that lying harpy downstairs has poisoned mine!' She smooths the eiderdown in front of her. 'On my lap as usual, if you please.'
  Milo puts the tray where requested, then unfolds the napkin and lays it across Cressida's chest, saying, 'So much to tell you! Honest! Lots!'
  'Well, goodness, Beloved. I'm all ears!'
  'I followed the Captain!'

XI

Cressida nearly chokes on a slither of cod. 'You ... *what*?'
  'Ya ... ya don't mind, do ya?' asks Milo.
  'Mind? No! I'm ... oh, I'm *thrilled*! Oh, Beloved, tell me what happened.'

'I … I dunno where to begin, innit.'

'At the beginning, Beloved, I usually find that's best.'

'Well, I went downstairs with the food parcel …' begins Milo.

XII

'… and that's why he needs this!' finishes Milo, grabbing the Phoenix.

'I'm speechless, Beloved,' breathes Cressida. 'And, as Dee will tell you, that's a rare occurrence. My head is spinning with … oh, Floating Islands and monstrous creatures – oh, we still don't know what MFC is exactly, do we?'

'Nah! But we *will* know! That's part of the deal! He'll tell me the story and I'll give him the Phoenix of Secrets to burn it and he'll –'

'Burn!' gasps Cressida. 'You … you missed *that* bit out, Beloved.'

'Oh … did I?'

'He wants to *burn* … my beautiful object.'

'He *has* to! The smoke – it'll travel in the direction of the Floating Island of Heart.'

'But … oh, Beloved! You know how special the Phoenix is to me. A gift. From your mum. My little Fliss. She chose it with her own little hands. Paid for it with her own pocket money. It meant so much to her. Have you forgotten everything I told you this morning?'

'Nah, but –'

'I think you *must* have, Beloved. Why, it's the only excuse you could have for possibly suggesting I allow the Captain to … to burn –' Cressida snatches the Phoenix from Milo and clutches it to her chest. 'Didn't my story of your mum mean *anything* to you at all?

'Yeah, but –'

'I'm sure it couldn't have, Beloved. My story has paled into insignificance compared to the Captain's. But my story is about your mum, Beloved. Your own flesh and blood! Your mum gave me this Phoenix as a gift and wrote me a letter – the letter! I wanted you to read it! Remember? But … oh, I'm sure you're not bothered to read a letter from your very own mum. Not now the Captain's story has taken over your brain –'

'Nah! Nah! I wanna read it! Please! It was over here you said – Here it is! On lavender paper. Please can I read it?'

'Well …'

'Pretty pleeaasse.'

XIV

'Very well, Beloved. You've twisted my arm. Read your mum's letter. And if ... well, after reading it, you still think the Phoenix should be sacrificed to the Captain's quest, then ... well, I will be guided by you. Deal?'

'Deal!'

— Twenty-nine —

I

My Dearest Cressie,

            This is the first letter I've ever written so it might not be very good.

But I've always kept a diary so, I suppose letter writing is very similar. Except ... well, you're going to read it, dearest Cressie.

I've tried to choose my words carefully, like you always told me.

And my first carefully chosen word is 'sorry'.

Sorry it's taken me so long to write. Yes, I know I could've phoned but I was afraid. That's right. Afraid that, if I heard your voice, I might start crying all over again and, this time, never stop.

I miss you so much, Cressie. The day Dad and me left you and Avalon Rise was the saddest day of my life. Whenever I close my eyes I see you standing on the drawbridge and waving. You were calling out my name. I called back, 'I love you!'

I hope you heard me ...

'Did you?' asks Milo.
'No! Carry on, Beloved.'

II

We nearly missed the train because Dad had to stop at an off-licence and get a bottle of whiskey. I told him, 'You drink too much.' And he said, 'That woman has given you too many opinions.' That woman, of course, was you. I felt like saying,

— 122 —

'Yes! Cressie has given me opinions. And they've changed my life.
I look different. And I think different.' But I kept quiet and made
sure Dad and me caught the train.

By the time the ticket collector came around Dad was
sprawled across two seats and snoring. Spit was drooling down
his chin and he had a half cheese 'n' pickle sandwich stuck to
his shirt. The ticket collector thought he was a tramp and was
going to throw him off. I had to say, 'No, it's my dad.'

The ticket master shook his head and said, 'Well, if you need
anything, little miss, you just let me know.' And, oh, I felt so
ashamed, Cressie. I wanted to jump off the train at the next
stop and run all the way back to you ...

'She should've done, innit.'
'Don't stop reading, Beloved.'

III

We travelled all night. Cressie, I didn't sleep a wink. And the
wheels of the train made a steady rhythmic noise. And the more I
listened, the more it sounded like, 'Cressida Bell, Cressida Bell.' Yes,
Cressie! Over and over again the train was singing me a lullaby
of your name ...

'That's spectacular!'
'Keep reading.'

IV

We arrived in Manchester Station early the next morning. We took
a taxi to our lodgings – or 'digs' as Dad calls them – and settled
into our room. The house was run by a landlady called Mrs
Bunnage. She was friendly enough, but, oh, not at all like you! She
didn't bat an eyelid when Dad bossed me around. It was up to me
to put a stop to that. I said to Dad, 'I don't mind helping you,
but I am not your servant! And, what's more, I'm not going to
sleep in the bathtub any more!'

You should've seen Dad's face, Cressie. He was like a rabbit caught in car headlights ...

'What's that mean?'
'Well, Beloved, a rabbit gets so dazzled by the brilliant light that ... well, it can't move. It's frozen. Bedazzled!'
'So Checker didn't get angry at all?'
'Read on and find out.'

V

Of course, Dad blustered and moaned a bit but, he didn't shout as you'd expect. I think, in a way, I'd scared him. So, that night, I helped Dad with his lines for the pantomime – I quite enjoy that anyway – but everything else (like cleaning shoes and ironing clothes) he had to do himself ...

'What *is* a pantomime exactly, Cressie? I'm not sure.'
'Why, Beloved, haven't you ever seen a pantomime?'
'Er ... nah!'
'Well, it's a theatrical entertainment, usually put on at Christmas. Full of sparkly scenery and dancing and ... oh, they're such fun! A lot of actors and comedians – like Checker Kick – do them during the winter.'
'Is it winter ...?' ponders Milo, peering at the letter. 'I thought Mum left you at the end of the summer season. Where's autumn got to?'
'Rehearsals, Beloved!' explains Cressida. 'Checker is there to start rehearsals. Five weeks, if he's lucky. And then he'll open in ... oh, what was the pantomime he was doing? Read on, Beloved! Read on!'

VI

The next day, Dad took me to the theatre where the pantomime was going to be performed. It's called the Royal Exchange Theatre. Very big and grand. Gold cherubs on the ceiling. Velvet curtains on the stage (red with gold tassels). I sat in the Green Room while Dad rehearsed ...

'What's the Green Room?'
'A place where actors relax, Beloved. So called because green is thought to be the most relaxing colour.'
'We still don't know the name of the pantomime?'
'You better keep reading then.'

VII

I didn't mind waiting in the Green Room. Not one little bit. I did all those things you taught me, Cressie: I drew in my sketchbook, practised my watercolours, read poetry and novels. Oh, I was never bored, Cressie. Not for one second. And that's all thanks to you.

And then ... oh, you'll never guess what happened, Cressie? The Wardrobe Mistress - her name's Mrs Lindy - saw my drawings and said, 'Why, what an artistic little thing you are! You can help me with the costumes backstage if you think you'd find it interesting.'

Interesting! What an understatement! I jumped at the chance. Imagine this, Cressie: me surrounded by costumes for rabbits and deer and, of course, the costumes for Hansel and ...

'Gretel!' Cressida claps her hands. 'That's the pantomime! *Hansel and Gretel!* One of my favourites. Those poor children. Lost in a forest. And a house made of gingerbread. And the witch ... oh read on, Beloved. Read on!'

VIII

I was sitting in the costume department, chatting with Mrs Lindy, when the Witch walked in. Oh, what a costume, Cressie! Being a pantomime, it's not your typical witch outfit. Mrs Lindy told me she wanted it to look like something out of an old

— 125 —

Hollywood movie: long black dress covered in sequins, long black gloves, masses of sparkling jewellery (all fake, of course). The witch also had a mass of auburn hair, long eyelashes, bright-red lips and ... a moustache!

'Moustache, innit?'

'It's a pantomime tradition, Beloved. Some of the male parts – like Peter Pan or Dick Whittington – are played by women. And some of the female parts – like the Ugly Sisters and Widow Twanky – are played by men. The actor playing the witch in this pantomime is called – oh, it's such an enchanting name – Valentino True.'

— Thirty —

I

I liked Valentino True instantly. We sat in that costume department for hours (his wig needed a bit of styling) and he told me all about himself. He's a bit older than my dad – he won't tell me exactly (vanity, eh?) – and loves Shakespeare. It's his ambition to play King Lear. Anyway, to cut a long story short, Valentino and Dad became good friends ...

'But Valentino True seems ... well, a nice guy.'
'He is, Beloved. But, unfortunately, he is also very weak. Easily swayed by people. And I'm afraid he succumbs to the bullying influence of Checker and –'
'Don't tell me! I'll read it!'

II

Before long they decided to form a double act! Kick 'n' True! That's what they're going to call themselves. Poor Valentino is straight man to Dad's joker. Of course, Dad thinks they're going to become huge stars. Can you imagine it? The Kick 'n' True show. Thirty minutes of Dad insulting every member of the audience and cracking jokes (so-called) about farts and bogies and smelly armpits. Yuk! I shudder at the thought. Poor Valentino. He doesn't know what he's got himself into.

But now for the good news!

At least ... I hope you think so!

Kick 'n' True have already got their summer season booked. And guess where? The pier near you! I was so thrilled when I heard. So was Dad because ... well, you can guess what he said, can't you? 'Ask that friend of yours if we can have a room for nothing again. Tell her you'll work for her like last year.'

Oh, Cressie, I feel *terrible* asking. Really I do. And I know there'll be three of us this year, not two. But ... oh, it *does* mean we can spend the whole summer together again.

And I *will* work for you! Honest! I'll do any job you want me to do at Avalon Rise. I've had a lot of practice at Mrs Bunnage's. I'm a dab hand at washing up and making tea, and poached eggs are my speciality.

Please say 'yes', Cressie!

I love you.

Your Fliss

'You said, "Yes", didn't ya!'

'Don't jump ahead, Beloved.'

'But I wanna know –'

'All in good time. Read the P.S.'

III

P.S. Saw this wooden Phoenix in a shop window. The shopkeeper told me it's a symbol of being born again. And I thought, if I stay at Avalon Rise once more, that's what will happen to our friendship. It will be born again! Oh, how I want that! How I need that!

P.P.S. Don't worry about how much it cost. Mrs Bunnage and Mrs Lindy gave me pocket money for helping them. And I would gladly spend every penny on my Cressie!

'Now ... you see, Beloved? What a very special gift the Phoenix is is? A symbol of friendship "born again". Your mum had such a gift for words – Oh, look at me! Brimming with tears.' She pats tears from her cheek, then grabs Milo's arms. 'Tell me, Beloved! Knowing what this Phoenix means to me – and to your mum – is it still worth burning to help the Captain? Is it? Is it?'

IV

The Captain needs it to burn so he can find the creature –
  But Cressie will be upset if he burns it because it's a gift –
  But the Captain's been searching for years and years –
  But Mum will be upset too because –
  But the Captain will be upset too –
  And it's the Captain's only chance.
  And I've got to help him!
  I'm his Promised One.
  I've got no choice.
  I've got to!
  Got to!

V

'Yeah!' Milo grabs the Phoenix. 'It's worth it!'

— Thirty-one —

I

'So be it!' breathes Cressida. 'Sometimes a sacrifice has to be made to help others. Now all I've got to do is ... unlock it.'

'Whaa ...?'

'The Phoenix's secret compartment, Beloved. I've put something very precious in it and – No, no, Beloved! Don't shake it. The thing inside the chest is very fragile. Oh, where did I put the key?' She points to the drawer in the bedside cabinet. 'Have a look in there, Beloved.'

'Right away.'

'Is it there, Beloved?'

'Er ... nah, Cressie.'

II

'Look on the window ledge.'

'... Nah, Cressie.'

III

'On the shelf?'

'... Nah, Cressie.'

IV

'On the other shelf?'

'... Nah, Cressie.'

V

'Oh, where is it? I can't let you burn the Phoenix with the precious thing still inside! Goodness, I was only cleaning it a few days ago.'

'*Where* did you clean it? Cressie?'

'It … it wasn't in this room.'

'The dining room?'

'… No.'

'The hallway?'

'No. It was … oh, yes! I remember now!'

'Where?'

'Dee's room! I was sitting on her bed, chatting away, and dusting the Phoenix. Silly me! I must have locked the chest and – That's it! Oh, yes, it all comes flooding back now. The phone rang! It was your mum, Beloved! Asking if you could stay. And I said, "Fliss, my dear girl, how strange you should ring because I was just cleaning your Phoen –"

VI

'Gotta ask her, innit!'

'Wh-who?'

'Dee! Ask her to search her room for the key.'

'Oh … well, yes, of course.'

'See ya, Cressie.'

'Oh … so quick, Beloved?'

'No time to lose, Cressie. The Captain needs that Phoenix. And he can't have it till you've taken your precious thing out. And you can't do that till you've found the key. So – see ya!'

'Wait, Beloved! Listen! It's probably best *not* to mention *why* you want the key. Just say … well, I'm giving the Phoenix of Secrets to you. That's all. If Dee finds out it's for the Captain … well, I shudder to think! And tell Dee the chowder was … scrumptious!'

— Thirty-two —

I

'The *key*,' ponders Dee, putting the dirty plates into the sink. 'Can't say I've noticed it.' She glances at Milo. 'Of course I'll look. But you'll have to wait though. I've got to wash up the lunch things first.'

'I can't wait – I can't! I CAN'T!'

Fizzzy Wasspzzz ...

'Losing your temper will gain you nothing!'

'... OK, OK!' Milo takes a few deep breaths to calm down, then asks, 'Where's the tea towel? I'll dry the plates.'

II

'Cressida Bell's always misplacing things,' complains Dee, leading Milo down the corridor to her room. 'She'd forget her dentures if they weren't super-glued to her gums. Oh, don't laugh. It's true! I spend all my days cleaning up after that temperamental doughnut. And do I get one word of appreciation? Fact: I don't!'

'You do! She told me to tell you the chowder was ... oh, what was the word? Scrumptious! That's it! Scrumptious!'

'Really?' Dee can't help a slight smile of satisfaction. 'Well, that's something, I suppose. Perhaps I'll cook the old mammoth something special for dinner. Things do get lonely without her frothing all over the place – Don't tell her I said that!' She opens the door to her room. 'In you go, Milo Kick.'

III

Test-tubes, innit!
   Charts on wall, innit!
   Telescopes, innit!
   Microscopes, innit!
   Everything so neat and clean and scientific.
   Just like –

IV

'A laboratory, innit.'

'Hardly, I'm afraid. But I've tried to make my living space as factually investigative as possible. No, no, don't touch anything, Milo Kick. You'll contaminate!'

'How we gonna find the key then?'

'*We* are not going to find it! *I* am going to find it. You can watch!'

'But –'

'This is *my* room! We do it *my* way. Or we don't do it at all.'

'... OK, OK.'

'And don't sit on the bed. I hate creased sheets.'

V

Me – standing in the middle of room.
   Dee – running her hands over bed.
   Me – thinking about Captain Jellicoe and Fliss and a Floating Island of Heart and Valentino True and the Phoenix of Secrets – so many stories spinning in me head. Like surfing all the channels on telly and –

VI

'Most of this equipment belonged to the Professor,' Dee informs him, getting to her knees and looking under the bed. 'That's what I called my male parent.'

'Ya mean your dad, innit?'

'Correct, Milo Kick. He was a scientist. The cleverest and most fact-hungry male of the species I've ever come into contact with. He wouldn't tolerate any froth whatsoever. Not one single bubble. It was the Professor who named me, you know.'

'Just … just keep searching, Dee. Please.'

'I'm perfectly capable of searching *and* talking, Milo Kick. The key is not *on* the bed. I am now searching *under* it. Satisfied?'

'Yeah. Sorry.'

'So do you want to know why the Professor called me Dee Dee Six or not, Milo Kick? Of course, if you have *no* interest in me whatsoever I'll just shut up and –'

'Nah, nah! Tell me if ya like. Go on.'

VII

'Because,' Dee explains, groping under the bed, 'after I was born, I was put in cot D, ward D, on the sixth floor of the hospital. Hence: DD6. A perfectly functional naming process. Certainly better than calling me Kylie or Britney.' She shoots Milo a quizzical look. 'Can you imagine calling me Kylie or Britney?'

'Nah,' chuckles Milo.

'I should hope not. The Professor called me Dee Dee Six and my brother Jay Dee Six because … well, bed J, obviously.'

'Didn't know ya had a brother, Dee.'

'Why should you? Not telepathic, are you? Not that I believe in telepathy, of course. Totally unscientific.'

'Is your brov older or younger?'

'He's seven seconds older.'

'Don't ya mean seven *years*?'

'No, Milo Kick, I mean *seconds*. Kindly refrain from telling me what I do and do not mean.' She gets to her feet and brushes dust from her hands. 'My brother and I are twins.'

VIII

'Twins!' gasps Milo. 'Ya mean ... your brov looks exactly like you.'

'Not *exactly*, no. We are similar.'

'Like fried eggs?'

'Fried eggs?'

'Ya said ya can't fry me eggs exactly the same as before, but you'll do them in a –'

'Similar fashion. Exactly, Milo Kick. An excellent comparison. Well done. Jay and I were indeed like similar fried eggs. Although, having said that, when we were growing up lots of people often mistook us.'

'Bet your mum didn't.'

'My female parent did not survive my birth.' Dee gets to her knees and starts running her hands over the carpet.

'Ya mean ... she copped it?'

'If that's what "not surviving" means in your rather bizarre vocabulary then, yes, she ... copped it. The Professor's tear ducts produced an enormous amount of salt water. But not for long. After all, he was a scientist. And you can't discover facts with your eyes full of saline H_2O. So he worked! All day. Every day! Move your feet, please.'

'Oh ... sorry.'

IX

'My childhood was full of endless "Eurekas!"' continues Dee. 'That's what scientists cry when they discover something. It means "I have found it!" When Archimedes discovered how a ship floats – "Eureka!" When Newton discovered gravity – "Eureka!"' Dee gives Milo a knowing smile. 'Of course, my discoveries weren't quite of that magnitude. The Professor was merely interested in the basic facts: qualitative analysis, quantitative analysis, flame tests for identifying metals, the principles of DNA, electrochemistry ... Why are you frowning, Milo Kick?'

'I ... ain't heard of any of that stuff, innit.'

'Most people haven't,' retorts Dee with a sniff. 'Their minds are too bubbly with froth. But it was the *facts* the Professor needed his children have. After all, he was training us to be his assistants – Move your feet!'

'Sorry, sorry.'

X

'The Professor was writing a book, you see,' Dee continues, searching behind a filing cabinet. 'It was called *A Manual for a Factual Understanding of Life Without Resorting to the Silliness of Froth*. The Profesor started writing it two days after Jay Dee Six and myself were born. Naturally, when we were baby male and female of the species he only managed a few pages a week. But as we got older, and we learnt to feed and wash ourselves, then the Professor could dedicate more time to his masterpiece.'

'And ... he trained ya to be his assistants?'

'Correct, Milo Kick. We travelled the country, collecting data and carrying out experiments in the Labmobile – Feet! Feet!'

'Sorry. What's the Labmobile, Dee?'

XI

'It's where we lived. A caravan the Professor had turned into a mobile laboratory. Most of the equipment you see in this room comes from the Labmobile. Jay Dee Six and I used to sleep in bunk beds. Him on top, me on bottom. We used to cook our food in a Bunsen burner flame and drink from test tubes. Every night the Professor would read us Michael Faraday's Laws of Electrolysis or William Thomson's Laws of Thermodynamics – Don't tell me. You haven't heard of them either?'

'Er ... nah.'

'Well, you don't know what you're missing.

Sometimes, even now, over fifty-five years later, I can still hear the Professor's voice when I lie in bed and – Oh, they were such happy days. I mean that in an unfrothy way, of course. There's a photo of us. There. On the wall. See?'

XII

It's black and white. Corners all yellowed and crinkly. A caravan parked in a ... a forest. Yeah! Trees 'n' bushes. And there – a man! He's wearing a white coat like a doctor. Look at his hair! Cut like Dee's is now. And – there! Standing in front of him! Two kids. They're both wearing white doctor coats too. And they've both got black hair cut the same as him. One is holding a test tube. The other a clipboard.

XIII

'Which one's you, Dee?'

'Oh, surely you can tell ... No, perhaps not. We're fourteen years old there and, up until that time, we were very much alike to the untrained eye.' She gazes at the photo and sighs. 'We're in Sherwood Forest. Studying the hibernation patterns of certain woodland animals. It is late autumn. If the photograph was in colour you'd see the trees were undergoing a chemical change.'

'Turning red, ya mean?'

'Correct.' Dee sighs again and points at the child holding the test tube. 'That's Jay Dee Six. It was soon after this photograph was taken that he started to ... well, metamorphose.'

'Meta-what?'

'To *change*, Milo Kick! *Change!*'

— Thirty-three —

I

'Change? How, Dee?'

'Oh, you don't want to know.'

'I do. I do.'

'But ... what about finding the key?'

'Tell me how he changed first.'

'Well ... the first sign I got was early one morning,' Dee tells him. 'We were taking some samples from a pond. I glanced up at Jay and he was looking at the trees and ... well, just smiling. I said, "Jay Dee Six, what facts have caused you to have that expression on your face?" And he pointed at the autum leaves and said, "They're ... beautiful!" Well, I felt like slapping him around the head with a wet surgical glove. "That's froth, Jay Dee Six," I told him. "If the Professor hears he'll ... well, I don't want to think of the consequences. Now, fill that test tube with fish poo and we'll do some experiments."' Dee takes a deep breath and glances at Milo. 'But, a week later, something ... oh, something truly disgusting happened.'

II

'What, Dee?'

'Oh, you don't –'

'I do! I do! Pretty pleeaasse.'

'Oh, I see you've learnt Cressida Bell's tricks already.' Dee sits on a wooden stool by the workbench. For a moment she thoughtfully touches a microscope, then says,

'It was late one night. I was in my bunk bed. Through the window I could see a full moon. I was just debating whether to get my telescope and gather some crater-based facts when ... a noise from the bunk above! Jay Dee Six is awake! And I can hear a page turning. He must be gathering data for the Professor's book, I think. So I get out of my bunk and look above and ... Oh, I can barely say it!'

'What, Dee?'

'It's too ... horrific!'

'Tell me! Tell me!'

'Jay Dee Six was reading ... *poetry*!'

III

'Poetry! Is that ... *all*?'

'*All!*' gasps Dee. 'Isn't that enough? Oh, I was so ashamed of him, Milo Kick.' I said to him, "How can you betray the Professor like this. Poetry is the worst kind of froth!" And do you know what he replied, Milo Kick? What disgraceful words came from his mouth?'

'What?'

'He said, "It makes me *feel* things!"' Dee covers her mouth as if she's about to be sick. 'My own male of the species sibling! *Feeling* things! Oh, the shame! The shame!'

IV

'What did the Professor say?' asks Milo.

'Well, I tried my best to keep it from him,' replies Dee, getting up and pacing the room. 'The Professor had to concentrate on his work. The last thing he needed was to start worrying about ... frothiness in his own genetic offspring!' Dee becomes quite breathless as she continues. 'I hid Jay Dee Six's poetry books! And the novels! And the plays – Yes! He was reading drama now. Sometimes he'd start mumbling lines from plays and I'd poke him hard

— 139 —

and say, "Stop that before the Professor hears!" And then – oh, yes! It snowed!' Dee stamps her foot with frustration. 'And that snow, Milo Kick, was the beginning of the end!'

V

'How, innit?'

'The Professor, always on the lookout for facts, declared, "This is the perfect opportunity to study sub-zero conditions." The whole forest had become white with frozen H_2O. The Professor set up the microscopes and test tubes and explained that snow occurs when water droplets in the clouds form ice crystals which collide and, as they fall, these ice crystals form snowflakes. The Professor then told us three fascinating snow facts.' Dee counts them off on her fingers. 'One: the largest recorded snowflake – or, strictly speaking, hailstone – weighed 765 g, or 1 lb 11 oz, and fell in Kansas USA in 1970. Two: in 1921, in Colorado – again in the USA – 1.93 m, or 76 inches, of snow fell in a single day. And three: no two snowflakes are the same. When looked at under a microscope, every single snowflake has a unique pattern –'

VI

'Magic!' gasps Milo.

'That's just what Jay Dee Six said!' exclaims Dee, pointing at Milo. 'The Professor nearly hit the roof. And rightly so. "There's nothing 'magic' about it," he says. "Or wonderful. Or amazing. Or any of those frothy words. It's just a fact."' Dee paces the room faster and faster. 'There are arguments! Jay Dee Six shouting, "You've got to have a sense of poetry, Professor. Otherwise things don't have any meaning!" The Professor picks up a test tube and stormed out of the Labmobile.

'I say to Jay Dee Six, "You've upset him now."

'He says, "That man needs to *feel* something."'

'I ask, "Why?"
'"To be *alive*!"' exclaims Jay Dee Six.
'"Froth!" I yell at him. "Froth! Froth! FROTH!"'

VII

Dee is getting breathless now, her eyes blazing. 'I was so angry, Milo Kick. Livid! I couldn't talk to my twin for three hours. I did some experiments on frozen squirrel droppings. Jay Dee Six sat by the window … gazing at the snow like a big girl's blouse! Honestly, he was becoming as soppy as a box of frocks. Eventually the Professor comes back. I show him the results of my experiments. Neither of us speak to Jay Dee Six. Later the Professor says, "Jay Dee Six, communication between us all will cease until you de-froth your brain cells." I hear Jay Dee Six producing salt water in his eyes that night. I hope … well, I hope he'll come to his senses! But the next day – Oh! Oh!'

'What, Dee? What?'

VIII

Dee stares out of the window at the ocean. 'The next day Jay Dee Six and I went exploring the forest. I was collecting snow samples and putting them in test tubes. And then, in the middle of a small clearing, we see something … amazing!'

'What?'

'It was a … Wizard!' For a moment she gazes into nothing, her whole body trembling. 'The most … amazing Wizard,' she says softly. Then, suddenly, she clicks back into robotic mode and gets to her knees. 'Now, we really *must* find this key!'

IX

'Oh, nah, Dee!' pleads Milo. 'You can't stop the story there! Tell me more!'

'Not now, Milo Kick!' she snaps. 'Talking about this …
disturbs my calm too much. Besides, you keep getting in
the way. I can't possibly search the room properly with
you in it. Why don't you explore the beach some more
while there's still daylight left.'

X

Still daylight –?
Oh, look! The sun's already getting lower.
And – oh, the Captain! I should go back to see him.
It's just that … oh, I want to find out about the Wizard and –

XI

'Go! Milo Kick! Go!'
'All right, all right. Don't get ya knickers in a twist!'
'Kindly keep my underwear out of this. And make sure
you keep that hat on. Too much sun can make you ill, you
know. Keep in the shade. Drink fresh water. Don't rush
about.'

— Thirty-four —

I

'The key is … *lost*, ye say?'

'Not … *lost* exactly, Cap. It's in Dee's room somewhere. She'll find it.'

'What if … she don't?'

'She will.'

'But she might not! The key might've slipped between the floorboards and – oh, without the key, Cressida will never give ye the Phoenix of Secrets, laddy! And I'll be sailing the seven seas for the rest of my born days! The Floating Island of Heart is always moving, ye see. One day here, the next day there. And if I don't find the Island … oh, that creature will never be destroyed.' And, suddenly, the Captain is punching at the rock face of the cave. Punching as hard as he can, hair lashing, saliva dribbling, eyes wide: 'Curse ye! CURSE YE!'

II

The Captain – he's hurting his hand!
Grazing his knuckles.
Gotta stop him!

III

'Don't, Cap!'

'Wh-what …?'

'You're bleeding!'

'Bleed –? Oh, laddy!' The Captain gazes at his hands as

if he's just woken up. 'What … what have I done …?'

'Sit down, Cap. I'll help you! Here!'

'Thank ye, laddy.' The Captain brushes tears from his eyes. 'I don't know what gets into me sometimes, laddy. Really I don't. I think of that hideous creature and … oh, I lose all reason.' He attempts a smile. 'I'm fine now, laddy. Don't ye worry yourself about me.'

'But your hand –'

'Oh, it be fine, laddy.' He nods towards the wooden chest. 'You'll find a bottle in there, laddy. Bring it to me, will ye?'

IV

Open the chest and –

Look! Old boots. A vest. And –

The harpoon!

Look how sharp it –

'Ye see the bottle, laddy?'

'You mean –' Milo holds a bottle of whiskey in the air '– this?'

V

'Aye! Open it, laddy!'

Milo grabs the cap and tries to unscrew it. 'It's a bit tight!'

'With ye muscles? Should be easy! Come on. Be a man … That's it! Well done, laddy. Now pour some of the contents over my poor damaged skin.'

Milo does so and …

VI

'Ahhh!' cries the Captain. 'It stings, laddy. Stings – Ahhhh!'

Milo stops pouring.

'Nay, laddy. More! Sometimes ye gotta hurt to do good.

It be cleaning my wounds for me – Ahhh – More! Ahhhh! That's enough now, laddy. Thank ye.' Once more he indicates the wooden chest. 'There be some bandages in there, laddy. Will ye –?'

'Sure thing, Cap.'

VII

Slowly, Milo wraps a bandage round Captain Jellicoe's left hand.

'Ye must think me a foolish old man, eh, laddy. Losing me temper like that. But sometimes … I get this feeling in me and … and … oh, words – they fail me, laddy. I just cannot describe what my temper be feeling like.'

'Fizzy Wasps!'

'Eh? What's that, laddy?'

VIII

'When I get wound up by something I get this bzzzzzzzzz in me head. It trembles me head like … like a washing machine in fast spin. And … I feel all this building up inside me belly like I'm going to go BANG!'

'Aye, laddy! That's just how I feel when I think of the creature of endless nastiness. But why do ye call it … Fizzy Wasps?'

Milo explains. 'Mum took me to see a doctor, ya see. Had to tell him what me temper felt like. All I could think of was … well, once I took a bottle of Coke from the fridge. And, before I opened it, I dropped it. Got all shook up, innit. When I took the lid off it went – Whoooosh!'

'Aye, laddy, it would.'

IX

'And then, another day, someone at my school kicked a football at this wooden shed. It hit a wasps' nest. And I watched as … all these wasps swarmed out. Thousands of them. Millions. All buzzing and angry. And … well, I put the Coke thing and the nest thing together. And that's what my temper feels like. Fizzy Wasps, innit!'

'Tell me, laddy … when ye lost ye temper with me earlier. When I asked ye about – oh, who was that wild laddy?'

'… Mojo.'

'Aye. The mention of his name. And that girl … Trixie. Both their names got ye Fizzy Wasps a swarming in ye head?'

'Yeah! Zillions!'

'But why?'

X

'Don't wanna talk about it!'

'But there must be a reason this Mojo and Trixie –'

Fizzzzy Waspzzzz

'– cause such anger –'

XI

'YOU'RE DOING IT AGAIN, AIN'T YA! SHUT IT! SHUT IT! I DON'T WANNA TALK ABOUT MOJO OR TRIXIE EVER AGAIN! THEY'RE NOTHING –'

Calm! Calm!

'– TO ME –'

Calm!

'– and … I … I … oh … oh … I'm sorry, Captain. I didn't mean to … oh, I wish … I wish … oh, I wish I didn't have the Fizzy Wasps. Honest, Captain!'

XII

'Oh, laddy … I know exactly what ye mean. I wish I wasn't controlled by my Fizzy Wasps too. They make me say things I regret … hurtful things to people I care for. And then … why, I just feel twice as angry as I did before. So I say worse things. It just goes on and on.'

'Yeah! That's it! Exactly.'

'In that case … we must learn to *tame* our Fizzy Wasps, don't ye think?'

'Yeah! Yeah!'

XIII

'A toast!' exclaims the Captain, raising the bottle in the air. 'To taming our Fizzy Wasps!'

And then he takes an almighty swig.

And another …

Another …

Another …

XIV

The Cap – he's draining the bottle and –

Smash!

– he's thrown the bottle!

'Get me another drink, laddy.'

'In the chest?'

'Aye!'

XV

The Cap – he's draining the second bottle.

The Cap – he's staggering round the cave.

The Cap – he's getting drunk.

The Cap – he's gotta stop, otherwise he won't be able to –

XVI

'Tell me, Cap.'

'Whaat's thaaat, laaaaddddyy?'

'About MFC! What is it? What did it do to you?'

'Oh, laaaddy …' Another swig. 'Oh, laaaaaddy …' Another swig!

'Stop drinking, innit.'

'Buuut I've *goooot* to driiiink, laaaaddy. It's the only waaaay I can numb the paaaain of thinking of that accursed –' He trips over his own feet and nearly falls. 'Ooooof!'

XVII

'So … where does the story of MFC start, Cap? Tell me!'

'Wheeere doooes it start, laddy …?' The Captain tries to focus his eyes on Milo. 'Why, laddy, it starrrr … oh, when I was *ye* age.'

XVIII

'My age!'

'Ayyee,' says the Captain, his hands reaching out for Milo. 'I haaaad hopes … when I was yeee age … And thaaaat wash theee starrrt off iiit, laaady – I HAD HOPESHH AND PLANSHH!'

And with that, the bottle falls –

Smash!

– and the Captain collapses –

CRASH!

– into the driftwood boat!

XIX

'Cap!'

Milo rushes over and sees –

XX

The Captain – he's unconscious, innit!
  The Captain – mouth blowing bubbles.
  The Captain – snoring!

XXI

Gonngg!
> *Is that the –?*
> *It is!*
> *It's the gong!*
> *Very faint but – oh, I'm gonna be late for dinner.*
> *Run!*
> *Run!*

XXII

Crunchcrunchcrunchcrunchcrunchcrunchcrunchcrunch
crunchcrunchcrunchcrunchcrunchcrunchcrunchcrunch
crunchcrunchcrunchcrunchcrunchcrunchcrunchcrunch
crunchcrunchcrunchcrunchcrunchcrunchcrunchcrunch
crunchcrunchcrunchcrunchcrunch …

— Thirty-five —

I

'You're late, Milo Kick.'

'I'm sorry ... I –'

'Breathless too.'

'Been ... run ... ning!'

'Well, I gathered that much!' Dee snaps, glaring. Then she relaxes a little and sighs. 'Oh, I'm not angry with *you*, Milo Kick. I'm angry with *this*.' She indicates the table set for dinner: candelabrum, knives and forks, plates, serviettes.

'It looks ... ready for ... nourish ... ment, Dee,' pants Milo.

'Thank you, Milo Kick. But, forgive me for saying, I didn't prepare it for *your* appreciation. I prepared it for ... *her*!'

II

'For Cressie, innit?'

Dee slumps into a chair and cleans her spectacles on the edge of the tablecloth. 'After you left this afternoon, I searched for the key a while –'

'Did ya find it?'

'No! I didn't!' Dee puts her glasses back and continues. 'And, perhaps, if you don't mind, I can talk about something bothering *me*, and not *your* petty concerns.' She takes a deep breath to calm herself. 'I came down to start dinner and, all of a sudden, the house seemed so ... so ...' She struggles to find the word. '... incomplete!' she finally manages. 'Avalon Rise should have Cressida Bell moving around in it. It should have her stick going tap-tap and the smell of her perfume. Oh, I know what you're thinking.' Dee gives Milo a defiant stare. 'I'm getting frothy.'

'A bit, yeah.'

'It's not froth, Milo Kick!' Dee slaps the table, rattling cutlery. 'It's fact! Cressida Bell and Dee Dee Six go together like –'

'Fish 'n' chips?'

'Well, I prefer to think of us as copper and tin.'

III

'What d'ya mean?'

'When you mix copper and tin together,' explains Dee, 'it becomes a totally new thing, neither copper nor tin. It becomes bronze. And, at the moment, there might well be copper in Avalon Rise. And there might well be tin in Avalon Rise. But there is certainly no –'

'No bronze, innit!'

'Correct, Milo Kick.' Dee casts her gaze over the table once more. 'And that's why I've prepared Chef's Special.'

IV

'Chef's Special?'

'Cressida Bell's favourite dinner,' explains Dee. 'For starters: onion soup with gin. Main course: beef braised with Guinness. Dessert: sherry trifle.' She indicates an old menu on the mantelpiece. 'It's from the original menu her Papa designed. Whenever Cressida Bell and I have one of our little ... tiffs, I always cook the Chef's Special and that sulking show-off smells the aroma and comes down those stairs and –'

'You're mates again, innit.'

'Correct, Milo Kick.' Dee frenetically cleans her glasses once more. 'Cressida Bell must've smelt the Chef's Special, Milo Kick! Why isn't she here? Do you think … she hates me?'

'Nah! Never!'

'Then why isn't she tapping her way down those stairs?'

'Do you … want me to go up and find out?'

'Oh … will you?'

'Yeah!'

V

Knock! Knock!

'Enter, Beloved.'

VI

'You knew it was me, then?' Milo strides up to the bed and plonks himself on the edge of the mattress. 'Hang on!' He sniffs. 'What's that pong?'

'Rosewater!' Cressida tells him, holding out a large crystal decanter. 'Oh, fill your nostrils, Beloved! The most enchanting aroma! I always dab this on my pulse points when I'm feeling a bit … well, crumpled. It revives my spirits no end.'

That's why she can't smell the dinner, innit.

Everything pongs of –

VII

'Such beautiful perfume!' gasps Cressida, dabbing more behind her ears. 'Nothing brings back memories like smells, you know. The smell of mincepies and turkey always reminds me of Christmas. And … oh, let's see! Yes! The smell of freshly dug earth always reminds me of that day part of the cliff plunged into the ocean …' She holds the crystal decanter out again. 'And do you know what this reminds me of?'

'Nah! But, Cressie, downstairs is –'

'Your mum!'

'Wh-what?'

'This rosewater is your mum's smell.'

'But … why?'

'We made it.'

'You … *made* it! That rosewater!'

'Every single drop, Beloved.'

'Gimmie a whiff, Cressie!'

VIII

'That summer … oh, there were so many roses,' continues Cressida as Milo smells the perfume. 'Oh, yes, Avalon Rise had a garden then. It wasn't the windswept wasteland you see now. There were geraniums bright as rubies. Hollyhocks tall as steeples. Lilies like orange butterflies and – more than anything – roses! Oh, how I loved them. And that summer – you see, for me, it will always be *that* summer – the roses had never been so glorious! Hundreds of them. Thousands. And I was outside watering them when I heard her voice –'

'Me mum!'

'My Fliss!'

IX

'So ye *did* let her come back for a second summer. I knew ya would. Her and Checker and Valentino. Ya let them stay for nothing.'

'Naturally, Beloved. What else could I do? I wrote Fliss a little note saying, "I will give your dad and Valentino one room and you – yes, *you*, my own little Fliss – shall have a room all to yourself!"' Cressida's nose twitches and she gives a sudden sniff. 'Is … is that onions I can smell …?'

X

Oh, no!
Not yet!
Wanna hear more about Mum!
The rosewater!
That'll take her mind off onions.
Shove decanter under her nose and –

XI

'Can't smell anything oniony, me,' Milo assures her, snuggling close. 'Just roses! Mmmm! Smell the lovely scent. That's it! Deep breaths! Good. Now … tell me about Mum!'

— Thirty-six —

I

'Imagine this!' Cressida declares, waving her arms in the air. 'I'm in a garden full of roses! And your mum – my adorable Fliss – one year older, running towards me across the cliff tops, crying out, "Cressie! Cressie!" I drop the watering can and glide across the drawbridge to greet her! We embrace. Spinning around and round! "Your hair's so long!" I tell her. "And what a lovely dress you're wearing. Oh, Fliss, you're a proper young lady now!" And we continue spinning and crying and laughing!'

'But … where's Checker?'

II

'There he is!' Cressida points, the smile vanishing from her face, as if the man has just appeared at the foot of the bed. 'Staggering towards us. Still wearing the same silly clothes. Only now, if anything, he's fatter. Balder. And his nose is twice as red. And – there!' Again, she points. 'Walking just behind him! You see?'

'Valentino True?'

'Bravo, Beloved! Mr True's tall and well built. He's wearing a dark suit, white shirt, cravat, and his hair is thick and tinged with grey. Most distinguished. And, of course, he's got a moustache. And – you'll never guess what, Beloved?'

'What?'

'It's Mr True who's now carrying the suitcases. It's Mr

True who's being bossed around! "GET A MOVE ON, VAL!"
I hear Checker grunting at him. "YOU'RE MOVING AS
FAST AS A STICKY BOGIE DOWN A HAIRY NOSTRIL!"'

III

'Ha!'

'Beloved!' gasps Cressida. 'Don't laugh at such
vulgarity! Please! Especially when it's directed at … well,
at a man such as Mr True.'

'So … Valentino is an OK sort of bloke, then?'

'Well, listen to this and see what you make of him.'
Cressida takes a deep breath. 'Imagine this: it's later that
night. I'm sitting in the living room enjoying a cup of
cocoa with my little Fliss. Through the open window… oh,
the stars! So many! And a full moon. Utterly, utterly
romantic. Except for – "IRON MY SHIRT, VAL!" "CLEAN
MY SHOES, VAL!" "WASH MY SOCKS, VAL!" Oh, what
a voice that man had! I'm surprised Neptune himself
didn't climb out of the ocean and complain. I ask Fliss, "Is
your dad *always* like this with Mr True?"

'"Always, Cressie," she tells me. "The other day, Val
forgot to buy Dad's daily bottle of whiskey and Dad
shouted at him, 'YOU'RE AS MUCH USE AS A
CHOCOLATE TEAPOT!'"'

IV

'Ha!'

'Beloved!'

'Sorry.'

V

Cressida continues, 'I said to Fliss, "But why does Mr True
put up with it? Have you asked him? Have you … tried to
help the poor man at all?"

'"Of course I have, Cressie," replies Fliss. "Honest.

After all, I know what it's like to be treated like that. One day soon after they'd decided to become the Kick 'n' True double act, Val and me went shopping. Oh, we had a really good natter, Cressie. But when we got back Val and Dad had an argument. "Stop talking to the kid," I heard Dad yell. "You'll make her feel she's important! And she's not! Hear me? She's nothing!" And, well … Val and me haven't really had a moment together since –"' Cressida's nostrils twitch and she gives a violent sniff. 'Beef!' Sniff. Sniff. 'I'm sure … yes, I'm *positive* that's beef!'

VI

Oh, no!
  Not yet!

*Wanna hear more about Mum and Checker and Val –
Rosewater!*

VII

'Can't smell anything beefy, me,' says Milo, snuggling
even closer and sprinkling rosewater over the sheets. 'Just
roses! Mmm … smell the lovely roses, Cressie. That's it!
Deep breaths. Good. Now … tell me about Mum.'

VIII

'Imagine this!' declares Cressida. 'That night, on my way
to bed, I knock on Mr Kick's door. It's opened by Mr True.
He's wearing an emerald-green smoking jacket. Very
refined. Behind him I see Checker unconscious on the two
beds. They've been pushed together once again, you see.

'"Don't tell me he's making *you* sleep in the bathtub, Mr
True," I say.

'"Oh, I don't mind, Madam," he says. "Checker needs
his sleep. He's the brains of the act, after all." "Nonsense!"
I say. "Come downstairs and have a nightcap with me, Mr
True. I want to talk." We go to the living room. I pour him
a brandy, then ask him bluntly, "Why are you with that
disgraceful man, Mr True? He's a vulgar brute and you are
… a real artist, I'm sure."

'"Oh, I am, Madam –"

'"*Miss!*" I inform him. "*Miss* Bell."

'"It's hard to imagine a leading lady like yourself
without a male co-star, Miss Bell. Have you never … loved
a man?"

'"I loved my dear Papa," I tell him. "And compared to
Papa, every man seems a bit-player. But enough of me! Tell
me about you! Why are you with that vulgarian?"

IX

'"Times are hard, Miss Bell," he explains with a sigh. "And

the great roles – nay, *any* roles – have, thus far, eluded my grasp. Of course, I am in constant training, both physically and spiritually – for greatness, but until the spotlight falls on me … well, bills have to be paid! Clothes have to be bought. A mouth – indeed, this mouth now speaking – has to be fed. And even though – yes, I admit it, Miss Bell – even though I *dread* every moment I'm with that artistic hoodlum, the money is most … shall we say 'satisfactory'?"'

X

'So … he's just doing it for the dosh, innit?'

'Well, to put it quite crudely, Beloved, yes. But … oh, I understood! Really! You see, most of his life he'd been involved in the arts. He'd run away from home at fifteen with a friend – and since then … disappointment after disappointment! Auditioning for roles he never got. Year after year. He tried his hand at anything, you know! The circus – oh, yes, he was a trapeze double act for a while. That flopped too. But it made Mr True physically very … shall we say, impressive. In fact, I caught sight of his stomach muscles one morning and, believe me, they had more definition than a dictionary.' Another sniff! 'Is that …? Yes! A whiff of vanilla. Which can only mean a custard! Which means – oh, could it be sherry trifle?' Sniff. 'Yes! Yes! I'm *sure* … there's a touch of trifle in the air.'

XI

Oh, no!
  Not yet!
  Rosewater!

XII

'Can't smell anything trifley, me,' Milo assures her, sprinkling perfumed liquid over the pillows. 'Just … oh, mmm, lovely roses, Cressie! That's it! Deep breaths. Good ... Now, tell me more! More!'

XIII

'Mr True and I hatch a plan to rescue Fliss!' she tells him, clutching the sheets with excitement. 'It is near the end of the summer. I'm upset thinking of Fliss leaving. One night Mr True takes me to one side and whispers, "You must buy Fliss from her dad, Miss Bell! You hear? YOU MUST BUY HER!"'

— Thirty-seven —

I

'*BUY!*' gasps Milo.

'Yes, Beloved. *Buy!* The moment Mr True says it ... why, it all seems so obvious! Money is all Mr Kick desires. Fliss can't be of any financial benefit to him. Just the opposite. She's *costing* him money. So I say to Mr True, "How much should I offer?"

'"Not so fast, Miss Bell," he warns. "Checker might be greedy but he's also ... well, proud! We've got to be clever. We've got to – or rather, *I've* got to – plant the seeds in his mind. Got to make him feel it's *his* descision. Leave it all to me. In the meantime –" he put his fingers to his lips "– mum's the word!"'

II

'A few days later,' continues Cressida, reaching out for Milo's arms and gripping tight, 'Mr True says, "Success! Checker agrees Fliss can stay here ... but – and listen very carefully, Miss Bell – he doesn't want to talk about it at all. Not one word. The money side of it embarrasses him, you see."

'"So it should," I say. "Selling his own daughter is disgraceful."

'"This is the plan, Miss Bell," Mr True tells me. "On the day we leave, you are to put the money in a brown envelope. I will leave a suitcase by the reception desk. While we eat breakfast, you are to put the envelope in this suitcase."'

Milo asks, 'But … how much did Checker want for her?'

Cressida leans forward and whispers the sum in Milo's ear.

III

'TEN THOUSAND QUID, INNIT!'

IV

'Shhh, Beloved!' warns Cressida. 'We don't want the whole of Cornwall to hear!'

'Sorry, Cressie, but … well, that's a lot of dosh.'

'Peanuts, Beloved. I would've given ten times that amount to help your mother.'

'So … you did it?'

'Naturally, Beloved.' She leans closer still, her breath whisper-heavy with secrets. 'On that last day, while Mr Kick and Mr True were having breakfast, I slipped the brown envelope into the suitcase by the reception desk.'

'But what about my mum? What did *she* know?'

'Nothing, Beloved! How could I tell poor Fliss her own flesh and blood was willing to sell her? No, no, that would never do. I told Fliss that her dad – out of the kindness of his heart – was willing to let her stay and that she … well, she wasn't to say a word about it one way or the other because her gratitude would embarrass him. So, on that last day, she just says, "Bye, Dad", and Mr Kick says, "See ya, kid." And that, as they say, was that! I had my Fliss in Avalon Rise – Oh, what bliss! Utter, utter bliss!'

'You were happy together, then?'

V

'Happy! We were delirious! Euphoric! Fliss said, "I want to remember this summer for ever!" That's why we made perfume from the roses, Beloved. We boiled petals in a huge

— 163 —

saucepan. Avalon Rise was rose-scented heaven – Oh, let me smell the rosewater! Quick! Ouick!'

Milo holds the perfume under her nose.

VI

'Oh, Fliss!' cries Cressida ecstatically. 'It's like she's in this room! Oh, what a time we had! Every evening we'd do little party pieces round the piano downstairs.'

'Party pieces?'

'Oh, you know, Beloved. Sing songs, recite poetry, tell stories, generally entertain each other. Don't tell me you haven't got any party pieces?'

'Well … nah. At home I just watch telly or play computer games!'

'Ugh!' Cressida shivers all over as if ice-cubes have been dropped down her nightdress. 'What a horrible thought, Beloved. Truly. Locked in your own little world. Not sharing anything with anyone. Ugh!' Another shiver. 'You must *share* your experiences with other people, Beloved. That's what … well, what *art* is all about. One mind talking to another. Getting inspired by each other. Why, if it wasn't for your mum – my precious Fliss – I would never have done the painting in your room.'

'How come?'

'Your mum *inspired* me, Beloved. One night, as my party piece, I told the story of King Arthur and Merlin, and your mum said, "Why don't you paint it, Cressie? The story means so much to you. Do the scene where the boy Arthur talks to Merlin in the cave! Oh, you'll do such a terrific job of it! Let's go out and search for a cave tomorrow. You can do some sketches and –"' Cressida's voice catches in her throat. 'Oh! I'm brimming now!' She dabs tears from her cheeks. 'Just thinking about it … the memories, the memories.'

Milo snuggles closer and gives her arm a gentle squeeze.

'What a comfort you are, Beloved!' she tells him.

VII

'So … did you go cave hunting, Cressie?'

'What –? Oh, yes. Although, of course, I knew exactly where a cave was. I used to play there as a child.' She blows her nose. 'So very next day we walked along the beach to the cave and … Oh, of *course*!' Her dark glasses glint and flare in the setting sunlight. 'It was *that* day!'

'What day?'

'Why, Beloved,' she says, gripping his hand so tight Milo feels a knuckle go pop. 'It was the day we found … the Mermaid!'

VIII

'Mermaid! H–how?' Milo is jiggling with excitement now, tugging at Cressida's nightdress. 'Tell me! Tell me!'

'Well, we were walking along the beach towards the cave and –' she sniffs. 'Oh, that *is* onions.' Sniff. 'And beef –'

'Nah, Cressie! Nah!'

'It *is*, Beloved.' Sniff, sniff! 'Dee has made Chef's Special!' She pushes back the blankets and swings her legs out of the bed. 'Where's my dressing gown?'

'But the Mermaid –?'

'Dressing gown! Dressing gown!'

'Here!'

'Come on!' Cressida heads for the door. 'Oh, Chef's Special! Dee has cooked it and now – oh, harmony is restored to Avalon!' She rushes out into the corridor. 'Dee!'

'Cressie!' Milo rushes after her. 'Tell me a more about the Merm –'

'Not now, Beloved.' Cressida breezes down the stairs. 'Dee!' She bursts into the dining room. 'DEE!'

— Thirty-eight —

I

'CRESSIDA BELL!' For a moment it looks as if Dee's about to rush into Cressida's arms. But she manages to restrain herself and coolly inquires, 'What brings you down?'

'Oh, Dee!' sighs Cressida, sitting at the dining table. 'Stop playing games! You know full well what has tempted me out of my boudoir.' She sniffs. 'This glorious aroma!'

'Oh. That,' says Dee dismissively. 'Well, there happened to be a lot of onions going to waste in the larder. Not to mention some beef in the fridge. So I thought, Why not use them all up?' She makes her way to the kitchen. 'I'll get the soup as you're here.'

'She has a heart of gold, Beloved! Really she does – Oh, sit down! Sit!'

Milo tucks himself into his seat, tugs at Cressida's sleeve. 'But I want to know about the Mermaid!' he whispers. 'Was it alive or dead?'

'Well, the Mermaid was –'

'Onion soup!' announces Dee, returning with a steaming tureen.

II

Oh, nah! Wanna know about the Mermaid. But ... oh, but ... Oh, look at Cressie. Slurping soup like there's no tomorrow. Dee's pouring her a glass of –

'Oooo, champagne, Dee!'

'I brought some up from the cellar.'

'Mmmmm … 1876 vintage!'

'Correct, Cressida Bell.'

'Papa's favourite.'

III

And the Wizard! Want Dee to tell me about him too but … oh, look at her. Sipping soup like she's not affected by the taste at all, but I can tell she –

'Ya like it really, don't ya, Dee?'

'What on earth do you mean, Milo Kick?'

'The food! The booze! Ya think it's yummy!'

'Yummy!' gasps Dee, shocked. 'I've never heard such an outrageous suggestion in all my life.' She points her spoon at the soup. 'This is merely fuel for me. That is all. I cook meals like this because Cressida Bell requests I follow the Avalon Rise menus, even though we haven't had a guest – except for you, of course – in donkey's years. Personally,' she goes on with a disdainful sniff, 'I'd be quite happy making do with a few multi-vitamin tablets washed down with a glass of tap water. And as for the champagne … Well, the body requires liquid. That's all.'

Cressida squeezes Milo's knee under the table and gives him a secretive smile. 'She's got a heart of gold really,' she mouths. 'Pure gold.'

IV

They're getting tipsy, innit!

'Enjoying your beef in Guinness, Beloved?'

'Yeah! It's spectacular.'

'Dee, your Chef's Special tastes exactly like Papa used to make it!'

'Not *exactly* –' begins Dee.

'*Similar*, innit!'

'Correct, Milo Kick!' Dee slaps the table with delight. 'Oh, the boy is learning so many facts, Cressida Bell. It's good to have him around!'

'Indeed it is,' agrees Cresida, raising her glass. 'A toast! To Milo!'

'To Milo Kick.'

'To me, innit!'

V

They're both getting drunk now.

Cressida's chatting away and spilling beef gravy all over her dressing gown. Dee's trying to make out she's sober but … well, her glasses are crooked and she's wobbling from side to side.

'You've drunk two bottles of champagne between you, innit.'

'It's a *magnum*, Milo Kick. Not a boshle.'

'*Boshle*, Dee?'

'Did I say boshle, Creshida Bell?'

'You did, Dee. Didn't she, Beloved?'

'Yeah! Ya did, Dee!'

'Oh, dear! The alchohol must be causing a chemical reaction in my brain.'

'It's made your false teeth loose!' laughs Cressida.

'I'll get the trifle,' slurs Dee, rising awkwardly to her feet. 'I can take my teeth out to eat that – Ha!'

'Ha!'

'Ha!'

VI

They're both out of their heads now, innit!

I'm enjoying this! Dee's trying to remain all logical and scientific and – look! Her glasses are crooked and she's got a big dollop of custard on the end of her nose.

VII

'Thisssh woman!' Cressida exclaims, clutching Dee's arm. 'She … she saved my life!'

'Oh, I did not, Creshhida Bell.'

'Did!' Cressida burps loudly, then drunkenly launches into, 'Sheven years ago … you came into my life and – oh, I was in a sherrible state at the trifle, Beloved. My eyesight was almost a slishe of beef! Blind as mushy strawberries, I was. All I could shee were shadows and mandarin slices and … Avalon Rishe was full of gravy stains and dust, and as for me – I was shtaggering round like a … a lump of lime jelly with kiwi fruit. And then … one day – oh, imagine thish! I'm outshide in the remnainsh of the roshe garden. I shee a stick-like figure walking towards me! It says, "If you are the woman known as Cresshida Bell then I've come to work for you!" Just like that, Beloved. My shaviour! She cleaned the gravey shtains from the houshe – Away dusty potatoes! And she … she … saved my – Ughmff!'

VIII

Cressida slumps forward and her head goes –
    Splat!
    – face first into the trifle.
    'CRESHIDA BELL!'
    'CRESSIE!'

IX

Milo and Dee help her sit up and wipe the custard and jelly from her face.

'Oh … Beloved! Dee!' Cressida licks her lips. 'The whole world is shuddenlyy … so … trifle.'

'Time you went to bed, Cresshida Bell. Come on! I'll help you – ooooo!' Dee wobbles uneasily. 'Time I went to bed too.'

'Want any help, Dee?'

'No … not necessary, Milo Kick. But –' she pats the top of his head – 'thank you for ashking. Come on, Cresshida Bell.' The two of them zigzag towards the door. 'I'll do all the washing-up in the morning, Milo Kick.'

'I'll do it if you like, innit.'

'Oh, blesshh!'

'No, no, Milo Kick. You're our guest!' She staggers a couple of steps into the hallway, then calls back, 'Oh, there is *one* thing you can do!'

'What? Anything.'

'Take that unopened magnum of shampoo down to the shellar. It needs to be – oh, keep still, Cresshida Bell – kept in a cool dark plashe. Put it on the rack at the back. In the shlot marked 1876 … Oh! Yes! The door to the shellar is under the shtairs. The light swish is –'

'Tug the shtring, Beloved!'

'OK, OK,' Milo assures them, chuckling to himself. 'I've got it! You two go to bed.'

'Oh, blesshhh!'

'Goodnight, Milo Kick.'

X

Me – opening cellar door.
   Me – pulling string for light.
   Me – going into –

XI

The cellar is cool and damp. The walls are grey stone, discoloured with moss. There are wine racks – mostly empty – along every wall, and a few barrels scattered across the floor. Milo makes his way to the back wall – as instructed – and searches for the slot with the correct date.

XII

Every slot must be the year they were made!
   1873
   1874
   1875

1876 –
Here it is!
Slip the bottle in and –
Hang on!
What's this –

XIII

Scratched into the stone wall
is the following inscription:

Fliss + Griff
4
ever

XIV

Mum!
    Mum and –
    Griff?
    Who's Griff?
    Whoever he is –
    They're both in a heart!
    Love!
    That means …
    Fliss loved Griff!
    Mum loved –
    Who?
    Who?

XV

Milo rushes up to Cressie's room –
    Knock!
    Silence.
    Milo opens door and –

XVI

Dark, innit!

And –
   Snoring!
   Oh, no! No!
'Cressie?' he calls into the room. 'Cress –'

XVII

'Milo Kick! Whash yooo up to?'

   Dee pokes her head up out of her room.

   'I ... I need to talk to –'

   'Well, not now, Milo Kick! Too late! Both ... Cresshida Bell and I are – ooo, why can I see the whole world shhpinning? I'm sure that's unfactuallll ...'

   Dee closes her door.

XVIII

Me – lying on me bed.
   Me – full of questions.
   Who's Griff?
   When was that heart scratched on the cellar wall?
   Oh, so many questions.
   Questions about ...
   The Mermaid on the beach.
   The Wizard in the forest.
   What is MFC?
   What did MFC do to the Captain?
   I need to know the answers.
   I have to know!
   But ... oh, can't be now!
   It'll have to be ...

XIX

Tomorrow ...
   Tomorrow ...
   Tomorrow ...

Fourth Day

— Thirty-nine —

I

'Cap!'

'Wh … whaa?'

'Wake up, Cap!'

'Ughh … Where I be?'

'In your driftwood boat, innit.'

'B-boat? That means – Sea! I be at sea!'

'Nah, nah! You're in a cave! Oh, pull yourself together, Cap. You drank too much last night and now you're –'

'Who … who be you?'

'Oh, sober up! Cap! Please. It's me. Milo.'

'Milo –? Wait! It's … it's all coming back to me now! I … I was talking to ye last night, was I not? And then I – oooo, my head feels like a pickled herring! A cup of tea is what I be needing – ooo, aye! Laddy, will ye make it for me? Ye will find some teabags in the wooden chest. And … oh, there's a box of matches! There! Ye see? Light the fire. There be water in the kettle already.'

II

'Feeling better now, Cap?'

'Much better, laddy. Ye make a fine cuppa and no mistake. And thank ye for bringing such a big food parcel. Why, I haven't had a breakfast like this since … well, I don't know how long. And … what's wrapped up in this silver foil here.'

'It's lunch.'

'Lunch! Why, laddy, what be the time?'

'Nearly one, Cap.'

'But … ye mean I've slept the whole morning and – Laddy! Why are ye here at this time? Ye be should be making ye way to Avalon Rise for mealtime! That clockwork woman will hit the roof if her routine be disrupted.'

'Dee ain't cooking lunch today.'

'Ain't cook –? Why, laddy what's happened?'

III

'Oh … where to begin? So much to tell ya! OK! Here goes! Last night Cressida and Dee kept drinking all this champagne? Glass after glass. Got really sozzled. Went to bed early. This morning I wake up and look out me bedroom window and … hang on! The sun's in a different place! It's higher and the light's more yellow. I look at the clock and it's half-past eleven!'

'Half-past *eleven* –! Why, laddy, what about breakfast?'

'Dunno! Didn't hear the gong or anything.'

'What did ye do, laddy?'

'Dressed quick as a flash, innit. Rushed downstairs and … no one! Empty! I call out "Dee! Cressie!" No answer! All feeling a bit spooky now. And … well, I really wanted to talk to Cressie. Couldn't wait for her to tell me about Griff.'

'Griff? Who be that, laddy?'

IV

'Dunno! That's just the point. You see, Cap – oh, she's been telling me this spectacular story. About me mum. And Mum's dad. That's me grandad. His name was Checker Kick. And … well, one day – oh, guess what Cressida and me mum found on the beach? A Mermaid! Spectacular, eh? I wanted to ask Cressida more about the Mermaid. And this Griff person. Cos I saw Mum's name and his in a heart and that says boyfriend and girlfriend stuff to me. So I rush to Cressie's room and shake her awake. Guess what she says? "Not now, Beloved. I feel quite hung-over." So I rush to Dee's room. Ya see, she's been telling me another story as well! About her dad – she called him the Professor – and her brother called Jay Dee Six, who likes poetry, and one day they found … Guess what, Cap? A Wizard. Like Merlin, ya know? So I shake Dee awake and guess what she says? "Fact: I can't cook breakfast. Fact: Milo Kick must go to kitchen and cook his own breakfast. Fact: there's some food wrapped in silver foil in the fridge that will suffice for lunch. It can be eaten either hot or cold. Fact: please hang the DO NOT DISTURB sign on my door!" Then she closes her eyes and goes back to the land of nod. So I made breakfast: just toast and stuff. Then I got lunch from the fridge and rushed here as fast as I could.'

'And why'd ye do that, eh, laddy?'

'Why'd I do *what*, Cap?'

'*Rush* here.'

'So you can tell me ya story, of course.'

'Ha!' spits the Captain. 'It seems to me ye be more interested in all these other stories.'

'Nah, Cap.'

'Aye, laddy! More interested in Cressida's story of your mum and Dee's story of her brother to be bothered about *my* story.'

V

'But I am, Cap. Honest! Your story's more … more spectacular than Cressie's story and Dee's story put together. Please tell me.'

'Well …' murmured the Captain, stroking his beard thoughtfully. 'I suppose we *did* have a deal.'

'Exactly. A deal! Oh, Cap, what does MFC stand for? Please tell me. Pretty pleeaasse!'

'Well … if ye really want to know.'

'I really really want to know.'

'It stands for Mighty … Oh, I'm still not sure ye be interested?'

'I'm sure! I'm sure! Mighty what?'

'Mighty Fizz …'

'Yeah?'

'MIGHTY FIZZ CHILLA!'

— Forty —

'Mighty Fizz Chilla! Oh, Cap! Please tell me more! You can't stop now.'

'Well ... look in the wooden chest, will ye?'

'Yeah, yeah. Anything.'

'Ye will find a black box in it. The word "EVIDENCE" is written across the top. Ye see, I always knew my story would seem far-fetched. So I've been collecting evidence of what I'm about to tell ye ... Found the box, laddy?'

'Yeah! Here!'

'Put it at my feet, laddy ... That's it! Now sit ye there – on that rock! Good, laddy. Now what shall I show ye first ...? Mmmmm. Aha! Of course! Look at this, laddy! It's a drawing I did of the town where I was born ...'

II
'It looks like ... something out of a picture book, innit!'

'Well, aye, laddy, I guess it does at that. A nice, old-fashioned, cozy sort of picture book. In fact, that was the name of the place. Cozywick. My ma and pa were both born in Cozywick. They opened a fish 'n' chip shop. They called it "I KNOW MY PLAICE, THANK COD". And when I be born … oh, laddy, they be as cozy as any Cozywickians have ever been. And then … then …'

'Yeah?'

'Oh, laddy, it's hard for me to talk about this bit. Look ye! My eyes become moist at the mere thought of what happened to … to …'

'To?'

'My pa!'

'Your dad! Well … what? What happened to him?'

'Why, laddy … he *vanished*!'

III

'Vanished! How?'

'Oh, laddy, ye don't want to be hearing my sorrows.'

'I do! I do!'

'Well … it happened like this: I be only a little baby at the time. It was a bright, sunny day. Most days in Cozywick were bright and sunny. Ma and Pa put me in my pram and took me for a walk. They walked out of "I KNOW MY PLAICE, THANK COD", down Comfy Armchair Avenue, up Middle-of-the-Road Street. All the time neighbours were going, "Oooo, what a lovely baby you've got." And Ma and Pa were beaming with pride. And then Pa said, "Come on! Let's climb over the hill!" And Ma said, "Nay! We can't! We mustn't."'

IV

'But … why, innit?'

'Because the other side of the hill was outside Cozywick. Ye see, laddy, no one who lived in Cozywick had ever left Cozywick. It was … well, the price we paid for total and utter Cozydom. But that day – for some inexplicable reason – Pa got it into his head that he wanted to see what was on the other side of the hill. And the more Ma said, "Ye mustn't!" the more Pa said, "I want to!" Oh, I just don't understand my Pa at all, laddy.'

V

'I do!'

'Ye *do*, laddy?'

'Yeah! It … it's like with me and Mum, innit. When we moved to Ocean Estate and I saw Mojo. The more Mum told me to stay away from him, the more I wanted to be his mate. It must have been like that for your pa, Cap. The more people told him not to look on the other side of the hill … well, the more he wanted to.'

'Aye, laddy. I guess ye must be right.'

'So your pa … I bet he climbed the hill, didn't he, Cap?'

'Aye, laddy, that he did.'

'So he got to see what was on the other side.'

'Oh, laddy, he did more than that! He went *down* the other side!'

'Down! Oh, Cap, what did he see?'

'Laddy, we never knew.'

VI

'Why? Didn't he tell you.'

'Nay, laddy, he didn't. In fact, he never said another word to any of us.'

'Why, Cap, why?'

'Because my Pa never came back! Ma waited, rocking me gently in the pram and calling his name. Day became night. Night became day. Still Ma waited. Finally, though, she gave up and went back home. She fed me and put me in my cot to sleep. And she sat by the open window in her bedroom, gazing at the distant hill, hoping against hope that Pa would return.'

'But ... he never did?'

'Nay, laddy, he never did.'

VII

'So ... Cap! You never knew ya Pa! Just like I never knew me dad.'

'Why, laddy, that's right! The thought's only just occurred to me, but ...aye! Ye and me both grew up Pa-less! And as for my poor old ma ... why, she became a wreck of a woman after Pa disappeared. I couldn't mention him in any way. If I did ... why, Ma would just burst into tears and say, "Miserable, me! Oh, miserable me!"'

VIII

'Me too! With me mum! I told ya this, Cap.'

'Ye did?'

'Yeah! At least I'm ... well, I'm *sure* I did. Mum – she gets upset if I so much as mention Dad. So ... well, I don't mention him at all any more.'

'Oh, laddy, our stories be more alike than I ever imagined.'

'Yeah! Spectacular! Go on!'

— Forty-one —

I

'As I got older, I started to help me ma in the fish 'n' chip shop. People said my battered haddock was the best they'd ever tasted. No one fried chips the way I did! People loved them! Ma would sit in the corner of the shop and watch me with ... oh, such pride. "Look at my son," she'd say to the neighbours. "What a little angel he is."

II

'Angel! That's what Mum used to call me!'

'Because ye wanted to please her.'

'Yeah.'

'Because ... ye love her.'

'Well ... yeah.'

'And ye still love her?'

'Yeah! Course. She's me mum.'

'But ... oh, it's tricky, eh, laddy, to please ye mum when ye want to do things she don't like?'

'Yeah! It does ya head in! Was ya head done in, Cap?'

'Not at first, laddy! Like ye, at first I was happy to do anything to make Ma smile. And then ... oh, how to tell this next part? Aha! Of course! I'll show ye this. Look at this, laddy. A page from my diary. I wrote it when I was about ye age.'

III

I be feeling really grown up now. Shaved for this first time today. Not much. Just fluffy bit on my upper lip. I've got a hair on my chest too. Feeling so excited about the future. Oh, how I yearn, body and soul, to meet someone to love. What an adventure that would be. To love!

IV

'Ya *shaved*. At *my* age.'

'Aye, laddy.'

'Spectacular!'

'But, laddy, ye have a bit of fluff on ye top lip.'

'Ya think so?'

'Aye!'

'So I might be shaving soon?'

'I might even buy ye a razor.'

'Spec-tac-ul-ar!'

V

'But, laddy, what about the other thing in the diary? Love? Have ye no questions to ask about that?'

'Oh … sorry, Cap. What … about ya love stuff? Did ya get that?'

'Well, I thought I stood a good chance, laddy. After all, I was young at the time and very cute.'

'Ha! Ha! Ha!'

'What's so funny?'

'Thinking of you … young and cute! Ha!'

'Well, let me tell ye this, laddy, and listen good: everything old and uncute was once not old and uncute. One day, ye will be as old and uncute as me, ye know.'

'That's … scary, innit.'

'Aye, laddy, I'm afraid it is. And there's not a word I can say to make it less so.'

VI

'So … what happened next, Cap?'

'Not sure I want to tell ye, laddy, if the thought of me needing love makes you laugh.'

'I'm … I'm sorry, Cap.'

'We all need love, laddy. We all need someone to hug and hold and tell our secrets and stories to. Sometimes we need it before we know what it is we be needing. We just know something be missing from our lives. And if you can't understand that … well, there be no point in me carrying on.'

VII

'I … I *do* understand, Cap. Really. Please carry on. Tell me about love stuff.'

VIII

'Well, picture the scene. It's late at night. I be nineteen years old now. I'm just closing up the fish 'n' chip shop. The sky is full of stars. The moon is full. Ma is upstairs waiting for me to go up. But this night, laddy – this particular night – I did not go. And d'ye know why?'

'Why?'

'I heard *it*.'

'What?'

'Singing!'

IX

'Singing! What sort of singing, Cap.'

'Why, the most magical singing ears ever did hear. The kind of voice that makes the birds shut up and pay attention. The voice came from everywhere and nowhere at the same time. As if … aye, as if the very starlight itself had decided to burst into song. I can hear it now, "Someone – ooooooooeeeeeee – find me – ahhhhhhh – and love me – ahhhhhhheeeeeee …" And … oh, I knew I had to find the singer. Ye see, laddy, even though I'd always been happy with Ma, I was beginning to feel … oh, it be hard to put into words … beginning to feel … feel …'

'Something was missing, innit!'

X

'Aye, laddy! That's it exactly. Something was missing. I didn't know what it was. But when I heard the voice –'

'Ya knew that was it!'

'Aye! So picture the scene, laddy: I'm searching the streets of Cozywick all night long. But the singing … oh, the singing never got any closer.'

XI

'So … you didn't find the singer?'

'Not that night, nay. I went home to bed. But the sound of the voice stuck to me like … like limpets to a whale. I dreamt about it. I woke up humming it. And all the next day … oh, I couldn't stop thinking about it. One of my customers said, "What's wrong with you?" And I replied, "I'm in love with someone I haven't met yet." And, that night I went out to search the streets again.'

'Did ya hear the singing, Cap?'

'Nay, laddy. That magical voice was nowhere to be heard. And … oh, what agonies I was in. To know that, somewhere, a person existed that I knew had to be part of my life. That, without them, my days would be as dry and worthless as a salted peanut in the Sahara Desert.'

'Oh, Captain … I know how ya feel.'

'Is that how ye felt with this … this –'

'Mojo?'

'Aye, laddy. Mojo!'

'Yeah! I wanted to be his mate so much.'

XII

'And ... oh, laddy, I've just thought of something. Ye mum told ye to stay away from this Mojo, didn't she?'

'Yeah.'

'Well, that's just what my ma said to me about the magical voice. She said, "That voice will be a bad influence on ye."'

'That's – oh, Cap! That's *exactly* what Mum said about Mojo. She said, "He'll be a bad influence on you."'

'And did ye totally ignore ye mum, laddy?'

'Yeah! And did ya ... oh, Cap, did ya totally ignore ya ma too?'

'Aye, laddy.'

'Spectacular!'

XIII

'Picture the scene: me, every night, searching the streets of Cozywick. The moon changed from full, to crescent, then to a white eyelash in the sky. And still no return of that magical voice. And then after a week of searching, a week of no sleep, I collapsed to the ground, exhausted.'

'Ya ill, innit.'

XIV

'Aye, laddy, I be making myself ill. When I wake up – picture the scene, laddy! – I'm in a strange bed. Where be I? I look round. Other beds. And nurses –'

'Hospital, innit!'

'Aye, laddy. And in the bed opposite – oh, look ye, laddy. The most beautiful lassy I ever did see. She's asleep. And her hair – oh, laddy! Her hair is green. And her skin glows as if she's slooshed herself in a bucketful of moonlight. A nurse comes over and takes my temperature. "Who is that green-haired lassy yonder, Nursie," I ask.'

'What does she say, Cap?'

XV

'The nurse replies, "No one knows! That young woman was found floating down the river on a piece of driftwood. She was delirious. Singing the same song over and over again –"'

'The song ya heard!'

'Aye, laddy. For it was she. And then I realized why I'd never found the voice that night. She'd been ever moving on the current of the river. Always just out of eyesight. The nurse continues, "She can't remember anything about who she is. All she knows is her name: Miranda!"'

'Miranda!'

'Aye, laddy! Such a beautiful name, don't ye think? And, as Miranda slept, I drew her. Oh, where is that drawing? Aha! Here! Look ye, laddy! Look at the love of my life. Look at my destiny. My fate.'

— Forty-two —

I

II

'She's … got a lot of curly hair, innit!'

'Aye, laddy. A lot of very pretty curly hair. And then … oh, then it happened. She started to sing in her sleep. "Someone – ooooooeeeeeee – find me – ahhhh – and love me – ahhhhhhheeeeeee …" I sang along with her. "Someone – find me – ahhhhh – and love me – ahhhheeee …" And, as I did so, her eyes clicked open. She grabs my hand and says, "You sing the same song as me." I tell her, "Aye, that I do!" And she says, "In that case, let us marry and live happily ever after. For I don't know where I came from or how I got here. But if we sing the same music, I will never be lonely again. Will you be my Lovey-Dovey Hubby?" And I reply, "Aye! If you'll be my Lovey-Dovey Wifey."'

III

'And so … you got hitched, innit?'

'Aye, laddy! Within seven weeks we were married and living in the most cozy little cottage in Cozywick. In fact, that's what we named the place: "Cozieplace Cottage". Here … I did a drawing of it –'

IV

'Er … cozy, innit.'

'Aye! As cozy as warm slippers on a winter's night. And Lovey-Dovey Wifey and me – oh, we were so happy. Our life together was … oh, shall I describe some of the things we did together, laddy?'

'Yeah, go on.'

V

'We'd sit by the pond in the back garden and feed the goldfish with bits of bread. The fish would make little bubbles as they nibbled. Oh, how Lovey-Dovey Wifey loved watching those fishy bubbles – What d'ye think of that, laddy?'

'Er ... yeah.'

VI

'We'd play tiddlywinks! Oh, what a game that is! Trying to flip those tiny tiddlywinks into a cup. Lovey-Dovey Wifey was much better than me. She always won and I had to make her a cup of cocoa as her prize – What d'ye think of that, laddy?'

'Er ... yeah.'

VII

'Every night, as we lay in bed, Lovey-Dovey Wifey and me ... oh, we'd say a little rhyme together. We wrote it ourselves. Shall I recite it for ye, laddy?'

'Er ... if ya like.'

VIII

'"I'm cozy and cuddly living with you.
I'm cuddly and cozy through and through.
Cuddly and cozy, that's us two.
Cozy and cuddly, loving me loving you."
What d'you think of my life with Lovey-Dovey Wifey, eh, laddy?'

IX

'Truth?'

'Truth.'

'Boring!'

'Boring?'

'Totally! I mean ... feeding fish. Playing tiddlywinks. Reciting that ... whatever it was! Your lives were so yawn-making! Didn't ya ever want something to come along and ... well, shake things up a bit?'

'Never, laddy! I could have gone on like that with Lovey-Dovey Wifey for the rest of my life. And, no doubt, I would have done. Were it not for this – Here! Read! It's from the local newspaper, the *Cozyville Gazette*!

X

Looking for Special Gifts

Visit Fin, Fur and Feather
– the boat of mythical animals.
Moored in the river for a short
period only.

XI

'Mythical animals?'

'Aye, laddy! And oh, I wanted to give my Miranda a gift for our seventh wedding anniversary and this seemed –'

'Hang on! Hang on!'

'Wh-what, laddy?'

'Where's ya ma got to?'

'My ... ma?'

'Yeah! I mean ... she didn't want you to get hitched with this Miranda, right?'

'Er ... aye, laddy.'

'And I bet she didn't want you to move out of the fish 'n'chip shop, right?'

'Er ... nay, nay. She didn't.'

'So what's she been up to all these seven years while you and your other half have been feeding goldfish and playing tiddlywinks and saying ya little poem?'

XII

'Mmm ... good question, laddy.'

'Well?'

'Well ... for a while, I tried to keep my relationship secret from Ma!'

'That's exactly what I did with Mojo, Cap!'

'Ye did! Good! I mean ... well, at least ye understand. And when, eventually, Ma found out all she kept saying, over and over again, was, "It'll end badly."'

'Mum said something like that about me and Mojo too, Cap.'

'Coincidence after coincidence, eh, laddy?'

'Yeah! It's spectacular!'

XIII

'So ... well, in the end, laddy, I'm afraid to say, I hardly ever visited Ma in the fish 'n' chip shop.'

'Cos every time ya did, ya both argued, right?'

'Aye, laddy.'

'And ... Fizzy Wasps!'

'Aye, laddy. Swarms of Fizzy Wasps.'

'OK, I'm with ya now, Cap. So let's get back to the story. Ya wanna present for Lovey-Dovey Wifey. This "Fin, Fur and Feather" place looks a good idea. Did ya go to the boat?'

XIV

'Aye! Picture the scene: it's after work. I walked down to the river. It's winter. My breath comes out in smoky puffs. And then ... There! A wooden boat, like a tiny Noah's ark, and covered in the most extraordinary paintings! Unicorns! Stars! Serpents! Moons! It makes me giddy just looking at them. There be no gangway on to the boat, so I had to jump on board. And then I hear it.'

'What, Cap?'

XV

'Strange squawks. Haunting howls. Weird whimperings
… All coming from deep inside the bowels of the ship.
And – there! Look ye, laddy! A door. And on it is pinned –
well, here, laddy! Here! Read it for yourself, laddy!'

XVI

WARNING!

*This Ship contains creatures you have only heard about in your
wildest dreams or in ancient myths and legends.
or from drunken old salors who thought were
talking gibberish.*

*Only knock if you are prepared for the totally unexpected
and can cope with sights that may curl your teeth or
turn your hair white.
Please think carefully about what you are about to do.
It could change your life.*

XVII

'Spooky, innit.'

'Aye, laddy. Spooky be the very word. I read the
message over and over again … Oh, what do do? What to
do? What, laddy? Tell me!'

'Ya have to knock!'

'So be it!'

— Forty-three —

I

'And … well, what happens, Cap?'

'For a moment, laddy, nothing. Except … oh, the animals shriek and howl and stomp their hooves and paws. Try to hear the sounds, laddy. Go on! Picture the whole scene, picture the whole scene … Wings flapping! Tails lashing! Horns cracking into wood! Slowly, the frenzy dies down and – The door! Look ye, laddy! It's opening!'

'By who, Cap!'

II

'An old man, laddy. His face is nothing but a mask of wrinkles. He's bald except for a few wispy strands of white hair. And … oh, look, look, laddy! He's wearing a long black coat and a shirt with a winged collar. He's got a a pair of small, square-shaped dark glasses on, and he's holding a walking stick made of … oh, nay!'

'What Cap?'

'It's made of glass! And his teeth … oh, nay! Nay!'

'What, Cap, what?'

'Gold, laddy! Solid gold! I've never seen such a bizarre human being in all my born days. Can ye see him, laddy? In ye mind's eye. Can ye?'

'Yeah! Oh … I *can*, Cap. It's spectacular!'

'The bizarre man says, "Welcome, brave young man. My name is Mr Chimera. Enter! But I take no responsibility for whatever peril you find within."'

'Go in, Cap! Go in.'
'I do, laddy, and … oh, nay! Nay! NAY!'
'What? What?'

III

'Cages, laddy! Cages and … glass tanks everywhere. The light is very dim – just a few oil-lamps – but I can still make out the shadowy shapes inside and … Oh, laddy, I've never seen the like. Each cage and tank contains a creature of such … Oh, nay! Nay! NAY! NAY!'

'Tell me, Captain! What can ya see?'

IV

'The first creature has the body of a snake and the head of a monkey. When it opens its mouth it makes a noise like a crying baby and the patterns on its scaly skin change colour.

'Mr Chimera whispered in my ear, "That's a Scissorfrash."'

'Spectacular, innit!'

V

'The second creature has the body of a pigeon, the head of a pig and the legs of a frog. When it sees me it winks and starts purring like a cat.'

'Mr Chimera whispers in my ear, "That's a Swinotron."'

'Spectacular, innit!'

VI

'The third creature is in a tank full of water. It's like a bright-green jellyfish and, for a moment, there don't seem to be anything strange about it at all. Then – quick as a flash! – the creature changes shape and becomes a green shoe! Then … a green umbrella! Then … a green top hat.

'Mr Chimera whispers in my ear, "That's called a Morphowobbler."'

'Spectacular, innit!'

VII

'The next creature is so small I have to peer very close. It's about the size of my thumbnail and, at first, looks like … Aye! A spider! Then I see … oh! Yuk! Yuk!'

'What, Captain?'

'It's got the legs of … Oh, I can't tell ye, laddy.'

'Ya can! Ya must!'

'It's got the legs of a human baby. And each leg is wearing … fluffy pink socks.'

'Mr Chimera whispers in my ear, "That's an Arachnosockosapien."'

'Spectacular, innit!'

VIII

'The next creture is … oh, there be nothing in the cage. Nothing except … A noise! A sound like fingernails scraping down a blackboard.'

'Mr Chimera whispers in my ear, "That's the invisible Screechmonster."'

'Spectacular, innit!'

IX

'The next creature is the largest. It's about the size of a dog – in fact, laddy, it's got a dog's body. It's not in a cage or anything. Just tethered to a post by a rope around its neck and – oh, nay!'

'What?'

'Its head, laddy! It's got the head of a … Oh, nay! Nay!'

'Wh … what?'

'An ant! A huge ant's head on a dog's body. And as I stare at it – my eyes bulging wider and wider – this creature says, "Well, you ain't no oil painting either, buster!"'

'My Chimera whispers in my ear, "That's the Sarcastic Insectowoofer."'

'Oh, spectacular! Totally spectacular!'

X

'Well, glad ye think so, laddy. But … well, to be honest with ye, none of them seems to be a suitable gift for my Lovey-Dovey Wifey. I say as much to Mr Chimera and he asks me to describe what kind of person the gift is for. So I tell him, "She is the coziest, safest, calmest person in all the world."

'"Aha!" exclaims Mr Chimera, rapping the handle of his glass walking stick against his golden teeth. "I've got just the thing! Follow me."

XI

'Where to, Cap?'

'Into a dark room at the back of the boat. At first … I can't see anything. Then Mr Chimera's face hovers into view, like a pale moon. "Tell me, young man," he says, "have you ever heard of the … MIGHTY FIZZ CHILLA?"'

— Forty-four —

I

'Here it is!' cries Milo, jumping to his feet. 'At last! You're in the same room as Mighty Fizz Chilla! Go on, Cap! Go on! Go on!'

II

'Mr Chimera says, "Young man, I have travelled the seven seas more years than your eyes have blinked. I have seen sights and creatures beyond belief. Centaurs stampeding through the rubble of Sparta! Serpents sucking submarines to the ruins of Atlantis. The hundred-headed Hydra hissing at heroic Hercules. All these things I have witnessed. But nothing equals the majesty or the beauty of what I'm about to show you now."'

'It's the creature!' cries Milo. 'Describe it, Cap!'

'Don't rush me, laddy!'

'Er … sorry, Cap.'

III

'Mr Chimera says, "There are three kinds of Fizz Chilla. The Lesser Fizza Chilla: this has been seen several times off the shores of Wales and India and was once in the possession of Napoleon shortly before the Battle of Waterloo. The Common Fizz Chilla: this is the most frequently seen and has, at various times, been spotted in all the waters of the world. According to some, a Common Fizz Chilla was briefly in the possession of Julius Caesar,

Mary Queen of Scots, the Captain of the *Marie Celeste*, and the second and fifth wives of Henry VIII. The third kind of Fizz Chilla is the most rare, the most magnificent, the most wonderful. It is behind me now. It is called … MIGHTY FIZZ CHILLA."'

IV

'YESSSSS!' Milo punches the air with glee.

'Mr Chimera lights a candle,' continues the Captain, his voice becoming very hushed. 'He moves to one side and … oh, I can still see the candlelight as it flickered across a table! For there … oh, there it be!'

'What? What?'

'A cup and saucer!'

V

'A cup and …? I don't get it, Cap.'

'That's all I see,' explains the Captain. 'A bone-china cup and saucer. The cup is full of milky tea. And in the saucer is a custard-cream biscuit.'

'I … I still don't get it,'

'Nor did I, laddy,' the Captain assures him. 'So I look Mr Chimera in the eyes and say, "Are ye playing a joke with me?" Mr Chimera glares at me and grips my arm in anger. "A joke," he hisses. "You think I've been travelling the world for three thousand years – yes, three thousand! – for a mere joke?" He points at the cup. "In there is a baby Mighty Fizz Chilla. A descendant of the legendary Mighty Fizz Chilla who swam in the fountain at Pompeii! All baby Fizz Chillas – whether they be Less, Common or Mighty – live, for the first seven months of their lives, in milky, warm tea and feed on custard-cream biscuits. Now … do you want to see the creature or not?"'

'Oh, say, "Aye!", Cap!' urges Milo, restless with excitement. 'Please! Say, "Aye!"'

'I do, laddy … AYE!'

VI

'And? What's it look like, Cap?'

'I don't know, laddy, for … well, nothing happens. The tea remains calm. I look at Mr Chimera and frown. Mr Chimera explains, "You'll have to coax the creature out of the tea. It's a shy little thing and has to be persuaded! Tell the creature how much you want to see it. Make gentle cooing noises like talking to a human baby. Caress it with your voice and … well, it might show itself."'

Captain Jellicoe leans towards the fire, his eyes blazing. 'So I say, "Oooo, pretty Mighty Fizz Chilla … please show yeself … Please, pretty, pretty Mighty Fizz Chilla … I so want to see ye …"'

'And, Cap? What happened?'

VII

'It still refused to show itself, laddy. Oh, the tea swirls around and a few bubbles rise to the surface, but as for any sign of the creature … nothing!'

'Mr Chimera chuckles and says, "Mighty Fizz Chilla can be a shy little thing." And then he clutches my arms and gazes at me with those square, dark glasses. "But, I promise you this, young man, Mighty Fizz Chilla is the most incredible-looking creature ever to grace this planet!"

'I ask, "How incredible?"

'Mr Chimera clutches my arm even tighter and replies, "Combine all the incredibleness of all the other incredible creatures you've just seen. Then multiply that incredibleness by the number of stars in the universe. And that, believe me, is only *one millionth* of the incredibleness of Mighty Fizz Chilla. Now …" He lets go of my arm. "Do you want to see it or not?"

VIII

'I say, "Aye", of course.'

'Mr Chimera says, "Then buy it! And wait for it to reveal itself. And when that day comes – as one day it will, it must – you will gasp like you have never gasped before."'

'Oh, buy it, Cap,' urges Milo. 'You've just *got* to find out what it looks like! You've *got to*!'

'"How much do you want for it?" I ask Mr Chimera.

'And Mr Chimera replies, "The contents of your left trouser pocket, if you please."'

IX

'Wh-what?' gasps Milo. 'But … that's stupid!'

'Stupid or not it's what I gave him: a snotty handkerchief, a fish hook, a boiled sweet, a dead cockroach, a shoelace, a bus ticket and a piece of fluff.'

'"Many thanks, young man," says Mr Chimera, "I wasn't expecting such treasure." He hands me the cup and saucer. "Mighty Fizz Chilla is now yours. May your life be eventful."

'Here, laddy! Look ye! The receipt Mr C. gave me!'

X

> ### *Fin, Fur and Feather*
>
> Receipt No. 2,000,000,611,277
> 1 Baby Mighty Fizzy Chilla
> Price – contents of left pocket
> Paid in full
>
> Mr Chimera

'Mr Chimera also gave me an envelope marked "HOW TO CARE FOR YOUR MIGHTY FIZZ CHILLA". Here – read it.'

XI

MIGHTY FIZZ CHILLA
Some useful hints

1. Feed your baby creatures one custard cream (crumbled) per day.
2. Gentle coaxing will tempt it to reveal itself. Never force the creature to show itself (i.e. don't put anything – fingers or spoons etc. – into the tea) as this could harm the baby creature.
3. Keep the cup topped up with tea (because, of course, evaporation will occur).
4. When it is old enough it will 'hatch' from the cup.
5. After that – it's anyone's guess!

XII

'That night, laddy, I walk back home clutching the cup 'n' saucer as carefully as I can. I don't spill one drop of tea. "Lovey-Dovey Wifey," I call when I reach the front door. "My hands are full! Open up, Lovey-Dovey Wifey." The door swings open and – there she is! I can see her still! My beautiful, green-haired sweetheart. She asks, "What have you got there?" And I reply, "A surprise, my love." But what I should have said was, "A nightmare!" Because from that moment on … oh, aye, from that very evening, things started to go wrong, laddy. Horribly, horribly wrong!'

— Forty-five —

I

'How, Cap, how?'

'Picture the scene: I'm standing next to Lovey-Dovey Wifey in the living room. In front of us on the table are the cup and saucer. Lovey-Dovey Wifey and I are trying to coax the creature out of the cup. "Oooo, come on, little cute Fizzy Chillery, show ye little cuty self to Lovey-Dovey Wifey and Lovey-Dovey Hubby –" There! Ye see, laddy! It's working! Something's emerging from the tea.'

'What is it, Cap?'

II

'A feather, laddy! Now two! Three. More and more feathers until … oh, laddy! It's wings! A pair of beautiful white wings!'

'Ain't they stained by tea?'

'Nay, laddy! They're spotlessly clean. Oh, I've never seen anything so … so wonderful! Here! A drawing I made of it!'

III

'Spectacular, innit!'

'Aye, laddy! Lovey-Dovey Wifey crumbles some biscuit into the tea. A few bubbles rise to the surface as the creature feeds and – That's when it happened!'

'Wh-what?'

'Rain, laddy! Dripping on me head. I look up and – oh, it's the ceiling, laddy! The ceiling itself is raining!'

IV

'H-how, Cap?'

'It's that accursed creature, laddy! Don't ye see that? It's started turning my world upside down already! Rain trickled down the walls. It ruins our beautiful shagpile carpet. The telly shoots sparks. Light bulbs explode.'

'Like a horror film, innit!'

'A horror film it was, laddy! The most horrific horror film since Dracula met the Werewolf in Castle Frankenstein on *The Day of the Living Dead*. And that's when Lovey-Dovey Wifey says, "Oooops, I've left the bath running."'

'The ... bath, Cap?'

'Aye, laddy. You see, when I knocked at the door Lovey-Dovey Wifey was just about to have a soak and she left the taps on.'

'But, Cap ...'

'What, laddy?'

'Ya can't blame the creature for –'

V

'I know what ye are going to say, laddy!' The Captain holds his hands up. 'An overflowing bath! The creature can't be responsible for that! Right?'

'Well ... yeah!'

'Well ... *wrong*! Oh, laddy, ye be the first person I've ever told the whole story to. Please, I beg of ye, wait till I get to the end before ye judge anything. It's so important to me that I make ye understand. I *need* ye to understand me, laddy. Deal?'

'Deal!'

VI

'The next night Lovey-Dovey Wifey and me tried to coax the creature again. We couldn't wait to see what the entire thing looked like.'

'Nor can I, Captain!'

'So help me, laddy. Come on, "Oooo, little Fizzy Chilly ... how we want to see of your cuty little body."'

'Oooo, Fizzy Chilly, let me see ya –'

'There! Oh, laddy! Look something is emerging from the tea! It's wriggling and ... oh, nay! NAY!'

'What, Cap?'

'Look at this drawing!'

VII

'But ... what is it, Captain.'

'A tentacle!'

'Ya mean ... like an octopus?'

'Aye, laddy.'

'But what kind of animal can have wings *and* a tentacle?'

'I don't rightly know, laddy. Nor does my Lovey-Dovey

Wife. And, try as we might, we couldn't get the creature to reveal any more of itself. Not that night anyway.'

'So … when did it?'

'Seven days later.'

'What did ya see?'

'This –'

VIII

'Wh-what's that, Captain?'

'An alicorn.'

'A … what?'

'The horn of a … unicorn!'

'Unicorn! But … oh, Cap! Wings! Tentacle! Unicorn's horn! What kind of creature is it? I can't … I can't get me brain around what it might be!'

'Nor could I, laddy! But I tell ye this … while I look at the alicorn sticking up from the tea, the next bit of accursed creature horribleness takes place to ruin my life.'

'What?'

'Fog!'

IX

'Fog!'

'Aye! The house is filling with fog, laddy. I start to

cough! Lovey-Dovey Wifey starts to cough! It's so thick and black, oh, it makes my eyes water. What panic there is, laddy. And that's when I hear Lovey-Dovey Wifey splutter, "Ooops, I've left the sausages under the grill."'

'The … sausages?'

'Aye, laddy. You see, when I called out, "Lovey-Dovey Wifey! Look! Something new is rising from the tea", she was cooking our tea and left the sausages under the grill.'

'But, Cap …'

'What, laddy?'

'Ya can't blame the creature –'

X

'Don't say it, laddy, for yet again I know exactly what ye be thinking! "Burnt sausages! The creature can't be responsible for that." Right?'

'Well … yeah.'

'Well … *wrong*! Oh, please, laddy, let me tell ye the whole story before ye judge anything. We had a deal, remember?'

'OK, OK, Cap! What happened next?'

'Why next, laddy, I lost my eye!'

XI

'Your eye! How?'

'Picture the scene, laddy: Lovey-Dovey Wifey and I are sitting at the table playing tiddlywinks. Beside us is the creature in its cup. Lovey-Dovey Wifey is just about to flip a tiddlywink when … oh, the most disturbing thing so far emerges from the tea!'

'What!'

'This!'

'It … it looks like …'

'Aye, laddy?'

'A shark head.'

'Shark head it is! I cry out, "Lovey-Dovey Wifey, look!" Lovey-Dovey Wifey jumps and flips her tiddlywink too hard and – Splat! Into my eye.'

'You mean … you were blinded by a tiddlywink?'

'Aye, laddy! A tiddlywink turned me Cyclops!'

XIII

'But, Captain … you can't blame the creature for –'

'I can! I can!'

'It's just an accident, innit!'

'And accidents just happen? That what ye think?'

'Well … yeah!'

'Wrong! Wrong! A million times wrong! Accidents *don't* just happen! Things don't *just* go wrong for no reason. There is a reason! The most accursed reason of all! The reason is … MIGHTY FIZZ CHILLA!'

— Forty-six —

I

'But, Captain –'

'No buts, laddy! I can see in ye eyes ye be doubting my every word. But I'll prove it to ye yet! Here! Read this –'

**NEED HOME DECORATION
DONE CHEAP?**

Then contact

Jimmy Slapdash
at 64 Liberace Road

for free estimate
(followed by next-to-nothing service)

II

'Why ... why ya showing me this, Cap?'

'The house, laddy. It was in a terrible state. Water from the bath had made the floors and walls damp. Smoke from the sausages had sooted the ceilings. Decoration was urgently required. And, of course, I couldn't do it because –'

'Ya eye!'

'Aye! My eye! Apart from being half blinded, the shock had made me feel quite poorly. I was a bedridden Cyclops.

And Lovey-Dovey Wifey kept saying, "Oh, Lovey-Dovey Hubby, I need the house de-damped and de-sooted." So … ye tell me, laddy! What should I do?'

'… Get Jimmy Slapdash!'

III

'Picture the scene, laddy: I'm lying in my bed. A bandage round my left eye. I've taken some tablets – for the pain – so I be a bit … well, whoozy. And there! On the dressing table! The cup with the baby Mighty Fizz Chilla! Lovey-Dovey Wifey don't want Jimmy Slapdash seeing such an extraordinary creature, ye see! He might take a shine to it and steal it! And, of course, at this time, I still hadn't realized the danger of the creature. I, like ye, still believed in accidents and coincidences. So I lie in bed and stare at that cup … The tea trembles like it's about to simmer and – There! Look ye, laddy!'

'What?'

'This!'

IV

'Wh … what is it, Cap?'

'What's it look like, laddy?'

'I … ain't sure. The pattern on the skin – well, that's a bit like a tiger.'

'A tiger it is, laddy. A tiger's body! And, as I lie, day after day, I get glimpses of all these things. Sometimes a tentacle and horn. Sometimes a shark head and horn. Sometimes a tiger body, tentacle and horn. But, no matter how long I watch, I never see the complete creature. Or how the various bits of its body are connected. And, meanwhile, I hear … oh, hammering and sawing! The sound of Jimmy Slapdash decorating the house. And that's how I lie for seven weeks. Listening to banging. Watching the creature. Until … oh, *that* moment!'

V

'*What* moment, Cap?'

'I remember the time and date so well, laddy. It was seven o'clock in the morning on the 7 July and I was … Oh! oh, nay!'

'What? What?'

'The memory of it, laddy! It's like I'm back there! In that bedroom! Look at it, laddy! The cup! The tea's bubbling and swirling. Like it's boiling. The cup's shaking? Ye see it, laddy? Rattling in the saucer! Tea spilling! Rattling gets louder! And – there! A flash of wings! Tentacle! Horn! Shark! Wing! Horn! Shark! Faster! Faster Faster! And then … NAY!'

'What?'

'The cup explodes and – oh, NAYYY!'

'What?'

VI

'I hear the front door slam shut – oh, NAYYYYY!'

'What?'

VII

'The broken cup! Spilled tea and – oh, NAYYYYYY!'

'What?'

VIII

'I ran out of the bedroom! "Lovey-Dovey Wifey," I call.

"It's hatched!" But the house, it's – oh, NAYYYYYY!'
'What?'

IX

'Empty! The house is empty. No one and nothing! No furniture! No carpet! Everything gone! I rush downstairs and ... oh, NAYYYYYYY!!!'
'What?'
'There, laddy! On the bottom step! A letter – Here! Look! I've kept it all these years as evidence – Look ye! LOOK YE AND WEEP!'

X

Dear Lovey-Dovey Hubby,

Being with you is as boring as watching grass grow. In fact, watching grass grow is a mission to Mars compared to your totally tedious company.

If I have to stay with you another day I'll chew my way across the ceiling.

So I'm leaving!

I am in love with Jimmy Slapdash – and have been since the first day I saw him and he first said, 'You could do with a lick of paint too, luv, if you know what I mean.'

Well, I do know what he means and I'm off to get painted.

Goodbye for ever, you boring man.

Miranda

(no longer your Lovey-Dovey Wifey)

XI

'So ... Lovey-Dovey Wifey left you, Cap ... Cap? Where are ya ...? CAPTAIN ...? WHERE'VE YA GONE? CAP ...? CAP ...?'

— Forty-seven —

I

Me – running out of cave.
Me – squinting against sunlight.
'Cap?'

II

Me – running across beach.
Crunch.
Crunch.
Crunch.
'Curse ye ...'
There he is!

III

The Captain – he's standing up to his knees in water.
The Captain – he's stabbing his harpoon into water and screaming –
'Curse ye, creature of wickedness. I will find ye and destroy ye!'
'CAP!'

IV

Me – running up to water ...
Crunch.
Crunch.

V

Me – running into water.
Splash!
Splash!

VI

Me – straw hat blowing off!
Me – feel sun on me head!
Me – feel water in my shoes!
Me – spray in me face!

VII

'Cap! Stop it! Please!'

'It's out there, laddy! The creature! And I'm going to wipe it from the face of the earth for what it did to me – O, CURSE YE, CREATURE! CURSE YE! CURSE YE!'

Splash!
Splash!
Splash!

'But … what *did* it do to you, Cap?'

VIII

'What did it –? Oh, laddy, how can ye *ask* that! Didn't ye hear what I've been telling ye? While I was sick in bed, the two of them – my Lovey-Dovey Wifey and Jimmy Slapdash – they weren't decorating! Nay! They were stealing furniture! And my Lovey-Dovey Wifey ran off with that interior decorator and it's all because of – THAT ACCURSED CREATURE! YE WON'T ESCAPE ME! CURSE YE!'

'So … you think the creature's to blame?'

IX

'*Think!* I don't *think* it, laddy, I *know* it! Lovey-Dovey Wifey would *never* have left me were it not for … THAT ACCURSED CREATURE! YOU CAN'T HIDE FROM ME!

CAN YE HEAR ME? I'M GOING TO HUNT YE OUT AND HARPOON YE BETWEEN YE SHARK EYES … YE WICKED –'

'Calm down, Captain.'

'I'LL HARPOON YE IN YE TENTACLES –'

'*Please*, Captain. Remember what we said about getting angry. We made a toast! To tame the Fizzy Wasps! Remember? Please! Tame them now! Tame them!'

'CREATURE …'

'Tame the Fizzy Wasps!'

'I … oh, laddy … oh, oh!'

'You calmer now, Captain?'

'I … oh, aye. Calmer, laddy, aye … Help me back up to the beach, will ye?'

X

Splash!

Splash!

Crunch …

Crunch …

'Let's … sit for a while … laddy, eh?'

'Whatever you want, Captain – Here! Let me help you.'

XI

The Captain is panting and sweating and resting his face in his bandaged hands and I've got me arm round his shoulder and – ugh! They're so hairy!

XII

'Lovey-Dovey Wifey and me … we were happy, laddy. She wouldn't just call me boring … not unless she had been under the spell of that accursed creature.' The Captain stares at Milo with one tear-filled eye. 'Ye understand that, don't ye, laddy? *Please* say ye do. I want ye – oh, how I *need* ye to – understand.'

XIII

'Yeah, Cap,' Milo assures him gently. 'I understand! No one in their right mind would ever leave you. Why, you're the most thrilling and exciting person I've ever met. The accursed creature is to blame.'

XIV

The Captain heaves a sigh of relief, 'Oh, laddy,' he breathes, wiping the tears from his face. 'Ye are the greatest friend an old man could ever have.'

'And you,' says Milo, giving him a hug, 'are the greatest friend a young man could ever have.' Then he gives the Captain a cheeky grin. 'And I'll like ya even more if ya tell me what it looks like.'

'What *what* looks like, laddy?'

'The creature.'

'The creature! Oh, aye … well, if you're sure you're ready to hear such horribleness.'

'I'm ready! I'm ready!'

XV

'Well … where was I in the story? Mmmm … aye! The creature hatched from the cup. Now, I didn't get a good look at it because I went downstairs to get Lovey-Dovey Wifey –'

'Fast-forward, Cap! Lovey-Dovey Wifey is gone. What d'ya do? Go back upstairs?'

'Aye.'

'And?'

XVI

'The creature – it's nowhere to be seen. I look around! Behind the wardrobe. Under the bed. And then –' the Captain points '– there!'

'What, Cap?'

'A trail of tea!'

'Follow it!'

'I do!' The Captain walks along the beach. 'Come on, laddy! Picture the scene with me! Imagine it! Conjure it in your mind! We're following a trail of tea out of the bedroom – Ye with me, laddy?'

'I'm with ya, Captain.'

'Down the hallway ...'

'With ya ... yeah!'

'Into the bathroom – There! A smashed window!'

'It's got out!'

'Aye, laddy. I look outside and – there it is! Making its way across the grass to the garden pond! And – oh, it's horrible, laddy! Horrible. HORRIBLE!'

— Forty-eight —

I

'Describe it, Captain! Please!'

'It's about the size of … well, a fried fillet of cod! Its head is a shark. And sticking out of the top is the unicorn horn. And it's got the body of, oh, a tiger. And on either side – wings! And the bottom part of its body – why, laddy, five octopus tentacles wriggle and writhe and squelch – Look! I'll try to draw it in the sand for ye.'

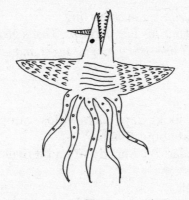

II

'Spectacular, innit!'

'Aye, laddy! For a moment, I just stare at it. Dazzled!'

'Like a rabbit in car headlights, Cap!'

'Aye, laddy! Exactly! Unable to move! I watch the creature wriggle and flap its way across the grass then – splash! – into the garden pond. I rush down and scream at it, "IT'S ALL YOUR FAULT! EVERYTHING THAT'S GONE WRONG IN MY LIFE! IT'S ALL BECAUSE OF YE!" And I try to catch it. But … oh, the creature is too quick for me. Like trying to catch an eel in a bathtub of olive oil. And … oh, listen, laddy! The creature is laughing at me. "Hee-hee-hee!" Such a nasty, spiteful laugh. "Hee-hee-hee!"' The Captain stops talking and looks at some driftwood by his feet. 'Mmm, perfect,' he murmurs, picking it up and running his fingers over its bleached smoothness. 'I know just where to put this.' He taps Milo's shoulder. 'Keep ye eyes open, laddy. I be needing plenty more driftwood if I'm ever going to finish my boat.'

III

His mood has changed so quick, innit.

Building the boat – it gives him something else to think about!

Stops him yelling and screaming.

Helps him tame his Fizzy Wasps. That's good.

Me – I don't like seeing him all upset and screaming.

So –

IV

'I'll help you look, Cap!' says Milo, scampering over the pebbles. 'What about this bit?'

'Just right, laddy! And there's a bit over there!'

'Got it!'

'And there!'

'Got it! Come on, Captain! Let's take them back to the cave. I'll help ya build the boat!'

'That's kind of ye, laddy. My damaged hands are still a little sore. And, while ye work, I can tell ye the rest of the most horrible story ever known to mankind. For if ye hair ain't turned white and ye teeth ain't curled yet … why, laddy, they soon will.'

— Forty-nine —

I

Milo grabs the hammer and –

Bang!

Bang!

Bang!

'How's that, Cap?'

'Mighty fine, laddy! And make sure the nails be not too long. Don't want them sticking though the other side. And make sure you hammer them in nice and tight. Don't want the wood coming lose halfway across the ocean – Ye sure ye don't want any help, laddy?'

'Nah, Captain! You lie there and rest.'

'Ye be looking mighty hot there, laddy. Look at ye T-shirt. Dripping with sweat.'

'Yeah, it's sticking to me, innit. Think I'll take it off.'

'Oooo, very macho, eh?'

'Yeah,' giggles Milo. 'What would Mum say, eh? Now, come on, Cap! The story! What happened after the creature splashed into ya garden pond and went, "Hee-hee-hee!"? Tell me! Please!'

II

'It tormented me, laddy. That's what it did!' The Captain takes a bite from one of the rolls Milo had brought and chews it thoughtfully. 'Every morning, when I be in the kitchen making breakfast, the creature would find a way in and spit water in my face – Mmm, I'm feeling a mite hungry. Where's that lunch you brought, laddy?'

'Here! In the silver foil! Catch!'

'What is it, laddy? Do ye know?'

'Nah.'

'Mmm … smells very scrumptious … Aha! Laddy! Look! It's slices of pizza!'

III

'Pizza!'

'Aye! And – oh, laddy, we can eat it with our fingers!'

'Yeah! Gimme a piece!'

'Here, laddy!'

'Mmm –' Munch, munch '– what a coincidence, Cap, eh? After all I've been saying about pizza 'n' fingers 'n' stuff.'

'Aye, laddy –' Munch '– a coincidence indeed … mmm.' Munch.

'Ya making –' Slurp! Munch! '– noises while ya eat, Cap.'

'Aye!' Munch! Slurp! 'So be ye, laddy.'

'Mum hates it when –' Munch! Munch! '– I do that!'

'Aye! I bet –' Munch! '– she does.'

'Mum would call us –' Munch! '– typical males!'

'Aye,' Munch. 'That she would!'

'Yeah.' Munch! Slurp! Slurp. 'Yeah!'

'Mmmmmyummmmy!' Slurp! Munch! Slurp! Chew! 'Yummy!'

IV

'YEAHMMMM!' SLURP! MUNCH! SLURP! CHEW! 'GOOD – MMMM – INNIT.'

'MMMM!' MUNCH! LICK! SLURP! CHEW! CHOMP! 'MMMYUMMY!'

'MMMMYEAH!' MUNCH! LICK! SLURP! 'HA!'

'HA! HA!' GIGGLE! SLURP! MUNCH! 'HA – HA!'

'HA! HA!' LAUGH! SLURP! SPIT! CHEW! 'HA – HA!'
'HA! HA! HA!'
'HA! HA! HA!'

V

And, for a while, Milo and the Captain collapse in hysterical laughter against each other.
'HA! HA! HA!'
'HA! HA! HA!'

VI

Gradually, they get their giggles under control, wipe tears from their eyes, swallow the last of their pizza, lick their fingers clean and –

VII

'This … this ain't gonna get the boat built, Cap,' says Milo, picking up the hammer and –
Bang!
Bang!
Bang!
'Don't stop, Cap! The story! More! What happens next in the story of the accursed creature?'

VIII

'Mmm … aye …' The Captain swallows his last mouthful of pizza and continues. 'Every afternoon, as I sat in the living room, the creature would find its way in and tickle my nose with its feathers and tentacles – You want some of this here juice, laddy?'
'Nah! But I do need a … a saw, innit.'
'A saw –? Oh, to cut the wood, ye mean.' The Captain points to a pile of tools in the corner. Ye will find it there, laddy. And if ye don't mind me saying so, laddy, you're looking a bit … well, flushed! Do ye think ye should slow

down a little?'

Saw!

Saw!

'Nah! Go on! Story!!'

IX

'Picture the scene! No matter how hard I try to keep the creature out, it always finds a way back in. Tormenting me day and night with its spitting and tickling and its childish, "HEE-HEE-HEE!"'

'Did ya try to catch it?'

'Of course, laddy. I laid mouse-traps with custard creams instead of cheese. Chased it round the house with butterfly nets. But I never, *never* got my hands on it! And all the time it was … growing!'

X

'Growing?'

Bang!

Bang!

'Aye, laddy! Before long it was the size of a cat! Then a dog! Then a –'

'Gimme the orange juice, Cap.'

'Oh … it's all gone, laddy.'

Milo sighs and –

Bang!

Bang!

'Story, Cap! More story!'

XI

'One day I wake up and … well, I knew what I had to do. I had to become the tormentor, not the tormented. The hunter, not the hunted. I had to –'

'Take control, innit!'

'Aye, laddy! I had to take control and –'

'Destroy the accursed creature!'

'Aye! Aye!'

Bang!

Bang!

Bang!

XII

'And so I went out into the garden. Oh, laddy, I can see it now! The creature – it be almost too big for the pond now. Its five tentacles squirming over the edges. Turning the once beautiful lawn to mud. Its cold shark eyes gazing at me. I grab a shovel and I yell, "I AM GOING TO DESTROY YE, ACCURSED CREATURE!"

Bang!

Bang!

'Go on, Cap! I'm listening!'

XIII

'I raise my shovel high and then – SPLOOSH!'

'What?'

'The creature flies up … out of the pond!'

'Chase it!'

'I do!'

Bang!

Bang!

XIV

'The creature can't fly too far! It needs water, ye see! And then – Splash!'

'What?'

'The creature's dived into the river.'

'Don't let it escape, Cap!'

Bang!

Bang!

XV

'I jump into a small rowing boat and I row after the creature and ...'

Saw!

Saw!

'... row and row ...'

Bang!

Bang!

'... and so my long hunt for the accursed creature begins –'

XVI

'What next, Cap? What next?'

'I'll tell ye, laddy. But before I do ... a question for ye, if I may?'

'Go ahead.'

Bang!

Bang!

'Ye promise ye won't get all Fizzy Wasps on me?'

'Yeah! We promised to tame 'em, didn't we?'

'That we did, laddy! But, ye see, I have a question about … Mojo.'

BANG!

BANG!

'Go ahead, Cap!'

XVII

'Well … from what ye said earlier, despite all the warnings from ye mum, ye *did* make friends with this wild thing, laddy.'

'In a way, yeah.'

'What d'ye mean?'

'Well …'

Bang!

Bang!

XVIII

'I kept following Mojo around. Trying to find a way to start chatting to him …'

Bang!

Bang!

XIX

'But I never could. I was a little … well, scared, I think … Mojo looked so spectacular riding through the estate on his motorbike. Doing wheelies and stuff. Smoking. Drinking … He's not gonna be interested in me, I thought … And then … and then …'

'Aye, laddy?'

'Well … Mojo – he made friends with *me*!'

— Fifty —

I

'*He* made friends, laddy?'

'Yeah! Ya see, one day, I was sitting at the bus shelter. The number eight bus stops there and ... oh, it goes to lots of spectacular-sounding places. St Paul's Cathedral, Oxford Street, Hyde Park Corner, Victoria Station.'

'And where were ye going, laddy?'

II

'Oh, nowhere! I never do. Mum wouldn't let me travel that far without her, innit. But ... oh, I like sitting at the bus stop and watching the people get on and off. Wondering what kinds of life they lead and –'

Bang!

Bang!

'– all the different things they've seen. It's peaceful at the bus stop too. I can just ... sit 'n' think and – there's a motorbike!'

III

'Wh-what's that, laddy?'

'It's Mojo, Cap! I'm at the bus stop and there he is, Cap! Mojo. Sitting on his bike and grinning. "Wotchya!" he says. I ... I look all round me. He must be talking to someone else. But there ain't no one else at the bus stop. Just me! So ... Mojo is talking to me, innit!'

Bang!

Bang!
Bang!

IV

'Mojo says, "What you looking so gloomy about, eh?"
And ... well, I couldn't speak. I just glared. Mojo says,
"Cat got ya tongue, mate?"'
   Bang!
   Bang!

V

'Mate! Mojo was calling me "mate"! I couldn't believe it!
Spectacular Mojo – he was trying to make friends with
me! ME!'
   Bang!
   Bang!

VI

'Mojo says, "Come on! I'll give ya a ride on me bike.
That'll cheer ya up." And so ... I get on his bike. And ...
whoooosh! Oh, it was so fast. Wind in me face. Wind in me
mouth. I clutched hold of Mojo for all I was worth. We
went down Bethnal Green Road. Past Mile End Tube
Station. Over the flyover at Bow. Totally and utterly
spectacular!'
   Bang!
   Bang!
   Bang!

VII

'Mojo said, "Meet me up the bus stop tomorrow. I really
like ya, man. It's like ... like we've known each other for
years and years, innit." And it was, Cap! It really was!'
   Bang!
   Bang!

Bang!

VIII

'Next day … Mojo said, "Ya know what – you're the best mate I've ever had, Mi." That's what he called me. Mi! So I said, "And you're the best mate I've ever had, Mo." That's what I called him. Mo!'

Bang!
Bang!
Bang!

IX

'Of course … I had to keep it secret from Mum. She'd've blown her top if she'd found out. She says, "Hope you weren't with that nasty boy, Sweetie?" I'd say, "Nah! Course not, Mum." Didn't like lying to her but … what could I do? Mo and me were mates … No more driftwood!'

'Wh-what?'

X

'Driftwood, Cap. Used up. I'll get some more –'

'I'll … I'll help ye –'

'Nah! Stay there, Cap.'

Crunch …

Crunch …

Crunch …

XI

Look! The sun's low 'n' bright red.

Must be getting late and –

Oooo, got a headache!

Crunch!

Crunch!

Here's some driftwood!

More! And – there!
More!
More!
More!
More!
More!

XII

'Look what I've got, Cap –'
He's asleep, innit.

XIII

Saw!
Saw!
Bang!

XIV

Need more driftwood –
CRUNCH!
CRUNCH!
OUCH!
Everything sounds so ... loud!

XV

SPLOOSH!
Crunch!
Head – it's going boom-boom.
Cwaaa.
CWAAA.

XVI

More drift –?
CRUNCH!
SPLOOSH!
Me – legs made of jelly.

Me – stomach going over and over.
And … oh, the sand is m
                    e
                      l
                        t
                          i
                            n
                              g
                                What's going on? I'm … oooo, the sand

Fifth Day

is turning into water and now I'm floating ...

— Fifty-one —

I

Ocean, innit! Me – in the middle! Not the big concrete place full of people. Not where we live. But the big wet stuff full of fish. I'm floating in the middle of …

> *Oh, a big, big ocean.*

II

Above – big, bright sun!
> *And lots of seagulls going –*
> *Cwaaa …*
> *Cwaaa …*

III

Me – kicking me legs to stay afloat.
> *Me – drinking salty water.*
> *Me – sun burning top of head.*
> *Me – screaming, 'SOMEBODY HELP ME. SOMEBODY –'*

IV

'– HELP ME!'

'Oh, listen to him, Dee! Don't worry, Beloved. We're here! We're –'

'Don't give him froth, Cressida Bell. He needs facts! Milo Kick! Listen carefully! You are in your room at Avalon Rise. In your bed. You are suffering from a touch of the sun. You are delirious. Can you hear me, Milo Kick? You are *delirious!*'

V

Look! A boat!
  It's made of driftwood, innit!
  No one's in it!

VI

Me – swimming over to boat.
  Me – climbing inside.

VII

Feel that!
  A breeze!
  The boat – it's
moving!
Moving
slowly

through the ocean. Look over the edge …
   Oh, so many fish. All different colours and –
   There!
   Someone's in the ocean!
   The boat – it's heading straight for them.
   'Don't worry,' I call. 'I'll save ya!'

VIII

Me – reaching over edge.
   Me – clutching a hand.
   Me – pulling person on board.
   It's a girl!
   About my age.
   She's got long red hair with a seashell clip in it and her dress is covered with dolphins and stars –
   'Mum!' I gasp. 'It's … it's you! Mum –'

IX

'– Mum!'
   'Oh, Dee. He's calling for his mum now! Don't worry, Beloved.'
   'Sip some more water, Milo Kick!'

X

'Oh, Mum – there's so much I wanna ask ya! Tell me about the Mermaid on the beach. Was it alive or dead? How big was it? And … your name in a heart with someone called Griff! Who was Griff? – Oh, tell me, Mum! Tell me!'
   Mum – she don't say a word.
   Mum – she just smiles at me.
   Mum – points at something.
   I look and see –

XI

Someone else in the ocean.
   The boat – it's heading straight for them.

'*Don't worry!' I call. 'I'll save ya!'*

Me – reaching over edge.

Me – clutching a hand.

Me – pulling person on board.

It's a man!

He's wearing a suit covered in white 'n' black squares and a frilly shirt and he's got a bottle of whiskey in his hand –

'Checker Kick!' I gasp. 'Checker –'

XII

'– Kick!'

'Dee! He's having dreams about that vulgar man. It's all my fault! Oh, don't panic, Beloved!'

XIII

'Checker!' I cry. 'There's so much I wanna ask ya! What did ya do with that ten thousand quid? It's a lotta dosh! Did you spend it all on booze?'

Checker – he don't say a word.

Checker – swigs from his bottle.

Checker – points at something.

I look and see –

XIV

Someone else in the ocean!

The boat – it's heading straight for them.

'Don't worry!' I call. 'I'll save ya!'

XV

Me – reaching over edge.

Me – clutching a hand.

Me – pulling person on board.

It's a man!

He's wearing a wig and a dress, like a pantomime dame, and he's clutching a brown envelope full of money –

'Valentino True!' I gasp. 'Oh, there's so much I wanna ask ya! Did you stay with Checker for long? Did you ever get the

part in a Shakespeare play like you wanted? Oh, why won't ya talk to me! Valentino! Checker! Mum! All of ya! Don't just sit there! Say some –'

Valentino points at something.

I look and see –

XVI

Someone in the ocean!

The boat – it's heading straight for them.

'Don't worry!' *I call.* 'I'll save ya.'

Me – reaching over edge.

Me – clutching a hand.

Me – pulling person on board.

It's a man!

He's wearing his white doctor-like coat and he's holding a book of poetry –

'Jay Dee Six!' *I cry.* 'Oh, am I glad to see ya! Come on, mate! Tell me about the Wizard. You walked into a clearing in a forest. Remember? With your sister? Remember? And you saw a wizard – oh, what was he like, Jay? Tell me! Pretty pleeaasse!'

Jay Dee Six points at something.

I look and see –

Someone in –

XVII

'– the ocean! Somone's in … gotta save them!'

'Oh, I've never heard such delirium, Dee!'

'I'll aim the fan at him a bit more! He needs cooling down, Cressida Bell! Here, Milo Kick, sip some more of this water!'

'It's Lovey-Dovey Wifey!'

'Who, Beloved?'

'Who, Milo Kick?'

XVIII

Lovey-Dovey Wifey is in the boat!

She fiddles with her curly green hair and humming a ... oh, it must be her 'someone love me' song.

'I've got a bone to pick with you!' I tell her. 'How could ya leave the Cap like that? And steal all the furniture too. That's way out of order. He thought the world of ya and ya treated him like ... like a piece of dirty chewing gum stuck to ya shoe.'

XIX

'Where's the Story taking us?' asks Lovey-Dovey Wife.
'Where's the Story taking us?' asks Mum.
'Where's the Story taking us?' ask Valentino.
'Where's the Story taking us?' ask Checker.
'Where's the Story taking us?' asks Jay.
'What d'ya mean,' I ask. 'What?'
And then all of them together, over and over again, ask, 'Where's the Story taking us ...? Where's the story taking us? Where's the story taking us ...?'

XX

'I dunno what ya mean!' I yell. 'Tell me what ya –'
Then I glance at the reflection of the boat in the water.
Across the side is written something!
Must be the name of the boat.
In the water it looks like:

ƳЯOTƧ

It's back to front obviously!
What is it the right way round?
Then I get it.
It's –

XXI

'THE STORY! IT'S ... IT'S THE STORY!'

— Fifty-two —

I

'Calm down, Beloved!'

'I'm in the *Story*! Where … are we going? Where … where's the *Story* taking us …? Where's the *Story* taking us –'

'You sure we don't need a doctor, Dee?'

'Do stop fussing, Cressida Bell. I told you, it's heat exhaustion. The Professor used to suffer from it frequently when we did our summertime experiments. All Milo Kick needs is rest, shade, a cool place, lots to drink and … a little peace and quiet! So try to refrain from frothing all over him. In fact, move your beached whale of a body so I can lay this damp towel on his forehead.'

'Mum! Mum!'

'Oh, listen to him, Dee! He's crying out for his mum.'

'What ya pointing at now, Mum? All of ya? What ya all –

II

– pointing at? Something ahead, eh?'

I look and see.

An island!

That's where the Story *is heading!*

It's taking us right to that Island and …

Oh! Look! I think it … yeah!

It's shaped like a heart. You hear me? IT'S SHAPED LIKE –

III

'... A HEART! IT'S THE FLOATING ISLAND CALLED HEART.'

'Deep breaths, Milo Kick!'

'OH ... THE *STORY*'S ON THE SHORE OF THE HEART!'

'Milo Kick is talking absolute nonsense, I'm afraid, Cressida Bell.'

'Nonsense it may be, Dee. But ... oh, it's pure poetry.'

IV

Me – climbing out of boat.

Me – standing on the beach.

Me – standing with Mum, Checker, Val, Jay and Lovey-Dovey Wifey.

The sun's so hot.

Burning the top of me head, innit.

And me lips are dry.

Tongue feels big.

And above –

Cwaaa ...

Cwaaa ...

Cwaaa ...

V

'Seagulls ... never seen so many, innit!'

'Oh, Beloved, the seagulls are outside.'

'You are in your room, Milo Kick.'

'Zillions of seagulls, innit! Hear them! Shrieking! Making me head hurt, innit! Seagulls! Sky getting darker with seagulls! And ... what ya all pointing at now?'

'Who are you talking to, Beloved?'

'He's delirious, Cressida Bell! How many times do I have to say –'

'Look! On the beach, innit! It's a trail of tea and –'

VI

'– custard creams! Let's follow it, everyone! Come on!

Me – walking across the beach.

Me – following a trail of tea and custard creams.

Me – being followed by Mum, Checker, Val, Jay and Lovey-Dovey Wifey.

Crunch.

Crunch.

Crunch.

And above –

VII

Cwaaa! Cwaaa! Cwaaa!

'Shut up! You hear me, ya seagulls! Shut – Ah! Now you're swooping at me! Clear off. Clear off –'

'There it is!' *says Mum, pointing*

'There it is!' *says Checker, pointing.*

'There it is!' *says Valentino, pointing.*

'There it is!' *says Jay, pointing.*

'There it is!' *says Lovey-Dovey Wifey, pointing.*

I look up and see –

VIII

'A cave! The tea and … custard creams …! They're heading into a cave …'

'Don't smother him, Cressida Bell.'

'But I want to hold him!'

'I'm going in the cave … It's getting darker … Oh, I'm scared!'

'Don't be scared, Beloved.'

'No, don't, Milo Kick!'

IX

I can just make out … stalagmites! Yeah! And stalactites! Moss on the rock! And – oh, look! Driftwood on the floor and –

Someone's feet!

X

Someone's standing in the shadows.
I can't see who it is.
'Who are you?' I ask. 'Who –?'

XI

'– are you?'
'It's me, Beloved! Your Cressie!'
'Fact: I'm Dee Dee Six!'
'I … I can't see your face! Come out of the shadows, innit! Come out! I can hear ya breathing! It's … it's a man! Yeah! You're a bloke, ain't ya! And – oh! Look, everyone! He's holdings a cup! A cup of tea!'
'Perhaps, he's thirsty, Dee.'
'Here, drink this, Milo Kick.'

XII

And in the tea I can see …
A flash of wings!
Tentacle! Alicorn! Tiger skin! Shark head!
It's MIGHTY FIZZ CHILLA!

XIII

'The Story *brought us here,' says Mum.*
'The Story *brought us here,' says Checker.*
'The Story *brought us here,' says Valentino.*
'The Story *brought us here,' says Jay.*
'The Story *brought us here,' says Lovey-Dovey Wifey.*
'Yeah,' *I say.* 'The Story *brought us here!'*

XIV

'Of course the Story *brought you here,' says the voice from the* *shadows. 'Where else would it take you?' He crumbles some custard-cream biscuit into the tea.*

Splash! goes the tea as the creature feeds.

'After all,' the man in the shadows continues, 'all stories lead to me. Haven't you learnt that yet? All stories lead to me.' And he starts to laugh. 'HEE-HEE-HEE … ALL STORIES – HEE-HEE! LEAD TO MEEEEEEEEEEEEEEEEEE!!!!!!'

— Fifty-three —

I

'NAH!' Milo sits bolt upright, dripping with sweat, clutching the sheets. 'NAAAAAAHHH – oh … Cressie? Dee?'

'Beloved! Are you awake?'

'He is, Cressida Bell!'

'I'm … in me bed, innit!' He flops back on to the pillows. 'Oh … I had a nightmare and … Oh, how'd I get here! Wh-what happened?'

II

'The facts,' says Dee, feeling Milo's forehead, 'are these: you were in the sun without the hat I gave you –'

'It blew off, innit!'

'You didn't drink enough. You ran about too much. In short, Milo Kick, you did all the things I specifically warned you not to. Result: heat exhaustion. You've been in a fevered sleep for –' she glances at her wristwatch '– twenty-two hours!'

'Twenty-two!' gasps Milo. 'But … I don't get it!'

'Beloved,' sighs Cressida, giving him a hug. 'The only thing you need "get" is that you're safe … Oh, your poor heart! It's beating so hard! Bless! Bless!'

'But … I don't remember walking back here.'

'You *didn't* walk back, Milo Kick.' Dee dabs sweat from his face and neck. 'You passed out on the beach and you were carried back.'

'Not by ...?'

'Oh, you *know* who, Milo Kick.' Dee fluffs up the pillows behind him. 'That weirdy-beardy!'

III

'Dee!' cries Cressida. 'How can you still call the Captain that! He saved our Beloved!'

'The Captain,' interrupts Dee, irritably, 'is *responsible* for this whole mess! Working Milo Kick like a skivvy. While he – that lazy-crazy – snoozed. And – more to the point – drank all the orange juice!' She puts a glass of water in Milo's hand. 'Sip this, Milo Kick! Liquid is your medicine now.'

IV

Milo empties the glass, then says, 'I'm ... I'm sorry, Dee. It must've really annoyed ya to see me with the Cap!'

'Oh, it's "the Cap" now, is it?' sneers Dee.

'Let Beloved speak, you brutal woman!'

Milo takes a deep breath and continues, 'I ... I lied to ya, Dee. At least ... well, I let ya think I didn't see the Cap. Or go into the cave. But I did. And I'm really, really, really sorry.'

V

'Apology accepted, Milo Kick.' Dee sits on the edge of the mattress. 'Let's not get all frothy about it – Wrist!'

'Eh?'

'I need to feel your pulse, Milo Kick! Wrist, wrist! Thank you.' She feels the beat of his blood for a moment, then says, in a softer voice, 'I am, of course, grateful the Captain was so ... *functional* last night. He carried you up the stairs. I'm not sure I could've done that. And, of course, Cressida Bell is about as useful as a one-legged man in a butt-kicking contest!'

— 247 —

VI

'I ... I ...'

'What, Beloved?'

'Well ... the Cap. He'll ... he'll be worried about me. I know he will. I don't like to think of him all alone in his cave and –'

'Then don't think about it,' interrupts Dee, letting go of his wrist. 'Because the Captain isn't in his cave. He's here.'

'Here!' gasps Milo. 'In ... in Avalon Rise?'

'Yes, Beloved! Oh, yes! The Captain's back where he belongs!'

VII

Dee gets to her feet. 'Well, I could hardly send him back into the wilderness after he ... helped you.' She pats the top of Milo's head gently. 'I had been so ... *curious*, wondering where you were. Oh, if only I hadn't got drunk and slept all day long I could've stopped you getting ill –'

'Nah, Dee! Don't blame yourself. Ain't your fault.'

'Well ... thank you, Milo Kick! But I have my own opinions about my own actions.' She coughs to clear her throat. 'Besides, it's thanks to the Captain that Cressida Bell and I were able to concentrate on tending you all last night and all today.'

'What d'ya mean?'

'The Captain has been our cook. And, at this very moment, he's downstairs preparing some light supper.'

'I wanna see him! Can I? Pretty pleeaasse!'

VIII

'In good time, Milo Kick! Just rest a bit more. That man ... oh, I know he has his good points and he thinks the world of you ... but he still froths things up for everyone around him. And you need calm.'

'Dee's right, Beloved.'

'Yeah ... OK! It's just good to know he's near by.'

'And it's good to know you're near by too, Milo Kick.'

And, with that, Dee leaves the room.

IX

'A heart of gold,' sighs Cressida. 'That's what she's got.'

'So have you, Cressie.'

'Why, Beloved, how utterly, utterly nice of you to ... Oh, look at me! Brimming up again!' She wipes tears from her eyes and snuggles close to Milo on the bed. 'Ooo, this is very cozy – Not making you too hot, am I?'

'Nah!' He snuggles closer to her. 'You still smell of that rosewater stuff – Oh, yesss! The Mermaid! Griff! Tell! Tell!'

'Aha!' chuckles Cressida. 'I was wondering when we'd get round to those two things. I seem to remember you rushing into my room yesterday morning and asking about Griff.' She sighs deeply and holds Milo's hand. 'Tell me, Beloved, is the sun setting?'

Milo glances out of the window. 'Yeah! Oh, you should see the sky, Cressie! It's bright red and yellow and ... it's spectacular!'

'Then the moment's right.' Cressie's voice is tinged with sadness. 'For, like this day, my story is coming to an end.'

— Fifty-four —

I

'Imagine this: I am on the beach with my beautiful Fliss. We're on our way to the cave so –'

'So you can do ya painting of Merlin, innit.'

'Bravo, Beloved! It's a hot day. The air … it's very still. No breeze at all. And then we see – Oh, look! Someone's lying on the beach. It looks like … yes! It's a woman and … a fish tail instead of legs. It's –'

'The Mermaid!'

'I'm clutching Fliss's hand so tight. We rush up to the creature and – oh! OH!'

'What's wrong? Is it dead?'

II

'No, Beloved! It … it was never alive. For now we can see … The Mermaid's hair is seaweed. Her eyes two shells. And the rest of her … sand and pebbles with fingers of broken driftwood. I've … I've never seen anything like it. And nor has Fliss. I can hear her gasp beside me. She asks, "Who … who could've made this, Cressie?" I tell her, "I have no idea … but it's … it's …'

'Spectacular!'

III

'Exactly, Beloved! Spectacular. Just the word I'm looking for. Fliss and I look at the Mermaid for … oh, it must have been hours. The sun sinks lower and lower. "We

should be getting back to Avalon Rise, Fliss," I say. But she won't leave the Mermaid. It's like she's hypnotized by it. "You must leave it, Fliss," I tell her. "The tide's coming in."'

'The sea – it'll … erode the Mermaid, innit.'

'Erode! Oh, Bravo, Beloved. I'm *so* glad you're remembering all these words. And … yes, that's exactly what happens to the Mermaid. The sea erodes the tail.

Then the belly. The fingers. And all the while, Fliss is weeping, "Poor Mermaid ... poor, poor Mermaid." As if it was a real living thing that was being eroded before our eyes.'

'Was ... nothing left?' asks Milo, softly.

IV

'Not a fish scale,' Cressida replies, hugging him closer. 'And that night your poor mum ... oh, she was so utterly, utterly sad. She goes out into the garden and gazes up at the stars. I say to her, "It was only sand and seashells, Fliss." Your mum says, "I know that, Cressie! But ... oh, did you see the expression on the Mermaid's face? So lost ... so lonely! Oh, who made it, Cressie? I've just got to find out. I've got to!"'

'And did she? Eh? Bet she did! Who made the Mermaid, Cress –?'

'Don't rush me, Beloved! Stories have to reveal themselves in their own good time.'

'Sorry ... Go on.'

V

Cressida takes a deep breath. 'The next day, once again we were on the beach, making our way to the cave, when we see – a horse! A horse with ... wings! It's the horse from the Greek myth. Pegasus! I'm clutching Fliss's hand so tight. We rush up to the creature and – oh! OH!'

'It's sand and pebbles, innit!'

'And rocks, Beloved. The horse is in a sitting position. And the wings are old surfboards. And the rest is sculptured sand and pebbles and seashells and ... oh, it's a masterpiece! A true masterpiece. But again the sea –'

'Erodes it!'

'And again –'

'Mum can't stop thinking about it.'

VI

'The next day – at last! – I make it to the cave. No creatures on the beach – although Fliss is looking everywhere. So while I sketch the stalagmites and stalactites, she's walking up and down the shore.' Cressida gives Milo's shoulders a squeeze and her voice becomes very hushed. 'I'm halfway through a sketch when I see – There! Look!'

'What?'

'In a shadowy corner of the cave. I move closer ... oh! OH!'

'What? What?'

'Why, Beloved ... it's a dolphin.'

VII

'Alive or dead?'

'Neither!'

'You mean ... another creation?'

'Just so, Beloved. And this one's all sand. It looks like it's jumping out of the ground itself! And then I see – Look!'

'What?'

'Blankets! Some empty crisp bags. A can of Coke! And then I realize ... whoever is making these things – they live here! In the cave! I rush on to the beach and call for Fliss. When she sees the dolphin and blankets she's so excited she can barely breathe. She says, "Let's wait here and see who it is." And that's just what we do. We wait.'

'And ... what happens?'

VIII

'Well, my belly starts to rumble for one thing. And, of course, I've got a guesthouse to run. Finally I say, "Fliss, we must be getting back to Avalon Rise. Dinner needs preparing – Come on!"'

'But Mum don't wanna leave, eh?'

'Just so, Beloved. She's determined to stay a little longer. I tell her, "Well, not too long." I come back here. To Avalon Rise. One hour goes by. Two … Three! Still no Fliss. Oh, I'm so worried, Beloved! It gets dark! I'm just grabbing a torch to return to the beach when … there she is!'

'Mum!'

'"Oh … Fliss! Look at you!"'

'"What, Cressie? What's wrong?"'

IX

'Her face, Beloved! It's shining like she's drunk a cup of starlight. Her eyes are twinkling like dew on roses. And I know what's happened! I don't even have to ask.'

'What, Cressie?'

'Whoever made those miraculous creatures had returned to the cave. And your mum – my precious Fliss – she was … *in love!*'

— Fifty-five —

I

'LOVE!' cries Milo, jiggling with excitement. 'Who was it? Who did she meet? Griff! Of course! It was Griff, wasn't it? Eh? Eh? It was Griff –'

The bedroom door swings open and Dee strides in. 'That man is just too much!' she declares. 'I'm trying to be patient but … oh, what a mess he's making in my kitchen! One baking tray burnt beyond repair. Pastry stuck to the ceiling!' She paces round the room. 'Cressida Bell! Get down there and do something. We'll *never* get dinner at this rate –'

'But … oh, no!' cries Milo. 'I need to know about Mum being in love –'

II

'Love!' splutters Dee, glancing at Cressida. 'Have you been exciting Milo Kick with more of your froth?'

'Well … Beloved and I have been talking, yes.'

'*Frothing*, you mean!' exclaims Dee. 'Doesn't *anyone* listen to *anything* I say? Milo Kick needs calm! Milo Kick needs rest! Where's the thermometer?'

'But Dee –' begins Milo.

'But Dee –' begins Cressida.

'No buts!' snaps Dee, shoving a thermometer in Milo's mouth. 'Now, Cressida Bell, get downstairs. Restore order to my kitchen before I throw that lazy, crazy, weirdy-beardy out again. Do you want me to do that?'

'No,' says Cressida. 'Certainly not.'

'Then get downstairs now!'

Cressie makes her way to the door.

'See ya later, Cressie!' says Milo, slumping back in his pillows.

'Indeed, Beloved,' says Cressie, closing the door behind her. 'See you later.'

III

'One degree above normal!' announced Dee, reading the thermometer. 'Now Cressie's gone perhaps you'll cool a bit. Have you been drinking lots of H_2O?'

'Yeah. It makes me pee a lot!'

'That means your kidneys are functioning exactly as they should ... Now move so you're sitting in the breeze from the fan ... That's it! Mmmmm ... dear, oh, dear.'

'What?'

'Oh ... I'm just thinking I'll have to fix the wall Captain Jellicoe damaged. Anything to get rid of that horribly romantic painting. Cressida might have some observational skills where rock formation is concerned, but Merlin's anatomy is totally unconvincing.'

'The Wizard!'

IV

'Wh-what's that, Milo Kick!'

'What I've been wanting ya to tell me about! The Wizard! Ya know? Ya and ya brother! In the forest. Ya both saw a Wizard ... Oh, tell me, Dee! Tell!'

'I don't want you getting excited again.'

'I'll get more excited if you don't tell! I *will* Dee! I will! I will! I will!'

'All right, all right ... so long as you promise to lie back, close your eyes and – no matter what I say – keep calm. Deal?'

'Deal!'

— Fifty-six —

I

'Fact: I am in the forest with my brother Jay Dee Six. Fact: we are both fifteen years old. Fact: in front of us stands a male of the species. Fact: He is dressed as a wizard. Several facts: he is about five feet tall, about one hundred and forty pounds, his hair is orange as burning sodium, his eyes are as blue as copper sulphate, his smile is as breathtaking as … a solar eclipse!'

'You … you fancied him!' chuckles Milo.

'How *dare* you!' gasps Dee. 'I did no such thing. I'm merely reporting the facts, that's all.'

'Yeah, yeah, sure. So … this bloke ain't *really* a wizard. Just *dressed* as one.'

II

'Correct!' Dee flops on the bed. 'He was wearing long robes that billowed in the breeze. A pointed hat. He was even holding a magic wand with a silver star on the end. His name was Avery Chance. He lived with his mum and dad on a nearby farm. He was rehearsing a part in a school play: *The Tempest* by William Shakespeare. Do you know this particular work, Milo Kick?'

'Nah.'

'Nor did I. But Jay … oh, he knew it. And Chance and Jay started talking about poetry and theatre and the magic of language. Right there! In the middle of a snowy forest. I say, "Jay Dee Six, we are supposed to be collecting factual information!" Avery Chance looks at me and do you know what he says? "Chill out, mate." Mate! He obviously thought I was a male of the species. Well, I'm so offended I walk away and fill my test tube with frozen rabbit poo.'

'What happens next, Dee?'

III

'I … I watch them. Jay Dee Six and Avery Chance. Oh, how they laugh together and converse. Like they've known each other for years and years. I can't bear to listen to them. I walk further away. But … oh, I can still hear them. Giggling. Gossiping. No matter where I go. I hear them! I hear them! Hear –'

'Keep calm, Dee.'

IV

'I'm … sorry, Milo Kick. It's been … one of those days.' She cleans her glasses on the corner of a sheet. 'Fact: that night Jay Dee Six says, "Avery wants to be an actor just like me. His mum and dad don't understand him. Just like you and the Professor don't understand me. Avery says he's not going to milk cows and feed chickens for the rest of his life. He's going to run away from home and become … a film star! Oh, he's so brave!"

'I say, "Go to sleep, Jay Dee Six!"

V

'But, that night,' continues Dee, 'I dream of Avery Chance. I dream he's holding me in his arms. I dream he's –' Dee stops herself and gives Milo an embarrassed look. 'Oh, dear … I'm frothing, I think.'

'You *fancied* him, didn't ya?'

'I … well –'

'*Fact*, Dee!'

'Yes, Milo Kick! I FANCIED AVERY CHANCE!'

VI

'Did ya … tell him?'

'*Tell* him!' gasps Dee, cleaning her glasses more
frantically than ever. 'Certainly not. I couldn't possibly run
the risk of the Professor finding out. He'd enough trouble
with Jay Dee Six without me adding to it.' She puts her
glasses back on. 'Every night, when the Professor was
asleep, Jay Dee Six would sneak out and recite poetry with
Avery Chance somewhere in the forest. I used to press my

nose against the window-pane, my breath misting the glass, wondering what it must be like to be … frothing in a midnight forest.'

'You should've followed him, innit.'

Dee gives Milo a knowing smile and puts her arms around him. 'Why, Milo Kick, that's exactly what I did!'

'Spectacular!'

VII

'It was the seventh night of their secret meetings,' Dee explains. 'It would also, I knew, be their last. The Professor, you see, intended to move the Labmobile to another location – miles away! – the very next day. So … after Jay slipped out into the night, a book of poetry clutched under his arm, I followed. I crept through the forest, keeping a safe distance. And then – There! The two of them. At the spot where we all first met. Sitting in front of a small camp fire and … frothing, frothing, frothing!'

'What did ya do?'

VIII

'I watched them. Oh, how Avery Chance's eyes blazed in the firelight. How his skin shimmered and … oh, his voice! So rich and deep and thrilling. Nothing but poetry and froth, of course. But … oh, how my heart beat to hear him say it. Then … they talk in whispers for a while. Jay Dee Six is nodding and – He's standing! Jay Dee Six is rushing off! Back to the Labmobile! I tuck myself behind a bush and … oh, Avery Chance is all alone now. He's packing up his books, and … and I want to speak to him so much!'

'Do it!'

IX

'I take a deep breath and step out of the shadows. My foot goes "crunch" in the snow. Avery Chance looks up and says, "What you come back for?" And then I realize. He thinks I'm my brother. I'm so taken aback that … oh, I can't move. I just stand there, motionless. Avery Chance says, "Look, Jay, we haven't got much time. Go back and pack a few things. Hurry! We've got to do it now! It's our only chance, mate."'

'They're running away, innit!'

X

'He walks over and wraps his arms around me. "You can't stay here, Jay! It'll destroy you. Your dad's a heartless machine. You're an artist! You know that?" And I want to say, Yes! I hear you. Me! Dee Dee Six! Let us *all* run away together.'

'Why didn't ya, then?'

XI

'Because the next thing Avery Chance says is, "And that sister of yours is even worse. She scares me to death. An ice-cube has got more warmth. You've got to get away from her, Jay. You don't want to end up a robot like her, do you?"'

'Oh, Dee,' sighs Milo, squeezing her hand. 'I called you Robot-Woman and … I'm sorry, Dee. Really.'

XII

'Quite all right, Milo Kick,' replies Dee. 'Fact: I went back to the Labmobile. Fact: Jay Dee Six had already packed and gone. Fact: I went to bed. Fact: I was stuck with the Professor.'

'Did ya … hear from Jay again?'

'Oh, yes. He sent postcards –'

'**LADDY!**' roars Captain Jellicoe, bursting into the room.

— Fifty-seven —

I

'CAAPPP!!' roars Milo, bouncing off the bed and into the Captain's arms. 'I'VE MISSED YA, CAP!'

'I've missed ye too, laddy.'

'Well, don't let me get in the way,' sniffs Dee, getting off the bed. 'And please do not excite the boy, Captain Jellicoe. It's because of you he was ill in the first place.'

'Well, he looks as strong as a … a white shark now,' responds the Captain. 'And just as hungry.'

'Dinner's finally cooked, then, is it?' wonders Dee.

'Nay, lassy,' sighs the Captain. 'Dinner's finally ruined. I burnt the soup. Dropped the Cornish pasties. And the trifle wouldn't set. But Cressida and me – we have made a pile of tuna sandwiches. And there's a big bowl of crisps. And two bowls of peanuts. And a big box of chocolates. So – it's a party! How's that sound, laddy?'

'Spectacular!'

'Then, come on! All of us! Aye! Downstairs and PARRRTTTTYYYY!!!'

— Fifty-eight —

I

'Party pieces!'

'Eh, Cressie?'

'What's that, lassy?'

'Don't be foolish, Cressida Bell.'

'Oh, *please* be pleasant, Dee!' urges Cressida. 'Sitting here with everyone like this … my Beloved beside me on the sofa. Captain Jellicoe in Papa's old chair. All of us eating and gossiping and drinking … oh, it brings back such memories of the heydays of Avalon Rise! And we always used to have party pieces after dinner. One by one we'd get up and sing a song or tell a tale or … oh, anything. What d'ya say? Party pieces, "Yes" or "No"?'

'Yeah, Cressie!'

'Aye, lassy!'

'… Very well, Cressida Bell.'

II

'Me first!' cries Cressida, rushing to the piano. 'Now, it's a while since I played this so you'll have to bear with me. It's a song Papa wrote, called "Life Goes Boo!" And when it comes to the chorus, I'll point to each one of you in turn and you have to say "Who? Me?" – Oh, you'll soon get the hang of it. Ready, everyone?'

'Go for it, Cressie.'

'Launch that song, lassy.'

'Get on with it, Cressida Bell.'

III

*Listen to that! Cressie can play that thing brilliant, innit! Hands
shooting up and down the keys and – oh, look! Her feet bouncing
with the beat and –*

The Captain – his feet are bouncing too!
And Dee – even she's tapping a foot!
Hang on! Cressida's about to sing –

IV

'I always thought
I'd go to France.
Learn to dance.
Put a cobra
In a trance.
So many things
I thought I'd do
But of all those things
I've done too few –
Cos life has a knack
Of surprising you.
It just creeps up and yells out "Boo!"
It happened to me
So it'll happen to you!'
'Who? Me?'
'Yes, you, Dee!'
'Who? Me?'
'Yes, you, Captain, you!'
'Who? Me?'
'Yes, you, Beloved.
If it happened to me
It can happen to you
For life is a thing
That just goes –

'Chorus coming up,
everyone!
Get ready for me
pointing at you!'

'Ready, Cressie!'

'Ready, lassy!'

'Ready, Cressida Bell!'

V

'BOO!!!'
yells Milo.
yells the Captain.
yells Dee.

VI

Spectacular, innit!
All of us – even Dee – dancing!
And flopping into seats.

VII

'Who's next!' cries Cressida. 'Come on, Dee! *Your* party piece now!'

'Yeah!' encourages Milo. 'What is it, Dee?'

'Facts, of course,' replies Dee, her face flushed and gleaming. 'Ask me anything about ... well, anything except frothy subjects.' She takes a sip of sherry. 'Brain on legs, that's me! Come on! Ask! Ask!'

VIII

Cressida asks, 'What's the world's largest flower?'

'The giant rafflesia,' replies Dee instantly. 'It can grow up to 105 centimetres – that's nearly four feet – and weigh up to seven kilograms or 15.4 pounds. Next question! Quick!'

Captain Jellicoe asks, 'What sea animal be so transparent when born that ye can see its tiny heart beating?'

'The seahorse! Oh, these are far too easy. Milo Kick! *You* ask me something to tax my brain cells, please!'

IX

Milo asks, 'How many seconds in a year?'

'Leap year or normal?'

'Er ... normal?'

'31,536,000 – Correct?'

'Well, I ... I dunno,' admits Milo. 'Just wanted to know the answer, innit.'

'Well, ask me something you can verify, Milo Kick! Cressida Bell, back to you! Quick, quick!'

X

Cressida asks, 'What's the first line of the poem –'

'Froth!' snaps Dee, shaking her head. 'Try again!'

'Well …' Cressida thoughtfully sucks a chocolate. 'Got it! Name the moons of Jupiter –'

'Ganymede! Eur –'

'Wait!' Cressida gives a mischievous smile. 'Beginning with the *closest* to Jupiter and ending with the *furthest* away.'

XI

'Mmm!' Dee's eyes light up with the challenge. She thinks for a moment, then in one breath recites, 'Metis, Adrastea, Almanthea, Thebe, Io, Europa, Ganymede, Callisto, Leda, Himalia, Lysithea, Elara, Ananke, Carme, Pasiphae, Sinope!'

'Oh, bravo, Dee!' Cressida claps her approval.

'Yeah! Spectacular, Dee,' agrees Milo, clapping. Then he jumps to his feet. 'My turn!'

'What's your question, Milo Kick?'

'Not a question! My party piece!'

'Ooooo,' squeals Cressida. 'Such enthusiasm! What's it to be, Beloved?'

'I'm gonna …' Milo is breathless with excitement. '… touch the tip of me nose … with me tongue!'

XII

'Is that possible?' queries Dee.

'Be mighty breathtaking if it be,' responds the Captain.

'But … oh, Beloved!' complains Cressida, 'I won't be able to see this anatomical wonder.'

'You can *feel* it, Cressida! All of ya sit on the sofa … ! The Cap in the middle. Cressida that side! Dee that side! Now … Cressie! Gimme ya finger!'

'Like this …?'

'Yeah! Now … I'll put ya finger to me nose when the

tongue's touching it! Ready?'

'Ready, Milo Kick.'

'Aye, laddy, aye.'

XIII

Milo's tongue pokes out ... and out ...

Push it out further, innit!

'It's getting there, Milo Kick.'

'Keep going, laddy.'

'Oooo, Beloved!'

Milo's face is getting redder as he strains to get his tongue up to –

There, innit!

'It *is* possible, Milo Kick!'

'A true wonder, laddy!'

'Let me feel, Beloved ... Oh, I can feel your tongue! Your nose! Together! What an utterly, utterly *glorious* party piece! Bravo! Bravo! Bravo!'

XIV

Milo flops on to the sofa, stretching out across their laps. 'Yesssss!' he cries in triumph, then snuggles his head into Cressida's lap. 'You make a good pillow, Cressie.'

'Well ...' she giggles, stroking his head. 'I'll take it as a compliment.'

'Cap! Rub me feet, will ya? I like me tootsies being rubbed.'

'Aye, laddy,' says the Captain, massaging Milo's feet, 'it'll be a pleasure.'

'Dee, move ya bony knees a bit, will ya? They're sticking in me back!'

'Pardon me for breathing,' murmurs Dee, shifting her legs.

'This is … spectaacuulaar!!' Milo quivers with the sheer comfort of it all. 'I'm so … floppy! And … yeah, I'm glad ya all liked me party piece! Mo taught me – oh, that's short for Mojo. Told the Cap about him, didn't I, Cap? Mo could touch his nose with his tongue too and I said, "Teach me, Mo." We sat in McDonald's for hours one day. The day after he first spoke to me, in fact. Mo – he stuck his tongue out and showed me how to stretch it. Then I stuck my tongue out and Mo said, "More, Mi! You've got to get more muscles in ya tongue, mate." Oh, you don't wanna hear me rambling on like this.'

'Oh, ramble away, Beloved.'

'Aye, laddy, ramble.'

'Proceed, Milo Kick.'

— Fifty-nine —

I

'Well ... on the third day of being mates with Mo, he says, "Tell me about the girls you live with." I started chatting about Sarah and Jackie, but Mo, he was getting a little impatient. "Nah, nah," he says, "not them. The other one. With the curly hair." I say, "Trixie?" And I just sort of rambled on about her for a while, not really knowing what to say. Then I happened to mention the butterfly hairclip ... Oh, ya don't wanna hear about this!'

'We do, Beloved.'

'Aye, laddy, we do.'

'We do, Milo Kick.'

II

'Well ... Trixie had seen this hairclip she liked in a jewellers down near Brick Lane. It was shaped like a butterfly and ... well, it cost too much for her. She'd have to save all her pocket money for six months to get it. Anyway ... the next day – the fourth day of being mates with Mojo – he puts something in me hands. It's about the size of a matchbox and wrapped in golden paper. "What's this?" I ask. Mo says, "A present, innit!" And I'm so happy! Mo has bought me a present! My best mate Mo! I start to unwrap it. Then Mo says, "Hang on! It ain't for you. It's for Trixie! I want you to give it to her for me. Just say it's from an admirer –" Oh, this must be boring you all.'

'Certainly not, Beloved.'

'Nay, laddy.'
'Not boring in the least, Milo Kick.'

III

'Well … that night I gave the present to Trixie. She says, "Who's it from?" I say, "An admirer." And Trixie blushes all over and giggles and rips the wrapping paper off. Inside … is the butterfly hairclip. She puts it in her hair and asks, "How do I look?" And I say, "Humpfff", cos now I'm beginning to realize … Mojo weren't interested in me at all. He was only using me to get to Trixie! He wanted Trixie, not me … Oh, you don't wanna hear all this.'

'We do, Beloved.'
'Aye, laddy, we do.'
'Proceed, Milo Kick.'

IV

'Well … the next day Mo says to me, "Did she like it? Eh? The hairclip?" I say, "Humpff." Mo says, "I've been trying to catch her eye ever since I got back to the estate. I talked to her once but she said I was trouble and she had to keep clear of me. But if she likes the hairclip … well, she might think I'm not such a nasty piece of work. Tell her it's from me, eh? Say, 'Mojo bought it for ya and he wants a date.' Put in a good word for me, Mi. Tell her I've changed. I ain't what I used to be. I'm a good-boy Mojo now …" Oh, you don't wanna –'

'Do!'
'Aye!'
'Proceed!'

V

'Well … that night I looked at Trixie as she showed off her hairclip. Everyone wanted to know who gave it to her. Her mum. My mum. Jackie. Sarah. Everyone was going, "Oh it's so *romantic*! A secret admirer ... Who *is* it, Milo? You must put us out of our misery." And I felt so ... so wound up. Angry. Ya know? Mojo was *my* mate. I saw him first. How dare Trixie stick her big nose in! So I said, "It's from Mojo! Him and his mates are having a game – it's called 'Who Can Get a Date with the Ugliest Girl on the Estate' and Mojo reckoned you were the ugliest girl, Trixie ..." Oh ... oh ...'

'Oh, don't stop!

'Aye, go on.'

'More!'

VI

'Well ... oh, I shouldn't've done it! I know I shouldn't. Trixie bursts into tears and rushes out of the flat. Next thing I know – shouting! Outside! I rush to the window. Trixie has found Mojo and she's shouting at him, "How dare you play a game with me! How dare you play games with *anyone*! 'Ugliest Girl on the Estate' – you and your mates are sick! Sick!" Mojo tries to interrupt, but Trixie just throws the butterfly hairclip at him and screams, "MILO'S TOLD ME EVERYTHING! HE'S A TRUE FRIEND! YOU ARE ... UGHHH!" And with that, she walks away from him ...'

'And?'

'And?'

'And?'

VII

'Trixie comes back to the flat. Everyone comforts her. And, of course, Mum is annoyed with me for disobeying her and hanging around with Mojo in the first place. "You see!" says Mum. "I was right! That boy is a nasty piece of work! I *knew* you were seeing him ... all your 'Humpffs'. You've never made sounds like that before. Perhaps now you'll listen to Mummy! Don't go anywhere near Mojo." But, of course, now I didn't want to. Because I knew ... Mojo would have it in for me, innit! He would … hurt me if he could …'

   'And?'

   'And?'

   'And?'

VIII

'I stayed in the flat for three days. Too afraid to go out, innit. Then I heard that Mojo had moved away all of a sudden. His dad had got a job on the other side of London and Mojo had gone with him. So … so I left the flat and … I went down to the market to buy some chocolate and Coke … and … and …'

   'Mmm?'

   'Mmm?'

   'Mmm?'

IX

'MOJO! There he is! On his bike. He catches sight of me. I run! Mojo chases me. I run! I run! I run! All the way down Mare Street! Run! Run! But … well, I can't outrun a bike, can I? Mojo's just following me. Cruising speed. And he's laughing! Laughing … I'm too exhausted to run any more. Mojo gets off his bike … he … he grabs me and … and …'

   'Oh!'

   'Oh!'

   'Oh!'

X

'Mojo punches me. Hard. In the belly. I … I … can't breathe! "STOP!" I cry. But he don't –'

   'Oh, no!'

   'Nay!'

   'No!'

XI

'Mojo cracks my head aginst the wall. Kicks me. Punches

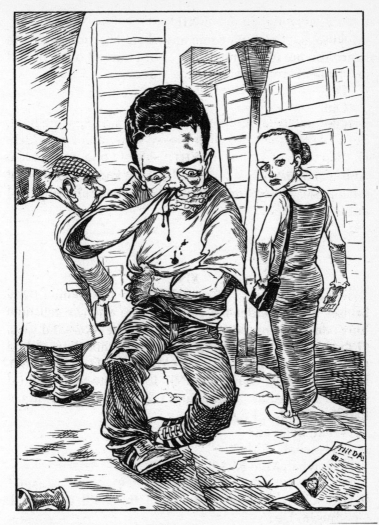

me again. Again … I fall to the ground … Mojo kicks me in my back –'

'Oh, Beloved.'

'Oh, laddy.'

'Oh, Milo Kick.'

XII

'Mojo says, "Don't ya come anywhere near me again. Ya hear? You are not wanted!" I ... I ... I hurt all over me ... I just ... lie there ... just lie there ... for ages ...'

'Oh!'

'Oh!'

'Oh!'

XIII

And ... no one helps! I ... just lie there and ... people just walk past ... They don't ask if I need help or anything ... I am ... all alone ...'

'...'

'...'

'...'

XIV

'When I get home ... I go straight to my room ... My bruises are all under me clothes so no one can tell how hurt I am ... Mum pops her head into me room and says, "I thought you were going to buy some chocolate –" And suddenly I'm yelling, "LEAVE ME ALONE! THIS IS MY ROOM! CLEAR OFF! GO ON!" It was the first time I'd ever ... shouted at ... Mum and I didn't mean to ... it just happened ... I ... I ... I ...'

'What, Beloved?'

'Aye, what, laddy?'

'Yes, what, Milo Kick?'

XV

'I ... I ... I'm feeling tired now. I think I'll go to bed. Goodnight, Dee.'

'Goodnight, Milo Kick.'

'Goodnight, Cressie.'

'Goodnight, Beloved.'

'Cap ... will you tuck me in?'

'I'd be honoured to, laddy.'

— Sixty —

I

'Comfy, laddy?'

'Yeah.' Milo nestles into the pillows. 'Thanks, Cap.'

'Ye be more than welcome, laddy.' The Captain sits on the edge of the mattress. 'Ye need ye rest after that mighty party piece. I haven't heard so many words tumble from one mouth since I met the Chattering Chimpanzee of ChimiChanja.'

'The … what?'

'Oh, just one of the many creatures I encountered while hunting Mighty Fizz Chilla.' He leans back next to Milo, his voice becoming a secretive whisper. 'I tell ye, laddy … some of the sights I've seen over the years … oh, they hardly seem possible.'

'Tell me some, Cap,' pleads Milo, resting his head against the Captain's tattooed shoulder. 'Go on.'

II

The Captain says, 'I've been chased by an angry polar bear across Antarctica's endless snow and made my final getaway on an iceberg the size of a house where I cooked a succulent fish for tea and watched a meteor burn in the midnight sky … Ye want to hear more, laddy?'

'Yeah! Tell me … the *best* bit of all ya adventures.'

'Why, laddy, the best bit was when I finally got the prophecy that led me to ye. Ye want to hear about that?'

'Mmmm, yeah.'

III

The Captain puts his arms round Milo, 'Picture the scene, laddy: I'm in a small boat no bigger than a canoe. I be paddling up a river. A big river, laddy. On either side – jungle! Trees with leaves the size of … why the size of the sheets on this bed. All my years of searching have led me here, laddy: the Congo River in the heart of Africa.'

'Spectacular!'

IV

'The river is full of the most amazing things – Look, laddy!' The Captain leans over the edge of the bed and points. 'Tell me what ye see. Look!'

'I see … carpet and –'

'Nay, laddy! You've got to use ye imagination. We're on a river. Look again!'

'Green …'

'Aye! The carpet *is* green. Now imagine the green of the carpet begin to ripple and swirl. Ye see that?'

'Yeah.'

V

'The carpet is a river! Listen, laddy. Trickling water. Splashing. Hear that?'

'Yeah! Yeah! I really do!'

'And there! Look!'

'What is it, Cap?'

'The elephant snout fish!' cries the Captain, pointing. 'See it? A fish with a long nose and – Oh, look! The nose is electric!'

'Yeah, I *see* it now, Cap! I really can!'

VI

'And there!' The Captain points somewhere else. 'The underwater antelope searching for fish on the river bed!

And there!' Pointing to a shadowy corner of the room. 'The walking catfish! It uses its fins like elbows! Ye see that, laddy?'

'Yeah, yeah!'

'Oh, can ye feel the heat, laddy? And hear the tropical dragonflies buzz and smell the smell of a million exotic flowers?'

'I *can*! I *can*!' cries Milo, for his skin is now prickling with sunlight, his ears droning with insects and his nose tingling with the aroma of foliage. 'I'll help ya paddle, Cap!' And Milo kneels on the other side of the bed and paddles. Spectacular here, innit!'

VII

'Look out, laddy!' roars the Captain, bouncing on the mattress.

'Wh – what is it?'

'A hippopotamus! It's underneath the canoe – Umph!' He nearly falls off the bed. 'Oh, they can be vicious creatures. Ye see it, laddy?'

'Yeah, yeah!'

'Quick, laddy! Let's paddle out of the way!'

Milo paddles as fast as he can.

I can feel the paddle in me hands, innit. Can see it splash in the water and … Oh, see the jungle whiz by in a blur of green –

VIII

'Well done, laddy. We're hippopotamus-free now.'

'That was close, eh, Cap?'

'Aye! The Congo River be full of suprises. Just when ye think it's safe something always – Oh, nay! NAY!'

'What now, Cap?'

'Look ahead, laddy! It's the rapids! The water's churning and splashing. And it's full of rocks and … Oh, nay! NAY!'

'What?'
'We're heading for a waterfall!'

IX

'Oomph – it's getting rough, Cap.'
   'Keep a grip on ye paddle, laddy.'
   'Like a roller coaster, innit!'
   'Mind that rock, laddy – ooomph!'
   'It's getting – oomph! – rougher, Cap.'
   'We can – oomph! – make it, laddy.'
   'Water spraying in me face, innit!'
   'Keep paddling! Keep – Look out, laddy! Here we go!
Over the edge of the waterfall! Hang on, laddy!'
   'Hang on, Cap!'

X

'EEEEEAAAAAIIIIIIIHHHHH!'
'EEEEEAAAAAIIIIIIIHHHHH!'

XI

'Oomph! We've made it, laddy! The bottom of the
waterfall and … Look, ye! We're in a peaceful lagoon! The
water's still as a mirror. And look at the birds! So many!
Swifts. Swallows. Martins. They all be plucking the insects
from the lagoon surface.'
   'It's so … calm, innit!'
   'Aye, laddy! Let's get to the bank of the river … There!'
Look at those flowers! Big as open umbrellas.' The Captain
puts his paddle down and swings his legs over the edge of
the mattress. 'Come on, laddy! Let's explore the jungle. Ye
feel the grass beneath ye feet, laddy?'
   'Yeah, Cap!'
   And … oh, I see everything … I see …
   I am there –

— Sixty-one —

I

The jungle all round me! So many colours and smells and sounds … Climbing over fallen trees and brushing insects from me face and –

'Look at that, laddy!'

'What is it, Cap?'

'Why, it's … it's the ruins of an ancient temple. Ye see the huge stones?'

'Yeah!'

II

We're making our way towards the temple, innit. The rocks look so old. Most of them are smashed. There's ancient writing on some and all of them have got moss and ivy growing on them –

'Monkeys!'

'Wh-what, Cap?'

'Can't ye see them, laddy? Hundreds of monkeys all over the temple. They're jumping up and down and shrieking and –'

'They don't want us here, do they?'

'Ye be right, laddy! The monkeys are protecting the ruined temple.'

'Perhaps … Oh, Cap, perhaps there's treasure inside!'

'Why, laddy, I hadn't thought of that, but … Aye! Ye might be right! What shall we do, laddy? Brave the monkeys and go inside or run away! The choice is yours.'

'Brave the monkey's, innit!'

III

We're making our way into the temple … The monkeys are still bouncing up and down and – Oh, they're really noisy, innit.

It's cooler in the temple!

Cap and me – we're walking down a stone corridor.

Footsteps, echoing all round me.

Sunlight coming through hole in roof.

'Look at this, laddy!'

'What is it, Cap?'

'Ancient writing on the walls! Like a form of hieroglyphics! Mmmm … oh, look ye, laddy. It seems to be representing mythical animals. A unicorn, and a … oh, a bull's head on a man's body? What is that! Aye! A minotaur. Ye see, laddy!'

I look at the wall and …

IV

'What kind of place is this, Cap?'

'No idea, laddy! But if ye be getting scared, we can always go back to the canoe and run away as fast as –'

'Nah! Nah! Let's go on! But … well, perhaps I should hold ya hand! Just in case ya get lost, of course!'

'Aye, laddy! Good idea.'

V

We move deeper into the temple, innit.

It's getting darker.
And … yeah! Cooler!
Sounds of jungle get fainter –
   'Laddy! Look! Another drawing of a creature! It's got a shark's head and a tiger's body and – oh, laddy! Can it be? Look! LOOK!'

VI

— Sixty-two —

I

'Mighty Fizz Chilla, innit!'

'Aye, laddy! Mighty Fizz – Oh, look! A monkey's grabbed my hand!'

'Mine too!'

'It's pulling me!'

'Me too.'

'Into … oh, laddy! We're in a chamber! Torches – that's *fire* torches – on the walls! And in the middle – Oh, look!'

'What?'

'A withered man. His face is so shrivelled it looks like a … oh, a skull, laddy. He's wearing a toga! Like from ancient Rome! And he's sitting on a throne made of solid rock! He looks so small and frail in such a big seat! And – oh, look! The monkeys are waiting on him. Serving him bowls of mangoes and grapes. Goblets of wine! One monkey is massaging his feet. Another is rubbing his temples. And now … oh, the man is looking at us! He's beckoning us forward! Shall we go, laddy?'

'Come on! Forward, Cap!'

II

We step forward and the monkeys gather round us – all making monkey noises. The man leans forward. I can hear his bones go click and pop and –

'He's saying something, laddy!'

'What?'

'The old man says, "What are you doing here? Piddle off!"'

III

The Captain says, 'We ... we didn't mean to trespass but –'

'Piddle off! Go on! Piddle!' *says the old man.*

'Who ... who are ye?'

'What do I look like?'

'An old man.'

'Then that's what I am. It's my name too. Old Man, that's me. Now ... piddle off.'

'But ... there's a creatures drawn on your wall –'

'There's lots of creatures! Piddle off!'

'But this particular creature I bought and –'

'Bought!' splutters the Old Man. 'So you've been on board "Fin, Fur and Feather", eh?'

'Aye! So ye ... ye know about that boat?'

'Know about it? ... Ha!' *The Old Man – he's leaning forward and grinning – ugh! So many teeth. And all of them like peanuts.* 'I built it! You hear? I built that miraculous ark.'

IV

'Ye built it? But ... when?'

'Oh, long before your time. Let's just say ... I taught Noah a thing or two.' The Old Man chuckles to himself. 'I was the first person to search the world for special creatures. And the first to sell them – How much did you pay for the Chilla? Eh?'

'Contents of my left pocket.'

'Cheap at half the price! Oh, I know what you're thinking? Why charge pocket-content prices? Well, it was *me* that introduced that particular pricing system. And let me tell you, it's proved more profitable than money ever could! I've got the pocket price – going back thousands and thousands of years. A certain Egyptian Pharaoh bought Pegasus for a toothpick, a coin and dirty comb. Have you any idea how much those three things are worth now? A fortune, that's what! Why, in twenty thousand years, a humble bus ticket or a half-sucked Polo mint might be sold for a king's ransom. All the contents of pockets are kept here. This is the Temple of Pocket Contents. The basement is full of this valuable treasure. I protect it and make sure ... well, let's just say I make sure the books balance.'

'The books balance?' The Captain chuckles and says, 'So you're Mr Chimera's accountant, are ye?'

'Oh, I'm more than that,' the Old Man replies. 'I'm Mr Chimera's dad.'

— Sixty-three —

I

'His *dad*, innit!'

'Yep! And, as such, I'm here to tell you – no refunds! That's always been the policy. So, even if you catch the creature, you'll never get the contents of your pocket back! Got me? Now piddle off. Hear? Piddle off!'

'But I not be wanting a refund! I be wanting to destroy it!'

'Destroy it!'

The Old Man's voice is so loud – look! The walls of the temple are shaking and bits are falling and all the monkeys are jumping about.

'You silly weirdy-beardy!' says the Old Man. 'How can you even think of destroying such a magnificent specimen.'

'Magnificent!' gasps the Captain. 'It ruined my life!'

'Ha!' spits the Old Man. 'I tell you this, weirdy-beardy, if my son offered you that creature – and, I hasten to add, at a criminally low price – then he must've thought you needed it! And, if you can't see that … well, you ain't got the IQ of a lettuce leaf. Now, piddle off and stop complaining.'

II

'I be willing to … *pay* for the information,' says the Captain. 'How does the contents of my right pocket sound?'

The Old Man is tempted! Look at him. Licking his lipless mouth with that – ugh! His tongue's like a rasher of bacon. But he still says –

'Piddle off.'

'The contents of my right pocket *and* my left.'

The Old Man's in a right pickle now. He wants to say 'Yes', I can tell. But –

'Piddle –'

'All my pockets! Shirt and trousers. That's seven pockets in all!'

III

'Deal!' The Old Man claps his hands together. 'But on one condition. I give you the answer in the form of a riddle. A little trick I learnt from a certain Sphinx just outside Thebes.'

'Well …'

'Take it or leave it!'

The Cap sighs and says. 'Deal, then.'

The Old Man – he's whispering something in a monkey's ear. The monkey rushes off and writes something on a piece of paper. The monkey hands the piece of paper to the Cap.

The Captain reads, 'Where land doth end and –'

IV

'It's the Prophecy, Cap!'

'Aye, laddy, the Prophecy it was. And – oh, I thank my lucky stars for it. For without that, I would've never come here and … met ye!' He ruffles Milo's ridge of hair. 'And we would never have become shipmates.'

'We *are* shipmates, ain't we, Cap!'

'Aye, laddy, the best and mightiest shipmates that ever were. And now … it be time for ye to get some shut-eye and –'

'Nah, Cap!'

'What's wrong, laddy?'

'Ya can't stop there.'

'I ... can't?'

'Nah! Ya told me the story would turn me hair white and curl me teeth. And ... well, that ain't happened.'

V

'It ... hasn't?'

'Nah! Oh, ya story's been full of thrills and surprises and I've enjoyed every second of it, but ... well, I expected more.'

'*More!*'

'Yeah! Oh, Cap, surely, in all ya years of hunting for the accursed creature, surely ya must've got *close* to it? *Surely* ya must've seen it in all its fully grown horribleness. Ya *must've*, Cap! Ya *must've*!'

VI

'Er ... Well ... of course I did, laddy.'

'Then tell me about it, Cap. Tell me the scariest, most hair-whitening, teeth-curling experience ya had with Mighty Fizz Chilla. Pretty pleeaasse.'

VII

'So be it, laddy. If that be what ye want –'

'It is!'

'And if ye nerves be up to the terror –'

'They are!'

'Then prepare to say goodbye to black hair and straight teeth. For I am about to tell ye the closest shave I ever did have with the accursed creature. And if this don't give ye goosebumps ... why, ye ain't got skin!' The Captain takes a deep breath, gazes into Milo's eyes and continues. 'It happened about seven years into my search. I had a small fishing boat at the time. Imagine it, laddy, imagine it! A fishing boat made of wood … a small cabin … Ye see it?'

'… Yeah, Cap!'

VIII

'And all around the boat … oh, the sea is very flat. Not a wave. Not a ripple … Ye see that, laddy?'

'Yeah!'

'The doldrums! That's what weather like this is called. I've been stuck in these doldrums for almost a week now.'

'And now I'm stuck with ya!'

'Aye, laddy. Now we're *both* on the deck of my boat and staring at –'

— Sixty-four —

I

Flat, blue sea.
  Flat, blue sky.
  No waves.
  No clouds.
  No wind.
  Nothing …
  'Oh, it's … eerie, innit, Cap?'
  'Aye, laddy, eerie be the word.'

II

The sun – it's scorching.
  The boat – it barely moves.
  Me – I'm sweating and gasping in the heat already.

III

'Laddy! Throw some of this over the side of the boat.'
  'What is it, Cap?'
  'It's a bucket full of custard creams. The accursed creature might still have a taste for them.'
  'Bait, eh, Cap?'
  'Aye, laddy. Bait!'

IV

I lean over the side of the boat and grab a handful of custard creams and –
  Throw!

Splish!
Splosh!
Splash!

V

The bickies float for a while, then slowly, slowly sink into the water.

    I throw in some more –
    Splish!
    Splosh!
    Splash!

VI

The Cap – he's gone into his cabin. I can see him studying a map –

    Throw!
    Splish!
    Splosh!
    Splash!

VII

Oh, it's so hot and … and humid! That's the word. Humid! I'm sweating so much all me clothes are stuck to me –

    Throw!
    Splish!
    Splosh!
    Splash!

VIII

The bucket is nearly empty now.

    Oh, I don't think this is gonna work. The accursed creature is either miles and miles away or it don't like custard creams any more –

    Throw!
    Splish!

Splosh!
Spla –
VOOOSSHH!!

IX

A shark's head.
   Huge!
   It just came out of the water and –
   Missed me hand by inches!
   I jump back.
   Stare!

X

The shark is eating the custard creams.
   Its teeth are big as carving knives.
   And ...
   Oh, there!
   Look!

XI

An alicorn!
   A glimpse of tiger fur.
   A flutter of feathers.
   A slither of tentacle.
   IT'S MIGHTY FIZZ CHILLA.
   And it ... it's ...
   Huge!

XII

Me – can't move.
   Me – trembling.
   Me – just watching ...

XIII

Munch!

Jaws chomp.
Teeth, teeth, teeth, teeth, teeth.

XIV

Slowly, I start to move …
   Me – I'm backing into a cabin.
   'C- C- Cap.'
   'What, laddy?' *The Cap is still totally engrossed in his map.*
'I'm a little busy –'
   'I've just … seen it, Cap.'
   'Eh? What's that …?'
   'Cap! We're gonna need a bigger boat.'
   And I point out at the ocean.
   'Look!'

XV

Mighty Fizz Chilla is swimming round us!
   Its teeth are glinting!
   Its alicorn is shining!
   Its tentacles are writhing!
   Its teeth are gnashing!
   Its wings are flapping!
   'Look at it, Cap! It's moving so quick. Like a torpedo.
Oh, Cap! I … I can hear it laughing too! Listen!'
   'HEE-HEE!'

XVI

*The Cap rushes out on to the deck and watches the creature as it
circles – watches the glinting and shining and writhing and
gnashing and flapping – and listens to the laughing …*

XVII

'ACCURSED MONSTER! STILL LAUGHING AT ME
AFTER ALL THESE YEARS, ARE YE? HOW I DESPISE
YE!!'

XVIII

And then I see –
   The creature stops circling.
   It turns towards the boat.
   Glint.
   Shine.
   Writhe.
   Gnash.
   Flap.
   'HEE-HEE!'

XIX

'CAP! LOOK! THE CREATURE IS ... OH, IT'S GONNA
ATTACK THE BOAT!!'

— Sixty-five —

I

SSSCCRAAASSHHH!!
  Mighty Fizz Chilla head-butts the boat.
  It goes up in the air –
  Whooosh!
  – then down –
  Splaashh!
  – like a roller coaster!

II

The Cap cries, 'EEIIAAAHHH!!'
  I cry, 'EEIIAAAHHH!!'

III

'Hold on to something, Cap! The creature is preparing for
another strike –'
  SSSCCRAAASSSHHH!!
  'EEIIAAAHHH!!'
  'EEIIAAAHHH!!'

IV

Water – it splashes everywhere!
  Water up me nose.
  Water down me throat.
  Water in me ears.
  But none in me eyes, so I can still see –
  'Oh, nah! NAH!'

'What, laddy?'

'Look, Cap! The creature's alicorn has punctured the boat. We've got a leak!'

'*HEE-HEE!*'

V

Water is slooshing round me ankles. The Cap grabs his harpoon and shrieks at the creature as it hovers just below the surface of the ocean –

VI

'HOW I HATE AND DESPISE YE, ACCURSED –'

'CAP!'

'Wh-what, laddy?'

'A tentacle has grabbed ya!'

'What? Oh, nay! AAIEEEEEE!!'

'Ya've dropped ya harpoon!'

Clunk!

'And, Cap … Oh, Cap, the tentacle is pulling ya over the edge of the boat.'

'AAAIEEE – HELP ME, LADDY!'

— Sixty-six —

I

I try to pull the tentacle off the Cap but –

Oh, it's so slimy and slippery. And every time I tug at it I see the tentacle gets tighter and –

'AIEEEEEE!!' goes the Cap.

'HEE-HEE,' goes the creature.

II

The Cap – his face is blood red now. The tentacle is so tight round his chest he can barely breathe.

And it's pulling him further and further over the edge of the boat –

'CAP!'

He just stares at me, eyes bulging, lips turning blue.

'HEE-HEE!'

And then –

III

I pick up the harpoon.

I strike at the tentacle.

Strike again!

Again!

Again!

IV

The tentacle loosens its grip on the Cap.

Eyes stop bulging.

Face less blood red.
Breathing starts.
'Don't ye stop, laddy!'
Again!
Again!

V

The tentacle slithers off the Cap.
Uncurls.
Slips back into the ocean.
'Oh, Cap! I thought I was gonna lose ya! I could never let that happen. What would I do without ya, eh? What would Milo do without his Cap?'
'And what would Cap do without his laddy, eh?'
We hug each other.
Then –

VI

'Where's the creature now, do ye think, laddy?'
'It's under the boat, innit, Cap. It's deep below and – AIEEE!'
'What's happened, laddy?'
'The creature – it's attacking us from below, Cap. The boat is wobbling all over the place and – AAIIEEE!!'
'AAIIEEE!!'

VII

'Look, Cap!' *I point at the deck.* 'Another puncture hole. It's accursed alicorn is –'
CRASHHH!
'Another hole, Cap – AAIIEEE!!'
'AAIIEEE!!'

VIII

'We're sinking, Cap.'

'Aye, laddy.'
CRASHHH!
'AAIIEEE!!'
'AAIIEEE!!'

IX

'Oh, Cap, water's splashing up to me knees now!
CRASHHH!
'AAIIEEE!!'
'AAIIEEE!!'

X

'Have we got any lifebelts, Cap?'
'Nay, laddy!'
CRASHHH!
'AAIIEEE!!'
'AAIIEEE!!'
Splash …
Splash …
Splash …

XI

'DON'T HIDE YE HORRIBLE SELF UNDER THE WATER!!' *cries the Cap, leaning over the edge of the sinking boat and stabbing at the ocean with his harpoon.* 'SHOW YESELF TO ME! COME ON! IT'S ME YE WANT TO TORMENT! SO LET ME SEE YE IN ALL YE HAIR-BLEACHING AND TEETH-CURLING HORRIBLENESS!! SHOW YESELF, CREATURE!'

— Sixty-seven —

I

Everything goes very still …
  No more crashing.
  No more splashing.
  Silence.
  Then –

II

A noise like a million skateboards zooming over gravel.
  It's coming from below.
  From the ocean.
  Louder …
  Louder …
  Louder …
  Then –

III

The sea begins to bubble.
  Like boiling water.
  And the noise gets louder.
  More bubbling.
  Louder …
  Bubbling …
  Louder …
  Bubbling …
  Then –

IV

An explosion of water!
    Like the biggest fountain ever.
    And –

V

Mighty Fizz Chilla hurls itself out of the ocean.
    'The creature, Cap!'
    'There it blows, laddy!'
    And we stare at –
    Wings flapping!
    Jaws snapping!
    Tentacles writhing!
    Alicorn gleaming.
    Tiger stripes dripping.
    'MIGHTY FIZZ CHILLA, INNIT!!' I cry.

VI

It rises higher …
    Higher …

VII

*The creature – oh, look at it! Look! It's horrible and scary, yeah,
but it's also … beautiful somehow. Look at it. The five writhing
tentacles connected to that magnificent tiger's body.*
    And the shark's head full of teeth, teeth, teeth.
    *And the massive swan wings – dripping water on me, like it's
raining.*
    And the alicorn.
    Oh yeah, it's horrible and beautiful and –
    'HEE-HEE!'

VIII

Mighty Fizz Chilla flies round and round the boat –
    'HEE-HEE!'

Wings go flap.
Jaws go snap.
Tentacles writhe.
Alicorn glints.

IX

'I HATE YE!'
  'HEE-HEE!'
  Flap.
  Snap.
  Writhe.
  Glint.

X

And, suddenly, the Cap is throwing his harpoon –
  Whoooshhh!!

— Sixty-eight —

I

The harpoon – it grazes the creature.
  The harpoon – it grazes the tiger body.
  The creature – it shrieks in pain!
  'HEEIAAAGHH!'

II

'Cap! The creature is hurt! It's so angry. Cap, you've scratched the creature and … Oh, nah! NAH!'
  'What, laddy?'
  'The creature – it's diving right at us!'

III

Teeth!
  Feathers!
  Fur!
  Tentacles!
  Alicorn!
  All aimed right at us!
  Like an attacking war plane!
  'HEEE-HEEE-HEEE!'

IV

I'm so scared.
  I'm trembling all over.
  I can't move and –

CRAAASHH! ^V

VI

Mighty Fizz Chilla slams into the bottom end of the boat.

A tidal wave engulfs us.

I hear the Cap go, 'AAIEEE –' Then gurgle, gurgle, cough, splutter.

I hear me go, 'AAIEEE –' Then gurgle, gurgle, cough, splutter.

VII

Water's in my eyes.

Can't see.

VIII

All I know is I've fallen flat on the deck and ... and ...

The deck is tilting up!

Up!

Up!

Up!

Like a slide.

And I'm sliding down it ...

IX

Me – I rub my eyes.

Me – I begin to see.

Me – I scream.

'NAAHHHHH!'

X

Mighty Fizz Chilla's head is at the bottom of the boat.

The bottom of the slide.

And its jaws are chomping, chomping.

And me and the Cap –

XI
'WE'RE SLIDING INTO THE CHOMPING, INNIT!'

— Sixty-nine —

I

'NAHHHHHH!'
　'NAYYYYYY!'
　Chomp.
　Chomp.
　Chomp.

II

'Oh, Cap! What're we gonna do... I can't get a grip on anything and –'
　CHOMP!
　CHOMP!
　CHOMP!

III

'Oh, Cap! I don't wanna be eaten by the creature. I don't wanna –'

CHOMP!

CHOMP!

CHOMP!

IV

'Laddy, listen! Close ye eyes! Don't look at it.'
　'But –'

'Just do as I say, laddy. Now! Close ye eyes and listen to the sound of my voice. Are ye eyes closed? Eh!'

'… Yeah!'

V

'The creature – it winks at me! I didn't even know that sharks had eyelids but … well, it winks, laddy. Like it's playing a game. You imagining this, laddy?'

'Yeah, yeah.'

VI

'And then … why, laddy, it just swims away. I hear its 'Hee-hee!' getting fainter and fainter … Ye hear that?'

'Yeah, yeah!'

VII

'The creature leaves me alone in the wreck of my boat and … well, soon I'm picked up by a passing ocean liner.'

VIII

'An … *ocean liner*!'

'Aye, laddy! And I spend six glorious months – free of charge – on a luxurious cruise getting my strength back.'

'Hang on! You went … *on a cruise*?'

'Aye, laddy. I cruised all round the Mediterranean and the Caribbean. I explored the Pyramids of Giza and the statues of Easter Island and … oh, such wonderful times I had.'

'Cap, can I open my eyes now?'

'Aye, laddy.'

— Seventy —

I

Milo finds himself sitting next to the Captain on his now very messy bed.

'Cap ... that was a thrilling story. And, yeah, if my hair ain't white and me teeth ain't curled then I count meself lucky. But ... well, can I say something, Cap?'

'Anything ye like, laddy.'

II

'Well ... perhaps, what happened to you – I mean, with Mighty Fizz Chilla and all that – perhaps ... well, perhaps, it ain't all bad.'

III

'What – what can you possibly mean, laddy?'

'Well ... your life before. In Cozywick, I mean. It was a bit ... well, boring.'

'Boring!'

'Yeah! Ya know, the same thing every day. But when Mighty Fizz Chilla came along – even though, at first, it all seemed really, really bad ... well ...'

'Mmmm, laddy?'

IV

'Well ... perhaps it was for the best in the long run. I mean, listen to yourself: cruise liners, Pyramids, Easter Island, not to mention the jungle and the Congo River. Why, you've seen the world, Cap. You've had adventures most people only dream about. And ... well, we met. And all of it happened because of –'

'Mighty Fizz Chilla!'

V

'Yeah, Cap! Exactly. So, perhaps, it ain't the accursed creature ya think it is, after all. Eh? What d'ya think?'

VI

The Captain scratches his head thoughtfully. 'Mmmmm ... I've never thought about it like that, laddy. But ... well, ye might have a point ...'

'Perhaps,' continues Milo softly, it's time to stop hunting the creature.'

'Mmmm ...'

'Will ya think about it, Cap?'

'Aye, laddy, that I will.' The Captain ruffles Milo's hair again. 'What a wonderful way of looking at things ye have. Perhaps ... aye! Now I've met ye – I *will* stop hunting the creature and settle down.' He gives the top of Milo's head a gentle kiss. 'Now, let's get tucked back up in bed. For – whatever I decide to do about Mighty Fizz Chilla – my story is all told. Just like yours.'

'Just like ... mine?'

VII

'Aye, laddy!' He tucks the sheets around Milo. 'Ye have told us what happened five months ago. Remember ye got hurt by Mojo and no one stopped to help ye. That be a terrible thing! I understand why that woke the Fizzy Wasps in ye –'

'But that ain't ... *everything*, Cap.'

'It's ... not?'

'... Nah.' Milo looks through the open window at the

star-filled sky. 'Mojo hitting me and no one helping was nasty, yeah, but … well, it's what it got me *thinking* about that really … changed me.'

'And … what did it get ye thinking about, laddy.'

'…'

'Eh, laddy?'

'Well, I –'

The door swings open and Dee breezes into the room. 'Captain Jellicoe, will you *stop* exciting the child this instant!'

— Seventy-one —

I

'But I be not!'

'Don't argue! I could hear the noise from downstairs. Honestly, anyone would think you were rehearsing a space battle from some science-fiction film. Not that I've ever seen a science-fiction film, of course. They're all pure froth from beginning to end, I'm sure.' She shoos the Captain out of the room. 'Besides, Cressida Bell wants you to help her clear away the party things. I made a start but ... well, I haven't had any real sleep in nearly thirty-seven hours so I need my bed!"

'But, Dee –' begins Milo.

'But, Dee –' begins the Captain.

II

'OUT!' snaps Dee, pushing the Captain into the corridor and slamming the door behind him. 'And as for you, Milo Kick –' she feels his pulse '– a good night's sleep is what you need. That's unless you want to be sent home a day early.'

'Nah!'

'Very well, then.' Dee tucks the sheets around him. 'Honestly, what a mess this bed is. What were you and Captain Jellicoe doing? Wrestling each other?'

'We were ... in a jungle.'

'I don't understand, Milo Kick.'

'The Cap's been telling me a story –'

'Stories!' cries Dee. 'Why does everyone like stories so much? They're just froth.'

'They're not! They're … thrilling! At least … the Cap's story is. So is the story Cressie's telling me about me mum. And so is the story *you're* telling me.'

III

'Me!' gasps Dee. 'I wasn't aware I was telling you a story at all.'

'You were. About Jay Dee Six.'

'That's not a story, Milo Kick. That's true. Pure fact from beginning to end. Totally froth-free.'

'Well, whatever it was … I was riveted, Dee.'

'You … were?'

'Yeah! Tell me what happened after Jay Dee Six ran away with Avery Chance. Please!'

'Oh … I'm much too tired, Milo Kick.'

'But I need to know! Pretty pleeaasse.'

'I'm afraid that particular trick won't work on me tonight. I'm immune from all pretty pleases, whether they be from you or Cressida Bell. And, besides, you need rest.'

'But I won't be able to rest wondering about Jay Dee Six and – Oh, tell me! Go on! Tell me! Please!'

'No.'

'Please.'

'No.'

'Please! Please! Please! Please! Please!'

'Shush! Shush,' says Dee, smiling despite herself. 'I've never heard so many pleases come from one mouth.' She looks thoughtfully at Milo, then says, 'I've just had an idea.' She dashes out of her room, then returns a few moments later with something in her hand. 'This will satisfy both our requirements.'

'What d'ya mean, Dee?'

'Postcards!' she replies. 'From Jay Dee Six!' She puts them in Milo's lap. 'If you read them ... well, you'll find out what happened next. And *I'll* be able to get some much needed sleep.'

'Spectac –'

'But *only*,' interrupts Dee, 'if you promise to read them *calmly*.'

'I will! Promise!'

'Then ... goodnight, Milo Kick.' Dee hesitates a moment, then stiffly bends and gives Milo a quick kisss on the shaven part of his skull. 'It's so ... *educational* having you here. Truly. Educational and ... quite special.'

— Seventy-two —

I

Dearest Dee,

I am in Paris with Avery. I know I should've told you I was going to run away but ... well, I just couldn't find the words. He is a genius! He's going to be a great actor! He's teaching me all he knows and I'm going to be a great actor too.

I'm working very hard as a waiter in a restaurant to earn enough money so we can start our own theatre company.

I'll write more when we have a hit play on our hands.

Love from your brother
Jay xxx

Their very own theatre company!
Spectacular!

II

Dearest Dee,

I know it's been years since I last wrote but ... well, I've been heartbroken.

These are the facts: I worked hard for five years and gave all my money to Avery. He said, 'Thanks, Jay, Now I'll start a theatre company and you and me will have lead roles in our first production.' That was the last I saw of him.

Fact: Avery ran off with all the money.

It took me a while to recover, but now ... oh, now I've met another genius. He's from Brazil and he wants to start his own circus. I'm going to work hard to get him the money. Also, I'm training to be a trapeze artist so we can both be the stars of the show.

I'll write more when we have a successful circus act on our hands.

Love from your brother
Jay
   xxx

Training to be a trapeze artist!
Spectacular!

III

Dearest Dee,

Well, you guessed it!

My Brazilian genius ran off with my money! I'm such a stupid, gullible fool.

Not any more, though!

I've met another genius! He's a mime artist from Rome. He says if he gets enough money he can create a show for the two of us.

I'm working very hard as a waiter in a restaurant and, of course, practising mime.

I'll write more when we have a successful mime act on our hands.

Love from your brother
Jay
xxx

Poor Jay! He keeps getting fooled!
I'm almost afraid to read the next postcard —

IV

Dear Sis,

I'm a mug!

You know what I'm going to say: my Roman Mime genius stole all my money.

I'm coming back to England, to try my luck in London.

I know I'm a great actor, I just need a lucky break, that's all.

Love from your brother

Jay

x

Oh, I hope he gets an acting job!
Poor Jay needs something to go right in his life …

V

Dearest Dee,

It's been twenty years since my last postcard.

Sorry about that! But I can tell you what's been going on in my life in one word: Failure!

No work!

Nothing!

Well, I once held a spear in a scuddy production of 'Julius Caesar' - But that's about it!

Someone suggested I should change my name. So … well, I have. I think it sounds more … theatrical! Who knows? It might get me the work I deserve. I'll sign off with how you should refer to me in future.

Love from your brother

Valentino True

xxx

Valentino True!
Jay Dee Six is … oh!

Me head– it's spinning, innit!
Valentino True – who knew me mum.
Valentino True – who stayed here.
Valentino True – who helped rescue Mum from Checker.
Valentino True is Jay Dee Six.
Dee's brother.
I've got to talk to Dee!
NOW!

VI

Me – rushing out of the bedroom.
  Me – bashing into –

VII

'Ooooomph!' goes Cressida.
  'Ooooomph!' goes Captain Jellicoe.
  They're standing in the middle of the corridor!
  They're holding each other.
  And they're –
  'Snogging, innit!'

— Seventy-three —

I

'Well … I …' blusters Cressida.

'Well … I …' blusters the Captain.

'Nah! It's all right!' insists Milo. 'I don't mind. Snog away. But … oh, I've gotta to speak to Dee! Right now –'

'Oh, Beloved, *please* don't disturb her.'

'Aye, she was very tired, laddy.'

'But … but …' Milo is restless with the need to talk about '… her brother!' he blurts out. 'Cressie! Her brother is –'

'Valentino True,' sighs Cressida, with a smile. 'Of *course* I knew. Oh, yes, Beloved, I knew.' She rests her hand on the Captain's arm. 'Brave Captain, will you excuse us! I think I need to explain one or two more things to our Beloved.'

'Pretty lassy,' responds the Captain, with a courteous bow, 'though parting is such sweet sorrow, I be taking my leave of ye if that be ye wish.' He kisses her hand. 'Thank ye for a wonderful evening. I shall prepare breakfast for ye in the morning.'

'Oh … I'll help you, dearest Captain,' Cressida assures him.

'I shall count the seconds until that moment.' And with that he goes into his room, still murmering, 'Aye, count the seconds … count the seconds …'

'Come, Beloved,' Cressida opens her bedroom door. 'Let me fill in a few gaps.'

II

Cressida is sitting on her bed, removing her make-up with vanishing cream, and saying, 'Oh, Beloved, I'm very weary tonight. So, if you forgive, I'll make this as brief as possible … Oh, where're the tissues?'

'Here, Cressie!'

'Bless! Bless!' She takes a tissue from Milo's hands and wipes cream from her face. 'After Jay ran away, poor Dee was left alone with her father, the Professor. Oh, what a terrible life she must've had! I wouldn't wish that on my worst enemy. Years and years with that … *machine* of a man! Helping him collect facts for his ridiculous book. Science, indeed!' She waves her finger in Milo's direction. 'Mark my words. Beloved: science might well *explain* things, but it takes *froth* to give things meaning – Oh, where's my moisturizing cream got to?'

'Here, Cressie, here!'

III

'Of course, one shouldn't speak ill of the dead,' says Cressida, rubbing moisturizer into her cheeks. 'And the Professor died a sad death, Beloved. One day, that Walking Brain of a Man, got up and couldn't remember what year it was. A week later he forgot what country he was in.' Cressida sighs deeply. 'Poor man was suffering from something called Alzheimer's disease. Bit by bit his mind was fading away. A lifetime of facts evaporating like a puddle in the desert. And Dee looked after him day and night. By the end, the Professor was like … like a baby. He had to be washed and fed and … oh, it *is* too sad, Beloved. Too, too sad. Too utterly, utterly sad.'

'So … he copped it?'

IV

'Just so, Beloved! Dee, of course, tried to make contact

with her brother. After all, Jay had to be told about the death of his father. Dee hadn't heard from him for quite a few years. So tracking him down proved a difficult task. Finally, she found him in a bingo hall in Newport Pagnell. Jay told her – or, should I say, Valentino told her – that working in a bingo hall was his punishment. "For what?" asks Dee. And that's when Valentino tells her how he once tricked someone out of ten thousand pounds.'

'Ten thou – You! He *tricked* you?'

'He did, Beloved.'

'But … *how* did he trick you? The money was for me mum and … well, ya got me mum. So how did –?'

V

'Because,' interrupts Cressida, 'Checker Kick never knew anything about the money. Oh, yes, Valentino persuaded him to let Fliss *stay* with me. But to *save* Checker money. That's all. After all, Checker was no longer using his daughter as a skivvy so … well, what possible use could she be to him. Fliss was just an added expense. Checker was glad to be rid of her. And Valentino –'

'Kept the ten thousand pounds for himself, innit!'

'Just so, Beloved! Two weeks after leaving Avalon Rise that last time, Valentino split from Checker and set up his own theatre company – Oh, Beloved, will you take my hairpins out for me.'

'Yeah, yeah.'

VI

'The theatre company failed, of course,' says Cressida. 'Like everything else in Valentino's life. Everything that poor man touched turned to failure. He was a Failure on Legs. Only now it was worse. He wasn't just a failure. He was a *guilty* failure. He became a shell of his former self: working in nightclubs, holiday camps and, finally, bingo halls – Put the pins on the dressing table, will you, Beloved? And while you're there, grab the hairbrush.'

'D'ya want me to brush ya hair?'

'Oh, bless. Bless!'

VII

'Dee says to Valentino, "You must go back to this female of the species whom you robbed of this money and work to repay it." Of course, Valentino nearly faints at the idea and cries, "Oh, I can't face her! I'm so ashamed! So, so, ashamed." And that's when Dee decided that *she* would repay her brother's debt.'

'So ... that's how Dee came here!'

'Just so, Beloved! And she's been with me ever since. And repaid the debt a million times over. For we became friends and friendship, believe me, is a priceless – Ouch! Be careful of tangles, Beloved.'

'Sorry, Cressie.'

VIII

'Dee wrote to her brother,' continues Cressida. 'She told him all was forgiven. That I bore no grudges. That he should join us here. Each time he wrote back with the same message, "I AM TOO ASHAMED." And each time his handwriting got wobblier and wobblier.' She shakes her head sadly. 'Booze, you see! Just like his old friend, Mr Kick, Valentino had taken to the bottle!'

'Whatever happened to Checker?'

'Heart attack. Dead! Help me into bed, will you, Beloved?'

IX

'I thought you and Dee were telling me two different stories,' says Milo, tucking the bedclothes around Cressida. 'But ... it's just *one* story, innit?'

'Just so, Beloved,' says Cressida, snuggling into the pillows and yawning. 'It was … just one story.'

'You look tired, Cressie.'

'I am, Beloved. But as so many stories are now coming together, I want to do one more thing before I succumb to the land of nod. Look in the bottom drawer of the bedside cabinet … Tucked right at the back you'll find a book wrapped in brown paper … You see it, Beloved? … See?'

'Yeah.'

'Remove the paper.'

Milo does so and, on the front of the lavender-coloured book, he sees the word 'DIARY' written in gold leaf.

'That,' says Cressida, 'belonged to your mum.'

X

'Mum's diary!'

'Just so, Beloved! And, in a way, it contains the final thread of the story. Or should I say all the stories? If I was more awake I'd tell it to you myself. But, on the other hand … Well, perhaps it's best you read it in your mum's own words! It starts … the day she met the love of her life.'

'Griff! In the cave!'

XI

'Promise me this, Beloved! Read it by the open window in your room. By moonlight and starlight, with the sound of the ocean in your ears! For the story your mum has to tell is … oh, such romance! Such utter, utter romance! Now kiss your old lump of a Cressie goodnight.'

'Goodnight, Cressie.'

'Goodnight, Beloved.'

'Kiss!'

'Kiss!'

— Seventy-four —

I

Monday 2 July
I've never had a day like today before. So many new feelings. I woke up one person and I'll go to bed another. As I sit here by the open window in my bedroom it's as if I'm seeing everything for the first time. The moonlight has never looked so dazzling, the ocean so big, the stars so brilliant.

I'm sitting by the window too, innit.

II

Oh, I don't want to forget anything about today. I want to preserve it for ever like ... like those roses me and Cressie turned into perfume. This book will be the written equivalent of that rosewater. For today, in a cave where a dolphin rose from the sand, I discovered love!

Love!

III

I waited alone in the cave for over an hour after Cressie left. I looked at the blankets on the ground, the remains of food (mostly hamburgers and chicken nuggets) and, of course, the dolphin. I tried to get some idea of who it was making the wonderful creatures –
Then I heard footsteps.
Someone was approaching the cave. I hid behind a rock.

crunch, crunch, went the footsteps. Louder and louder. And ...
oh, my heart was beating so hard I was sure whoever it was
would hear it. I took a few deep breaths and said to myself,
Don't get in a flap, Fliss. You have every right to be here. The
cave is public property and –

Then I saw him! Standing in the entrance to the cave.

Behind him, the setting sun blazed orange and seagulls swooped
and shrieked. His hair was long and as black as crow feathers. His
face was ... oh, so manly. So strong-looking. Yet soft too. Like
rock covered in velvet. The palest, smoothest velvet I've ever
seen. His eyes were like bits of broken glass, and peered sharply
from beneath hooded eyebrows. He was wearing very tight black
jeans, black boots and a black shirt, opened to the waist,
revealing a marble-smooth chest and a silver chain around his
neck. All in all, he was like something from another age, a past
full of cloaks and swishing swords and –

Oh, stop frothing, Mum!

IV

He was carrying some driftwood and two large shells. He spread
these things out on the floor, then sat on a rock, studying them.
'Look at that shell!' he says. And – oh, how my heart missed a
beat, because I thought he was talking to me. I was just about
to get up and reveal myself when he carries on, 'So many colours.
Like oil in water, eh? Other shells ain't bad either ... Mmm, yep,
yep.' That's when I realized –

He's talking to himself, innit!

V

He starts making a new creation out of the shells. Oh, how I
love to watch him work! The way his hands scoop up the sand,
shape it, pat it smooth. And all the time he's talking to himself.
'Put a pebble here! Yep! That's it ... good, good ... Now, move this

shell over here ... Yep, Yep!'

He's getting hot. I can see sweat trickling down his face and his hair is sticking to his forhead.

'Gonna be a sea-monster! Yeah! That's what ya gonna be!' He's talking to the thing he's making as if it's alive. 'Give you the head of a lion and the body of ... of? Of? A snake! Yep! Good, good -'

Then he stands up and takes his shirt off and — oh, my heart! I'm sure it's as loud as a bass drum. I've never been this close to any boy taking off his shirt before. Well, Dad used to, of course, but his chest was hairy and flabby and his belly was like a barrel, but ... oh, the torso before me now was so beautiful —

Wish she'd stop frothing!

VI

Then I see! A bruise! Two bruises! One on his arm. The other below his left shoulder blade! They look so painful and nasty that I gasp out loud —

'Who's there?' he cries. 'Come out! Come on!'

I'm so nervous I can hear my teeth rattling in my skull.

Slowly, I emerge from my hiding place and say, 'H-hello?'

'What ya doing here?'

'N-nothing,' I tell him. And I wanted my voice to sound brave and strong, but I'm afraid it came out like a pathetic girly squeak. 'I was just ... wondering who made ... all those wonderful creatures —'

'Well, now ya know, don't ya?' he sneers. 'So clear off!'

I couldn't move! My eyes were fixed to his skin. The curved caterpillar of his spine and ... those bruises! Oh, those bruises!

'What ya looking at?' he yells, trying to cover the black and blue blemishes. 'I ain't no animal in a zoo, ya know! Now, ya heard what I said. Clear off! I don't wanna be pestered by some silly little schoolgirl!'

'But I only want to talk to —'

'Clear off!'

'But –'

And he raises his fist at me! Yes! He raises his fist as if he's about to hit me. And I cry out and stagger back and – oh, I slip on some seaweed and I fall! I'm so confused. Why's he being so nasty to me? I just don't understand –

Someone's hurt him, Mum. Can't ya see that? The bruises! He's been hurt and now he's … got the Fizzy Wasps, Mum! He's got the Fizzy Wasps!

VII

I lie on the ground with seaweed stuck to my dress and … I cry! Just sob and sob. I'm crying about every bad thing that has ever happened to me. I can hear the sound of weeping as it echoes around the cave like a wild animal.

The boy – the young man I should say – looks horrified. He says, 'I'm … I'm sorry. It's just that …' And then he lets out a cry of despair and starts hitting his head with his fists. 'I'm bad!' he yells. 'I'm bad! Bad! Bad!' And he kicks the sand dolphin to smithereens.

'Stop,' I cry. 'Oh, stop! Please!'

But he's still hitting himself and yelling and then – oh, he kicks his new creation, the sea-serpent, to pieces as well. Finally, he collapses to the ground and buries his face in his hands!

Oh, why's he acting like this?

I don't understand!

I do!

VIII

I go up to him and lay my hand on his shoulder. He jolts like I've given him an electric shock. 'Please …' he says. And his voice is breaking with tears. 'Go away!'

'No,' I tell him. 'I'm not going away! Oh, look at your

creations!' I start collecting together shells and pebbles. 'They were so beautiful. I especially liked the Mermaid, you know. That sad look in her eyes. She wanted to be human, didn't she? She wanted legs. And ... oh, that's why she'd climbed up on to the beach. To experience a bit of what it feels like to run and skip and play. But, in her heart, she knew it could never be. She was born different and would always be so.'

And that's when he looked at me and – oh, those eyes. Glinting like black ice. 'My name's Griffin Dice,' he says.

Gonna get all lovey-dovey, innit!

IX

For a long time – hours? days? millennia? – we just gazed at each other. There was a lot of pain and hurt in his eyes, and ... oh, I wanted to ask so many questions (about his bruises and where he came from and what he was doing here), but I knew the time wasn't right.

Then, without saying anything, Griffin got up and started to make another sculpture. He pressed pebbles into a mound of sand and then looked round for something and – I knew what he wanted! The seaweed. I got it for him and thrust it into his hand. He looked at me and ... oh, we were speaking without using words. It was like we were telepathically linked. We existed in a world of feeling and emotion. He was part of me already and I was part of him. For hours we worked in silence, creating a creature with the body of peacock and two human heads. It's only when we stood back and looked at it that we realized one head looked like him and the other looked like me.

I said to Griffin, 'We should call it –'

Love, innit.

X

'Love!' agreed Griffin. 'But ... your eyes are blue! I wish we had blue pebbles instead of those white ones.'

'We could paint them! Look! I've got a paintbox here! We could choose a blue and paint the pebbles -'

'Colours!' He gazed at the tubes of oil paint as if they were treasure. 'Oh ... so many!' He read the names off the tubes. 'Alizarin crimson! Scarlet Lake!'

'And here – look!' I knelt opposite him. 'Cadmium yellow.'

'Monestial blue.'

'Madder red.'

And, as we looked at the colours, so we leant closer and closer to each other. And our voices became softer and softer ...

'Emerald green.'

'Zinc white!'

And that's when we kissed –

Yuk!

XI

Oh, I didn't want to leave him.

I wanted to stay in the cave and talk colours all night. But I knew Cressida would be worried, so I had to get back to Avalon Rise. I asked Griff to come with me, but he ... oh, he wouldn't. I promised to return in the morning with some food for him. He kissed me again at the entrance to the cave –

OK, OK, I get the point! Mum goes back and ... well, Cressie guesses she's in love ... flick page ... Yeah, Mum tells Cressie ... Cressie asks to meet Griffin ... Mum goes up to her room to ... well, write this! OK!

Next day ...

What happens next?

— Seventy-five —

I

Tuesday 3 July

Oh, how I missed him last night.

A minute away from him is an eternity. I'm sure I bored Cressie to tears talking about Griff. I asked if Griff could stay here, in Avalon Rise, and Cressie said, 'He's more than welcome, Fliss. I hate to think of anyone spending the night in a cave and eating ... junk food! Ugh!'

Oh, how I love my Cressie! I gave her a big kiss and a hug. And when we went to bed – oh, how could I sleep? All I could do was think about my Griff. Down there in his cave. All alone. I kept thinking, it's so close. If I shout his name he'll hear me. But instead I just blew kisses in his direction –

Gonna puke in a minute!

II

All night I dreamt of him.

Wonderful thrilling dreams -

Oh, skip all this! What next ...
Mum gets up ... breakfast ... Cressie says, 'Don't forget! Tell the boy he's more than welcome here.' ... Mum goes to cave and ... right! Read on!

III

I'd never seen anything so … breathtaking! For the cave was now full of his creations. Mermaids on the floor, rocks turned into winged creatures with seaweed hair, paintings on the walls. And – there!

My Griffin! Stripped to the waist and splattered with paint. And, as usual (oh, how quickly I've got to know all his habits), talking to himself, 'Put this here! Yeah! Paint it yellow – lemon yellow! Making this … all this for … for her. Been thinking of her all night … Oh, yeah! No sleep! Looking up to Avalon Rise and thinking, My Fliss! My Fliss!

Oh, my heart beat so fast!

He feels the same as me!

As gently as possible I stepped forward and said, 'Griff –?'

He spun round to face me.

'New colours,' he said. 'New things! Can't work fast enough. All because of you! Kiss me, Fliss! Kiss me!'

Oh, not again! Turn a page –

IV

We strolled along the beach together. He held my hand but said very little. His eyes are always blazing, alert, and he's always glancing at me to make sure I'm happy – which I am, of course. With him. Always, always. Words – we don't need them! We tell each other more in this silence than in a lifetime of babble. We see a crab scuttle over shingle and we look at each other and smile –

She does ramble on! Turn a page …
Aha! Here! Mum has persuaded Griff to go back to Avalon Rise …

V

He hesitates at the drawbridge. 'What's wrong, Griff?' I ask. He can't answer but ... oh, I see the fear in his eyes. Like a hunted animal about to be trapped. I say, 'You'll be safe here. Honest. Cressie is my friend. She won't hurt you.'

But other people have! Don't ya see that, Mum?
He's been hurt bad and now ...
Oh, I know what he's feeling.
I know!
I know!

VI

'What a handsome young man!' gasps Cressida when she sees him. 'And is that sap green on your cheek? Well, I do hope you've been putting my paints to good use! Now, go into the dining room, both of you! I'll fix you a bite to eat! You must be hungry.'
'Oh, yes, Cressie,' I say.
'Humpff,' says Griffin.

He thinks it's a trap! Don't know who to trust! He feels out of place. Feels he don't belong here. Wants to run back to his cave –
Oh, I know!
I know!

VII

Cressie brought us some pizza and a big bottle of sparkling mineral water. She sat at the table with us and tried to make conversation with Griff, but all he kept saying was, 'Humpff!' And he refused to use the knife and fork. Tomato sauce all over his shirt and face. And, what's worse, all over Cressie's beautiful lace tablecloth. I kept noticing Cressie look at it as the stains got bigger and bigger. Poor Cressie –

Nah! Not poor Cressie! Poor Griff!
It's Griff who feels out of place, innit!

VIII

'Griff is such a good artist,' I say, trying to fill the awkward silences. 'You should see what he's done in the cave. It's like an art gallery.'

'Ooo, I'd love to,' says Cressida. 'If it's anything like that Mermaid we saw – Oh, what a shame it had to be washed away. But the sand dolphin! I'm sure that's still there –'

'Ya saw it!' growls Griffin. 'Ya were in my cave too!' And then he glares at me. 'Ya didn't tell me that!'

'Well ... I ...' I began, but I couldn't think of what to say.

'Why can't people leave me alone?' Griffin yells. 'Always sticking their noses in!'

And, with that, he gets up (the chair crashes over behind him) and storms out of the house –

Let him go! Don't chase after him or anything. He just needs to cool down and get rid of the Fizzy Wasps.

IX

I chase after him!

Nah! Wrong!

X

Griffin shouts and tells me to 'clear off!'

Told ya!

XI

And I start crying. Cressie comes up behind me and wraps her arms around me. 'I'm sorry, Fliss,' she says. 'That's all my fault.' And then Cressie starts crying. I can see Griffin in the distance, standing on top of the cliff, his hair lashing in the wind, his shirt billowing around him. And even though I hate him for what he's just said and done, I still love him –

Sort ya head out, Mum!

— Seventy-six —

I

Cressie goes back to Avalon Rise. I wait on the cliff. Watch and wait for Griff. I sit on the grass. He keeps glancing over at me, but doesn't move. Hours pass. Slowly, like a wild animal, he walks back to me. He sits beside me. We don't say a word. He holds my hand. He kisses my fingertips. Again, words are unnecessary. I know he's sorry. All afternoon and into the evening we sit like that.

The sun sets. Stars fill the sky. And still he's holding my hand. Gradually, he lays his head in my lap. He ...

He trusts ya, Mum!

II

Then – I hear the soft rumble of distant thunder! I look up and see stars have been replaced by clouds. Cressie comes up and touchs my shoulder. 'Get inside, Fliss! There's a storm coming!'

'I can't leave him, Cressie!' I tell her. 'He's been up all night creating things and now – oh, look! 'He's totally exhausted.'

'I meant, <u>both</u> of your insides! Quick!'

'But he might get angry, Cressie.'

He will!

III

Cressie says, 'There's no choice! Look! The first drop of rain! I'm not leaving the boy out in this weather –'

'He's not a boy.'

'He is! And you – young lady – are still a girl! And both of you will do as you are told! Now, inside! Before the storm gets any worse. Come on, I'll help you carry him.'

Big trouble on the way, me thinks.

IV

Cressie puts Griffin to bed (she asks me to wait outside while she does this), then we both go downstairs. Cressie makes a pot of tea and we sit in front of the fire. Outside... oh, the storm is getting worse and worse! Thunder and lightning have started now!

'We don't know anything about him, Fliss,' Cressie says.

'I know I love him!' I interrupt. 'That's all I need to know.'

'But you've only just met him.'

'It feels like I've known him for ever.'

'But... where does he come from? Where's his family? I'm sure they must be worried. And those bruises! How on earth did he get those? He's too young to be alone –'

'He's sixteen!'

'He's still a baby as far as I'm concerned, Fliss. We'll have to phone the police or do something –'

'No, Cressie! You might scare him away. And if you do that, I'll never forgive you –'

I was interrupted by yelling! Coming from upstairs. It was Griff!

And then – oh, the sound of things smashing!

It's the glass ornaments, innit!
Griff – the thunder must've woken him up and he didn't know where he was.
Oh, he's throwing anything he can get his hands on.

V

We rush upstairs and – there he is! Standing on his bed. In his boxer shorts. Hurling the glass ornaments across the room! 'Let me out! Let me out!'

'The door wasn't locked, Griff!' I tell him. 'It's just a bit stiff. You're not a prisoner!'

'Where am I?' he yells.

'Griffin!' says Cressida as firmly as she can. 'You're in Avalon Rise. We had no choice. The rain – oh, listen to that thunder!'

'I like the rain!' he yells.

'Oh, my ornaments!' says Cressie. 'They belonged to my dear papa! A lifetime's collection –'

'Go away!' yells Griffin. And he picks up his clothes.

'Leave me alone!' He pushes past us and out into the corridor!

He rushes downstairs!

He struggles to open the front door.

'Stop, Griff!' I cry. 'The drawbridge is up anyway! You won't be able to get across! Please stay with us and –'

His eyes dart all over like a cornered animal. 'I don't need anyone!' he screams. 'Everyone lets me down!'

And then he sees the door to the cellar. He opens it and runs down.

He's so scared, innit!

He wants to be friendly, I know he does. But the Fizzy Wasps keep getting control and making him say and do nasty things...

What happens next? Mum tells Cressie to go to bed... Mum waits outside the cellar door ... Waits for hours ... Storm stops ... Then, plucking up her courage, she knocks on cellar door ... She hears Griffin mumble, 'Come in, Fliss.' She goes down and –

VI

He's huddled, fully dressed, in the corner. I can tell from his bloodshot eyes that he's been crying. I sit there on the stone floor next to him.

He wants to tell ya things, Mum. I know he does. Don't say anything. Don't rush him. Just let him say it in his own time.

VII

He says, 'My mum left me when I was two months old. She didn't want me. Dad had to look after me. But he didn't want me either. He kept hitting me. Lots. 'You ruined my life!' That's all he kept saying. I ran away for the first time when I was seven. They found me. Dad said he didn't want me any more. I was with foster parents for a while. But they just said I was trouble and they didn't want me either. In a kids' home for a while after that. Always getting into trouble. Didn't mean to. Just happened. But ... I loved making things. With Plasticine and stuff. Magical animals – things I dream about! Other kids used to smash 'em to bits. Then Dad said he wanted me back. But all he wanted was a servant! Someone to buy his cigarettes and cook his dinner and go to the launderette with his stinking clothes. Every time I refused he hit me. Couldn't take any more. I've run away for good now. I've run away and I ain't ever going back. I've ... I've never told anyone all this before, Fliss. Just you. It's our secret. You mustn't tell anyone. Not even Cressie. Cos ... it's just you

and me. Ya hear that? Just you and me! – LOOK!'
And he moves from the wall and –
There! A heart with –

The heart in the cellar! I've seen it! What happens next …?
Mum persuades Griffin to go back to bed … Mum goes to Cressie and says, 'You must promise not to ask Griff anything! I want him here, Cressie. I need him here! If he goes … then I'll go with him!'
What next?
What next …?

— Seventy-seven —

I

Wednesday 4 July

Griff was so sweet this morning. He'd stuck together some of the animals he'd broken and gave what he'd made to Cressie as a present.

He's saying sorry, innit.

II

It was a typical Griffin creation – a mixture of all sorts of animals. 'How ... inventive,' said Cressida. 'I'd never thought of putting that head on ... that body and – oh, with wings too! But, somehow, it all fits together. What a true artist you are. Thank you, Griffin. Now... your breakfast's on the table. Why don't you two eat it while I get on with some dusting?'

Cressie's staying out of their way!
Poor Cressie, she must be feeling so… ditched!
What happens next…? Turn page…

III

Thursday 5 July

I am in paradise! All day with Griffin. Collecting driftwood and seashells. In his cave helping him with his wondferful animals. Oh, I love –

Yuk! Next page –

IV

We eat dinner in his room. We watch the setting sun –

What about Cressie, Mum? You're ignoring her...
Next page!

V

Friday 6 July
Another day in paradise –

Yuk! Next!

VI

Saturday 7 July
Oh, how I love Griff –

Yuk! Next!

VII

Sunday 8 July
There isn't much time. I've got to write quick.

Something's happened! What?

VIII

It's nearly midnight and soon I'll be gone.

Gone?

And I need to write about what happened today first.

What, Mum? What!

— Seventy-eight —

I

I could tell cressie was in a mood about something when I first got up this morning. *(Yeah! You've been blanking her, innit! She saved you from Checker and, for two years, you've been like Mum and daughter and now you –)* But I didn't have a chance to talk to her about it because Griff wanted to get to the cave *(See what I mean, Mum?)* and continue with his work. He's making the biggest creature ever. It's got the body of a whale, the head of an eagle and the tail of a peacock. We're having such fun painting pebbles *(With Cressie's paint, don't forget!)* for the tail feathers. How time flies when I'm with Griff. *(Bet it's not flying for Cressie.)* And he's been in a good mood for days now. *(No one's asking him any questions, that's why.)* And he's finally admitted that he prefers to sleep in a bed than on the stony floor of a cave. *(Get on with it, Mum. What happened?)*

II

When it started to get dark, we walked – hand in hand, as usual – back to Avalon Rise. *(Yuk!)* Cressie put out dinner on the table and asked us if we'd had a nice day *(Oh, please, don't ignore her, Mum)* but Griff and me weren't in the mood for talking *(Poor Cressie)* and we just ate our soup in silence – although, of course, it didn't feel like silence for us. *(Bet it did for Cressie, though.)* Because I can read his glinting eyes like a book. *(Yuk!)* Just like he can read mine. *(Yuk! Yuk! Yuk!)*

    After dinner we go to his room and sit by the window. I can hear cressie coming up to bed. She raps on the door and pokes her head in. 'Come on, Fliss,' she says. 'Time for bed. Go to your room.' Usually, I just say, 'OK, Cressie,' and follow her out, but tonight (*Oh, no, Mum, don't argue with her*) I say, 'Just a few more minutes, Cressie.' (*Big mistake, innit.*) I can see Cressie's face go red with anger (*Told ya*), and suddenly she's shouting, 'Not a few more minutes! Now, young lady! You two are spending every second of the day together and you will not – I repeat not – spend every second of the night together too!' (*Cressie's upset more than annoyed! She's upset at being ignored and – oh, Mum! Just get up and go to your room before Griffin –*) 'Belt up!' shouts Griff. (*Too late!*) 'You ain't her mum!' (*Oh, nah! Nah!*)

III

'How dare you talk to me like that, young man!' cries Cressida, stamping her foot in anger. 'This girl is like a daughter to me. I love her like my own flesh and blood. And I've got to protect her (*Oh, don't say it, Cressie! You're annoyed! You don't mean it!*) from bad influences.'

'Oh, I get it!' roars Griff. 'I'm a bad influence, eh?'

'Well, you tell me!' exclaims Cressie. 'I ... I don't know anything about you. Where'd those bruises come from? (*Oh, no! No! Shut up!*) A street fight, no doubt! (*You're wrong, Cressie, wrong!*) And that means ... what? A gang? (*Nah!*) That's it, isn't it? (*Nah!*) You've been in a gang fight and now you're hiding from them! Well, I'm not going to let you suck my Fliss into your world of criminality! (*Oh, now I feel sorry for you, Griff! You ain't done anything and now –*) I want you out (*Nah, Cressie!*) of my house by morning!'

'Cressie!' I cry.

'Fliss – go to your room! Now!'

IV

I do as I'm told. I hear the door slam shut. Cressie's in her room. Griff is in his room. And I'm in mine. I bury my head in my pillow and weep (*Griff's gonna come to her room*) and then I hear a gentle rap at the door (*Knew it*) and Griff steps inside and - oh, he's dressed and (*He's gonna ask her to run away*) he says, 'We've got to leave, Fliss! Now! Together! The whole world is against us. I can't live without you, Fliss. Please.'

And, of course, Mum does! Oh, poor Cressie. Poor Mum. Poor Griff. Poor everyone. What a mess!

V

And now I'm in my room and my bags are packed and I'm about to leave. Griff says he'll jump across the moat with me in his arms. I'm leaving this diary here so ... well, Cressie, you can read it! I want you to know just how much Griff means to me. How much I need him. If you'd only given it more time, been more ... oh, just more patient and clever, things would've worked out so differently — Griff is whistling from below. He's already outside by the moat. I've got to go! Cressie, I will always love you. But, right now, I need Griff more. My life is going to be happy with him.

That's it! No more! Mum runs off with Griffin.
Cressie must've been gutted when she found out.
And where did Mum and Griff go?

VI

Oh ... I'm so tired now!
What a day ...
Get into bed ...
Turn off lamp ...
Stars ... Moonlight ...
And I'll ask more questions ... in the ... mor .... ning .... g
.... g ...

— Seventy-nine —

I

I'm back in the cave, innit.

In front of me is the figure in the shadows. He's still holding a cup with the baby Might Fizz Chilla splashing around in the tea.

I see glimpses of the creature –

Shark!

Tentacle!

Wing!

Tiger!

Alicorn!

II

The figure says, 'So... have ya twigged yet? Eh? You twigged why all the stories lead to me.'

'Nah!' I reply. 'Why?'

The figure steps forward.

It's Griffin!

His eyes shine like broken black glass. His hair is as black as raven's wings. And he's grinning.

'Put the pieces together, Milo,' he says. 'That's all you've got to do ... You've read your mum's diary. How did she describe my eyebrows?'

'... Hooded, innit!'

'And she loves me. And runs off with me – oh, Milo, ya can't be that thick! Surely you've twigged by now! Eh? EH?'

'Ya mean ...?'

'Aha! He's got it!' And he leans very close. 'I'm ya dad, Milo! You hear me?

I'M YOUR DAAAAAAAD!!'

Sixth Day

— Eighty —

I

'Dad!'
Milo – his eyes click open.
Milo – he sits bolt upright.

II

'Dad!'
The sun's rising, innit.
The sky's turning blue, innit.
The seagulls are shrieking, innit.

III

'Dad!' Milo's gleaming with sweat and his hands are shaking and he's clutching at the sheets and he's saying over and over again, 'Griffin is me dad! GRIFFIN IS ME –'

IV

DAD! DAD! DAD!
   That's why Cressie's been telling me all about Mum and Checker and – Yesss! That's where everything was heading! Griffin is me dad. And– oh, yess! Of course! I get me hooded eyebrows from him. And me jet-black hair.
   Griffin! Dad!
   I've gotta talk to Cressie!
   Got to ask her more about –

V

Milo hears a noise from downstairs. (*That must be Cressie helping the Captain make breakfast!*) He jumps out of bed. (*What's the time –? It's only seven o'clock!*) He gets dressed as quickly as possible (*Griffin! Dad! Griff! Dad!*) and rushes out into the corridor (*Dad! Griff! Dad!*) and hears –

VI

'... mean the world to me ... oh, my lassy ...'
That's the Cap! He's still being all lovey-dovey with Cressie again –
A giggle!
That's Cressie!
She's helping make breakfast, innit!
Feel guilty about interrupting their lovey-dovey stuff but I ain't got no choice.

VII

Milo rushes downstairs and into the dining room and sees –

VIII

The Cap and ...
DEE!

IX

Dee and the Cap!
They're smiling at each other.
They're hugging each other.
'Fact: you mean the world to me,' says Dee to the Captain.
'Oh, my Dee! My very own Dee,' says the Captain, hugging her tighter and leaning forward to kiss her –

X

'DEE!' shrieks Milo.
  Dee jumps and stares at Milo.
  'CAPTAIN!' shrieks Milo.
  The Captain jumps and stares at Milo.

XI

'WHAT … ARE … YOU … BOTH … DOING … INNIT?'

— Eighty-one —

I

'Oh, Milo Kick … let me … explain…'

'Aye, laddy … it's not … what it … looks like.'

Milo cries, 'Captain! You were getting all lovey-dovey with Cressie last night! I saw you! In the corridor!'

'Oh, laddy, listen to me –'

'And Dee!' continues Milo. 'You're supposed to be Cressie's best friend!'

'Oh, Milo Kick, let me explain –'

'AND YOU'RE BOTH DOING THE DIRTY ON HER!'

II

And, suddenly, the Captain is rushing past Milo and up the stairs – his hair and kilt lashing around him – and yelling, 'CRESSIDA! CRESSIDA!'

III

'Milo Kick,' pants Dee, 'you mustn't jump to conclusions before you know all the facts!'

'Were ya or were ya not about to kiss the Cap?'

'That's … a misleading fact!'

'Nah, it ain't! A kiss is a kiss!'

'Not necessarily –'

'The facts, you said! My question needs a simple "Yeah" or "Nah". Were you and the Cap about to kiss, Dee?'

'Well …'

'Answer!'
'Yes!'
'TRAITOR!'

IV

And, suddenly, the Captain is rushing back down the stairs and past Milo – his hair and kilt still lashing around him – and yelling, 'ADIEU –'

And he's out of the house!

'– ADIEU!'

V

'CAP!' cries Milo.

'CAPTAIN!' cries Dee.

And the two of them rush to the front door in time to see the Captain leap over the moat and –

'Umpphhh!'

– land on the other side and –

'ADIEU!'

– rush across the cliff!

VI

'What's he … up to?' ask Milo.

'I … I do not know,' replies Dee faintly. 'He … he's heading for the beach by the looks of it.'

'The cave!'

'Probably.'

'But … why? And what does "Adieu" mean anyway?'

'The dictionary definition is "goodbye"!'

VII

'Goodbye!' gasps Milo. 'But … Oh, nah! He can't be leaving just because I caught you two – Oh, Dee! I didn't want to scare him away! I … I was just surprised and –'

VIII

'YEEAAAAAAAAAAHHHHH!!!!'

'That's Cressie!' cries Milo.

'Cressida Bell!'

And they're at the foot of the stairs when Cressida appears at the top, her dressing gown and hair flapping all around her –

'What's up, Cressie?'

'What's wrong, Cressida Bell?'

'He's stolen it!' shrieks Cressida, clutching her bosom. 'That man – he rushed into my room and … Oh, I wasn't sure what he was doing! Then he rushes off! And when I feel for it – Oh, it's gone! GONE!'

'You mean …' begins Milo.

'JUST SO, BELOVED!' wails Cressida. 'THE CAPTAIN'S STOLEN THE PHOENIX OF SECRETS!!!'

— Eighty-two —

I

'But, Cressie, your precious thing –'

'It's still inside, Beloved!'

'Oh, it means so much to you, Cressida Bell!'

'Oh, it's not just the precious thing! Don't you both see? The Captain is yelling "Adieu" and if he sets sail … oh, we will never see him again. Never! Never! Never! Never! Never!'

II

Never see the Cap again!

Oh, nah!

Nah!

III

'Milo Kick,' says Dee, 'you've been helping Captain Jellicoe build his boat, haven't you? Do you consider it seaworthy?'

'Nah! It's full of holes!'

'Then Cressida Bell is correct. If he sets sail … we will never see him again. Because even if the Captain *wanted* to return, that boat will surely sink and – What are you doing, Milo Kick?'

IV

Me – I'm lowering the drawbridge.

Me – lowering it as fast as possible.

'Is that you lowering the drawbridge, Beloved?'

V

'Yeah! I've gotta stop the Cap! He can't just … go like this. I've gotta stop him.'

VI

The drawbridge – it's down!
  Me – running across!

VII

'Run, Beloved! Run!'
  'Go, Milo Kick! Do it!'

VIII

'STOP, CAP! STOP!'

— Eighty-three —

I

Me – running along edge of cliff!
  Me – rushing down steps to beach.
  Me – on beach and –

II

Crunch!
  Crunch!
  Crunch!

III

The sun is just above the horizon.
  The sky is tinged with orange and yellow.
  The seagulls are beginning to swoop and –
  Cwaaa!
  Cwaaa!
  Cwaaa!

IV

Me – rushing across beach.
  Me – slipping on wet stones.
  Me – heart beating fast.
  Me – sweat on me face.
  Me – blood pounding in me ears and –

V

There he is!

The Cap!
He's got a rope tied to the boat and –

VI

The Captain is pulling the boat across the beach.
  With each tug he makes a violent grunting sound –
'EEAAGH!'
Tug!
'EAAGHHH!'
– and the boat scrapes across the beach with a grating, rasping noise.
  Skissshhh!!
'EEAAGHHHH!'
Tug!
Skisssshhhh!!

VII

'CAP!' cries Milo. 'YOU'VE … GOT … TO … STOP!'

— Eighty-four —

I

Me – rushing after the Captain.
    Crunch!
    Crunch!
    Crunch!
    'STOP!'

II

'EEAAGH!'
    Tug!
    Skissshhh.
    'EEAAGGHH!'
    Tug!
    Skissshhh.

III

'CAP! STOP!'

IV

The tide is out so Milo starts running on pebbles –
    Crunch!
    Crunch!
    Crunch!
    – and on to muddy sand –
    Squelch!
    Squelch!

V

'Cap!' cries Milo. 'You've gotta … stop … You can't –'
Squelch!
Squelch!
'– can't *go*.'
Squelch!
Cwaaa!
Squelch!

VI

'LEAVE ME BE, LADDY!' roars the Captain. 'I'M NOT GOING TO LET THE ACCURSED CREATURE ESCAPE ME NOW! BESIDES, I SAW THAT LOOK IN YE EYE WHEN YE CAUGHT ME WITH DEE! YE DON'T WANT ME AROUND ANY MORE!'

VII

Tug!
'EAGGGHH!'
Skirssshhh!

VIII

'But … I *do*, Cap!'
Squelch!
Squelch!
'NAY, LADDY!'
'YEAH, CAP! OH, PLEASE …'

IX

The muddy sand is turning to water now.
Squelching becomes –
Splash!
Splash!
Splash!

X

The gulls sweep lower.
 Cwaaa.
 Cwaaa.
 Cwaaa.

XI

'CAP! DON'T ... LEAVE ME!'

— Eighty-five —

I

'I not be wanted here, laddy!'
   'You *are*!'
   'EEEAAGGHH!'
Tug!
Skissshhh!
   'CAP!'
   'EAGHH!'
Skissshhh!
The boat has touched water now!

II

Me – there's water around me shins.
   And the Captain's still tugging.
   And the seagulls are still shrieking.
   And the sun is still burning and –

III

'OH … STOP … CAP!'
   'EEAAGGHH!'
Tug!
Splash!

IV

Me – there's water at me knees now!
   And the Captain's still tugging.
   And the seagulls are still shrieking.

And the sun is still burning and –
The Cap's getting into the boat.

V

'CAP! DON'T LEAVE!'
  'ADIEU, LADDY!'

VI

'Ya ... ya can't leave me, Cap!' cries Milo, grabbing the back of the boat with both hands. 'Ya ... can't! Oh, Cap! We're friends! I ... need ya –'
  'Nay, you don't –'
  'I do! Oh, Cap ...'
  SPLASH!
  SPLASH!
  SPLASH!

VII

Water in me face now!
  And I'm coughing and spluttering!
  And the Captain – he's grabbing an oar!

VIII

'CAP!' Cough, splutter. 'CAP! DON'T LEAVE ME! THIS ... THIS IS WHAT I FELT FIVE MONTHS AGO!'
  'Wh – what d'ye mean, laddy?'
  'WHEN MOJO HIT ME –' Cough, splutter. 'REMEMBER? I LAY THERE AND ... NO ONE HELPED AND ... I WAS ALL ALONE!' Splutter, cough, splutter. 'AND IT MADE ME THINK ... OH, IT MADE ME THINK ABOUT ...'
  'Go on, laddy! Say it! SAY IT!! SAY IT!!!'

IX

'ME DAD!' cried Milo. 'HE LEFT ME TOO! DAD DIDN'T WANT ME EITHER! WHY? WHY DID DAD LOOK AT ME AND CLEAR OFF! I WAS HIS BABY! HE … HE DIDN'T LOVE ME! AND MUM WON'T TALK ABOUT HIM! AND I WANNA KNOW… ME DAD, CAP! OH, ME DAD! WHY DIDN'T DAD LOVE ME? WHY? WHY DIDN'T ME DAD LOVE HIS MILO?'

X

And, suddenly, Milo is weeping.

Weeping like he's never wept in his whole life.

Weeping as if the very air has grabbed him and is shaking him.

Weeping as if there's a wild bird trapped in his chest.

Weeping as if he wants to turn his whole body inside out.

Weeping as if his very tears want to create an ocean.

Weeping as if his tears want to water rainforests.

Weeping as if the Earth was a sponge.

Weeping as if his language was sobbing and he had a life story to tell.

XI

And the Captain jumps out of the boat.

XII

And the Captain sweeps Milo up in his arms.

XIII

And the Captain holds Milo like he's never been held before.

XIV

'There, there,' says the Captain, kissing the top of Milo's head. 'You've said it now!' And he wipes tears from Milo's face. 'Let's go back to the shore, my beautiful laddy.'

— Eighty-six —

I

'Oh, Beloved!'
'Oh, Milo Kick.'

II

Cressida and Dee are on the shore now.
The Captain puts Milo down between them.
For a while, Milo continues to sob.
The others kneel around him, holding his hand, stroking his hair, patting his back –
'You're safe now, Beloved!'
'Safe with us, Milo Kick.'
'Always, laddy, always.'

III

Milo says, 'Then ... you ain't gonna leave me, Cap? Leave me and hunt for the –'
And Milo looks at the Captain.
And sees –

IV

The Cap – his tattoos have washed away.
The Cap – his beard is half hanging off.
The Cap – his eye patch is gone.
The Cap – he's got two healthy eyes.

V

'CAP!' cries Milo. 'WHAT ...? WHO ...? HOW ...?'

VI

Cressida pulls the beard from the Captain's face. 'This man's name is not Captain Jellicoe, Beloved.'

'Then ... who ... is it?'

'Well,' begins the Captain, and now his voice has lost the seafaring accent, 'I've had many names in my time because, as an actor, I have been required to portray a number of –'

'Oh, get on with it!' snaps Dee.

'The name I was born with,' says the Captain, 'was Jay Dee Six.'

— Eighty-seven —

I

'JAY!' gasps Milo.

'My brother,' says Dee.

'But ... that means –'

'I'm also Valentino True,' says the Captain.

'VALENTINO!' gasps Milo. 'But ... oh, I don't get it ... I just don't ... get it!'

II

'Listen carefully and all will become clear, Beloved. Are you ready?'

'... Yeah'

III

'The story of this man –' Cressida reaches out and grasps the Captain's arm '– links together all the stories you've been hearing. He was born Jay Dee Six and he ran away with –'

'Avery Chance!' interrupts Milo. 'I know. And kept having failures 'n' stuff. He changed his name to Valentino True ... then ripped you off for ten thousand quid. Then ... then ... he became an even bigger failure, innit. And ... and Dee came here to pay off his debt. You both asked him to join you but he ... he wouldn't. He was too ashamed.'

'Bravo, Beloved. An excellent summary. So now –' another squeeze of the Captain's arm – 'perhaps, *you'd* like to bring your own story up to date.'

IV

'Oh, the shame of it!' cries the Captain, getting to his feet and waving his arms in the air. 'The humiliating shame. I was a drunken wreck of a thing working in a bingo hall. But it's what I deserved! My punishment! After all, I had swindled the kindest and most beautiful woman I'd ever met –'

'Stop frothing!' snaps Dee.

V

'Letters!' continues the Captain, turning his back on Dee. 'My sister and Cressida Bell wrote letters from Avalon. "Join us," they said. "All is forgiven!" But the shame was too great. It gnawed within me like a worm in the bud –'

'Froth!'

VI

'Years pass!' continues the Captain, shooting Dee a withering look. 'I drink more. I lose my job in the bingo hall. I have no money. My life is in ruins. Shattered. My glorious youth faded to nothing. I'm sleeping in a cardboard box. Oh, the shame, the shame, the utter shame! Finally, I know I have no choice. I must join my sister and the most beautiful woman, whom I betrayed. I must get on my hands and knees and beg for forgiveness. I must open my shirt and say, "Strike me in the breast, for it's what I deserve –"'

VII

'Stop!' snaps Dee. 'There's enough froth here to make a million milkshakes. The facts, Milo Kick, are these: my brother walked all the way from Brighton to here. Fact: I looked out of the window one morning and saw him collapsed on the cliff top. Fact: my brother is unshaven, dressed in rags, half starved. Fact: Cressida Bell and I carry him to Avalon Rise and put him to bed –'

VIII

'Fact!' interrupts the Captain. 'They saved my life.'

'Oh, Mr True,' sighs Cressida, tears in her eyes. 'Bless you, bless you.'

'Go on, Cap,' urges Milo. 'What happened next? How did you end up ... in the cave searching for the accursed creature?'

IX

'It is my way of ... well, *repaying* the debt I owed. You see ... all the time I've been here, I've been wondering how to make amends for my terrible, nay, my despicable actions. And then ... just over a week ago ... your mum rang Cressida. She said, "My boy needs help! He's changed! Something happened five months ago. I've got my suspicions what it is, but ... oh, my angel has become a monster. He won't talk to me any more. And he needs to talk ... You're the only one I can turn to, Cressie. Please help my boy like you once helped me."'

— Eighty-eight —

I

'So …' ponders Milo.
   'What, Beloved?'
   'What, Milo Kick?'
   'What, laddy?'
   '… it was a trick, innit!'

II

'A trick!' gasps Cressida.
   'A trick!' gasps Dee.
   'A trick!' gasps the Captain.
   'Well … yeah! The Captain living in the cave … the hunt for Mighty Fizz Chilla … all of that … just a lie!'

III

'Oh no, Beloved!' cries Cressida, grabbing Milo's hand and squeezing it tight. 'A million times no! Listen – everything I told you, of course, was true. And everything Dee told you was true –'
   'I deal *only* with facts!' insists Dee.
   'But *he* don't!' Milo points at the Captain. 'And what you –' pointing at Cressida and Dee '– both told me about the Captain – that ain't facts!'
   'But it's still *true*, Beloved! Why it's just as true as my story or Dee's story. You see, that's what stories do! They point out a truth we knew but … but …'
   'Never *knew* we knew, innit, ' says Milo softly.

IV

'Bravo, Beloved! That's it exactly! And the story of Captain Jellicoe and his hunt for Mighty Fizz Chilla ... oh, that might be *unreal*, but it's still *true*. Because the story made you *feel* things. It unlocked things in you. You *understood* what Captain Jellicoe felt when Lovey-Dovey Wifey abandoned him. You understood it because –'

'It's how I felt with ... well, with Dad, innit.'

'Bravo, Beloved.'

'Correct, Milo Kick.'

'Aye, laddy.'

V

'And we all worked so hard, Beloved. Me, Dee, Mr True. Preparing everything for your visit. Dressing Mr True as an old sea captain. Half-building a boat out of driftwood. And then ... getting you interested in the Captain. Tempting your out of your room. And the Captain –'

'I gave the performance of my life, didn't I, laddy!'

'I guess ... you did, innit.'

'And I tried to work things you told me into my story, laddy, and ... well, even my little mistakes became part of the story.'

'Like what, Cap?'

'Like ... well, like when you commented on the way the prophecy had been written. You remember the messy handwriting?'

'Oh, yeah, it was terrible, innit.'

VI

'That's because ... well, when I wrote it, laddy, I'd unfortunately had one too many sherries –'

'You were sozzled!' snaps Dee.

'All right, Dee, all right. I was sozzled, laddy. And you said the prophecy looked like it was written by –'

'By monkeys, innit!'

'Exactly, laddy. And so later on in the story I –'

'You made the prophecy written by monkeys, innit!'

'Exactly, laddy, and … oh, there's lots of things like that. The more you think about it in times to come, the more examples you'll find.'

VII

'Oh, Beloved! You're not… angry with us, are you?'

'Don't be angry, Milo Kick.'

'Oh, please, laddy. Don't.'

VIII

Angry?

Milo reaches inside him through every vein and artery –

Angry?

– every blood cell and nerve tissue –

Angry?

– every thought and memory and feeling. And no matter how hard he searches, there are –

IX

No Fizzy Wasps, innit!

X

'Nah … I ain't angry … You did all this because … because …'

'Because we *care* for you, Beloved!'

'Fact: we *care*, Milo Kick.'

'Oh, aye, laddy, more than all the stars in the sky, we *care*.'

XI

'I … I'll miss the Captain though,' says Milo. 'I … liked him so much. And … oh, I'll just miss him, that's all.'

'But I'm still here, laddy. As the great Shakespeare once

said, "One man in his time plays many parts." So ... well, the Captain is just as much part of me as Jay and Valentino. But, to make things easier, please, I beg of you, *always* call me Cap. In fact – everyone! My name is Cap from now on. For in a way, I *am* Captain of something very, very special.'

'But ... what?' asks Milo.

'Why, laddy ... I'm the Captain of the story.'

XII

Cressida gazes into Milo's eyes. 'And the Captain's story – just like all the stories you've been listening to – unreal and real together, they've all led you to this moment. The moment when the question you screamed out at the vast ocean will be answered.'

'Out at the –? Oh, ya mean about Dad!'

'Just so, Beloved! The final bit of this long puzzle of stories is about to fit into place. But to do that, we'll have to go to where it all began.'

'Where, Cressie?'

'The cave!'

— Eighty-nine —

I

They sit round a small campfire, their shadows rising huge and flickering on the cave walls.

Milo and the Captain, clutch blankets round them.

'And now,' says Cressida, her voice echoing, engulfing them all, 'you will hear the final part of this epic tale. And, as I speak, Beloved, I want you to … be part of it.'

'Aye, laddy, picture the scene!'

'Yeah! I will!'

II

'Imagine this!' cries Cressida, firelight glinting in the dark of her glasses. 'It's several weeks after my Fliss has run away. Oh, I've been so worried. Hardly slept a wink. And then, one night, the phone rings. I pick it up and a voice says, "It's me, Cressie!"'

'Mum!'

'Just so, Beloved! She tells me she's safe and well and … oh, so much news. She and Griff are living together. In some squat in south London. Brixton, I believe. They haven't got much money, but they're happy. I put the phone down. For the first time since Fliss ran away I feel … well, more relaxed about things. Perhaps everything will work out for the best and Fliss and Griff will live happily ever after.'

'But they didn't, did they, Cressie?'

III

'No, Beloved, they didn't.' Cressida takes a deep breath and continues. 'Imagine this: it's seven months later. The phone rings again. It's Fliss. But, this time, as soon as she speaks, I know there's something wrong! "What is it, Fliss? Tell your Cressie! Please!" Fliss says, "I'm going to have a baby – Oh, don't get me wrong, Cressie. I'm thrilled! I know I'm young but I want this baby so very much." I ask her what the problem is. And she says, "It's Griff! His changes of mood are so ... big! One minute he's kind and wonderful. The next he's ... oh, he's a wild animal. I can't talk to him any more."' Cressida sighs and warms her hands in the glow of the fire.

'Don't stop, Cressie! Please!'

IV

'Imagine this: it's a year later. The phone rings. It's Fliss. And – oh, she's so distressed. "It's Griffin's moods, Cressie! I can't stand it any longer! I love him but – oh, Cressie! Griff gets so violent! And I'm worried. Not for me but for –"

'Me, innit!'

V

'Imagine this: it's five months later. I'm asleep in bed ...'

And as Milo listens, the shadows on the rock begin to take shape ...

They engulf him like a blanket and –

VI

I can see it, innit!
  There!
  Cressida is asleep in her bed as –

— Ninety —

I

A noise!

At the window!

Cressie's eyes flutter open as –

*The noise comes again! Like really heavy rain, innit. Or rain
that's turned to ice – Oh, what's it called! Hailstones! Yeah!*

Cressie – she's getting out of bed.

Cressie – she's going to the window and looking out and –

'Fliss!' cries Cressie. 'My Fliss!'

II

Cressie – she rushes downstairs!

Cressie – she lowers the drawbridge!

Cressie – she rushes out into the moonlit night –

'Fliss!'

'Cressie! Oh, Cressie!'

*My mum – still young, but now ... yeah! I can see the mum
I know in there somewhere. Mum rushes into Avalon Rise. She
looks like she's been watching a horror film. Hair all messed up
and her eyes big and scared.*

*'Fliss! It's the middle of the night? What are you doing here?
Is something wrong –?'*

And then Cressie stares.

Stares at a bundle of rags Mum's holding.

Only it's not a bundle of rags!

It's a bundle of baby.

'This is my beautiful Milo,' says Mum.

III

Me, innit!

Baby me!

Baby me! Being kissed by Cressie.

'Oh, look at him!' squeals Cressie. 'He's got your blue eyes, Fliss.'

'He's got his dad's hooded eyebrows, though.'

'Griffin!' gasps Cressie. 'Is that why you're here? Has he been ... a brute again?'

Mum – she nods and goes to say something. But all that comes out is a strangled sort of noise and tears spurt from her eyes and snot dribbles out of her nose.

IV

Cressie takes me out of Mum's arms and tells her, 'Go and sit on the sofa, Fliss! I'll look after the baby for a while and I'll make you a nice pot of tea – Go on! Go on!'

V

Later now ...

The log fire is burning.

Mum and Cressie are snuggling next to each other and sipping tea.

Where's baby me got to?

Ah! There I am!

Asleep on the armchair! Sucking a dummy.

Mum says, 'The arguments just keep getting worse and worse, Fliss. Honestly, I don't understand Griff any more. It's like ... like he's two people. One of them is the dreamy, romantic Griff I fell in love with, who spends hours making me little sculptures out of cigarette packets and Coke cans. The other is the angry, shouting monster who ... gave me this!'

Mum lifts up the sleeve of her blouse.

A bruise!

VI

'Oh, Fliss,' cries Cressie, hugging her tight. 'I'm so sorry! Why didn't you tell me it was this bad before now?'

'I didn't know how to, Cressie! I felt so bad about running away and … oh, I felt I'd let you down somehow.'

'You were in love, Fliss! And love … oh, it's like a fever sometimes.'

'Well, I'm well and truly cured of that fever now. When Griffin did this –' she touches the bruise – 'I knew I had to get away. I sneaked out with Milo and caught the train here.'

VII

'Well, I'm glad you did! Avalon Rise was – and always will be – your home! Oh, it'll be such a thrill to have you back! And with a baby too! It's been so strange living here all alone.'

'Alone? But what about your guests?'

'Oh, Fliss, there are no guests. Not any more. The last ones left last year and since then … just empty rooms.' Cressie shrugs and tries to smile. 'I can't blame them. There's no pier, no town, nothing! Every year the wind and sea washes away more.'

VIII

'Oh, Cressie,' sighs Mum, 'why didn't you let me know? You must have been so lonely here.'

'Lonely! In a place full of glorious memories? Never! Besides, I've had plenty to occupy my mind. Look!' Cressie rushes out into the entrance hall, then returns dragging a large painting. 'I got this back from the framers last week.' She props the painting against the armchair. 'What do you think?'

'Cressie!' gasps Mum. 'It's Merlin and the Boy King! You did it!'

IX

'Took me ages to finish. Almost as long as you've been gone. And you see? Here? On the cave walls?'

'Griff's paintings!' cries Mum. 'And there! In the background – Griff's dolphin made of sand! Oh, Cressie, it's ... wonderful. Truly! A masterpiece.'

'Bless you, Fliss. Bless. I needed to hear that. You know what? I'm going to do more. A whole sequence of paintings showing the legend of King Arthur! Oh, yes! I've got plans and ambitions –'

Suddenly, the window blazes with light.

Car headlights!

A screech of car tyres and –

X

'FLISS!'

A yell from outside!

A man's yell!

'FLISS!'

XI

'Oh, no!' gasps Mum, clutching Cressie's arm. 'He must have guessed where I'd be and –'

'FLISS!'

It's Griffin! It's –

— Ninety-one —

I

'Dad!' cries Milo.

'Just so, Beloved.' The firelight blazes brighter than ever in Cressida's dark glasses. 'It is Griffin! Screaming and howling in the night. 'FLISS! FLISS!' And then – OH!'

'What?' asks Milo.

II

'Stones!' replies Cressida. 'He's throwing stones at the windows and screaming, 'LET ME IN! LET ME IN!' And then – OH!'

'What?'

III

'Thumping!' replies Cressida. 'He must've jumped over the moat and now – Thump! Thump! Thump! Fliss is whimpering with terror. Baby Milo is crying and crying. And then – OH!'

'What?'

IV

'Smashing! A window's been broken. And, suddenly, there he is! Throwing rocks from the other side of the moat!

'Go away, Griff!' yells Fliss. 'Leave us alone! It's over! You hear me?'

'NOOOOOOOO!' he cries. Such a howl of pain. My ear drums ring with it! The chandeliers tremble with it. And

then – OH!'
    'What?'

V

'Weeping! Griffin is weeping like a hurt child. I look out of the window and – There! Sitting on the roof of his car. Weeping and howling like a wolf at the full moon. And hitting himself! Hitting himself!'

'Oh, Dad,' sighs Milo. 'Dad. Dad!'

'And then, among the painful weeps and howls, words begin to take shape –'

— Ninety-two —

I

'I ... WANNA ... SEE ... MY SON! PLEASE! DON'T ...
DON'T TAKE MY LITTLE BABY AWAY FROM ME! I
LOVE HIM ... I NEED HIM ... OH, PLEASE! MILO ...! MY
MILO ...! MY MILO!

II

There are tears in Cressie's eyes.

There are tears in Mum's eyes.

Cressie says, 'Fliss, you and the baby go upstairs. I have to talk to him.'

'But Cressie –'

'He's like a wounded animal, Fliss! I can't leave him out there like that. Go to your room and lock the door. Everything will be all right.'

Mum nods and, hugging me very tight, she goes upstairs.

III

Cressie – she lowers the drawbridge!

Cressie – she walks over the moat!

Cressie – she goes up to my dad!

'Griffin,' she says, going to touch him.

IV

Dad – oh, he flinches away!

Don't, Dad! She's trying to help!

V

Cressie – she goes to touch him again!
   This time Dad keeps still.
   Cressie strokes his hair.
   Dad stops crying.
   And then –
   Oh, he slides off the roof of the car and into Cressie's arms.

VI

'I'm bad!' he sobs. 'Ain't I? There's something in me that's …
bad! Why do I do these things? Don't mean to …'
   It's Fizzy Wasps, Dad!
   Don't you see that?
   Get rid of the Fizzy Wasps and everything will be all right.

VII

'Shhhhh,' Cressie is stroking Dad's hair. 'You may have done
some bad things, Griff, but you're not bad.'
   'I … love Fliss.'
   'I know you do.'
   'I … I love Milo.'
   'I know, I know. And they both love you.' Cressie grabs his
head in her hands and looks him straight in the eyes. 'If I let you
in the house, will you promise – I repeat promise – to keep calm?'
   'Oh, yeah! Yeah!'

— Ninety-three —

I

Dad's sitting on the sofa.
    His face is still wet with tears.
    There are lots of scratches on his cheeks and chest.
    Oh, Dad, how could you hurt yourself like that? How could –
    Footsteps!
    Mum is coming downstairs.
    She's holding me.
    Mum – she stands in front of Dad.

II

'Hello, Fliss,' says Griff.
    'Hello, Griff,' says Mum.
    Both their voices are full of trembling things.

III

Dad stands up and takes a step towards Fliss and me.
    Mum takes a step back.
    Dad stops and says, 'Please!'
    Mum nods.

IV

Dad walks up and kisses her and then –
    Oh, he kisses me!
    Kisses me on the forehead!
    Kisses all me fingers!

And Dad says, 'I love you, little Milo. Oh, little Milo! Your Daddy loves you!'

V

Cressie says, 'Let's all sit down, shall we?'
    Griffin sits on the sofa.
    Cressie sits in an armchair.
    Mum sits on Cressie's lap. She puts me –
    There!
    I'm on the floor.
    Oh, look at my little face and my little feet and –

VI

Dad says, 'It's hard … for me to talk about … what I'm feeling. I … I don't really know myself.' He takes a deep breath and … oh, how difficult this is for him. 'When I used to stand on the beach … I'd look out at the ocean and – oh, the waves would become part of me. I could feel them in my blood. The animals too. I was a dolphin, a whale, a –'
    'Weeeeaaaahhhggghhh!'
    It's me!
    I'm crying!

VII

Dad goes on, 'And when … when I'm standing on the roof of the tower block, I look up at the sky and … oh, the clouds become part of me. I can feel them in my blood. Hurricanes and snowstorms pulsing through my veins –
    'Weeeeeaaahh!'
    'And … and the animals too! Pigeons! Sparrows! Blackbirds! I'm part of everything –'
    'Weeeaahhhhggghhh!'
    'Shhhh, Milo,' says Mum.
    Dad – he's looking really wound up now.
    But still he goes on –

VIII

'And … oh, I dunno, but sometimes I feel I've been born in the wrong place. At the wrong time. I should be –'

'WAAAAAAAAHHHGGGHHH!'

'Shhh, Milo,' says Mum.

'Shhh, Milo,' says Cressie.

'I should've been born a wild –'

'WAAAAAAAAAAAAAAGGGHHH!'

'Shhh, Milo.'

'Shhh, Milo.'

'– thing –'

'WAAAAAAAAAAAAAAAAAHHHHH!'

IX

'OH, SHUT THAT BABY UP!' yells Dad. 'SHUT IT!'

X

Dad – he's jumping to his feet!

Dad – his fists are clenched!

Dad – he raises them as if to hit me –

'NOOO!' cries Fliss.

'NOOO!' cries Cressie.

XI

And Cressie hurls herself in front of Dad.

And Dad – he pushes Cressie!

Cressie – she stumbles back over!

Cressie – she hits her head on the corner of the painting that's propped against a wall –

— Ninety-four —

I

'CRESSIE!' cries Milo.

'CRESSIE!' cries the Captain.

'CRESSIDA BELL!' cries Dee.

'Don't worry, everyone,' Cressida assures them. 'It wasn't a hard knock. I hardly felt it. But your mum ... oh, she screamed at your dad, "GET OUT! NOW! I NEVER WANT TO SEE YOU AGAIN! GO! GO!" And I could tell by the whimpering sound in your dad's throat that ... well, he'd scared himself by his own actions. So ... he ran out of Avalon Rise.'

'Where'd he go?' asks Milo.

'We assumed he went to the cave,' she replies. 'After all, the car he'd stolen remained outside. And your mum ... oh, she was an angel to me! The fall had shaken me a little, you see. So I took to my bed. And you know how I enjoy being made a fuss of.'

'You can say that again,' murmers Dee.

II

'But me dad – didn't anyone see him again?'

'Imagine this,' says Cressida. 'It's two days later. The middle of the night. I'm laying in bed when – OH!'

'What!'

'A noise at my window! Someone's throwing gravel up. I hear a voice hiss, "Cressie!"'

'It's me dad!'

III

Cressida nods and continues. 'The window's half open so he can hear me when I call out, "I'm not very well, Griffin! What do you want?"

'"To say goodbye," he calls back. "Don't bother getting up. I'm not worth it. I just wanted to tell ya ... I'm sorry! I would never hurt my little Milo. Ya know that, don't ya?"

'I tell him, "I thought I did, but I don't think I'm so sure any more."'

'It's the Fizzy Wasps,' sighs Milo. 'Ain't it, Cap?'

'I'm sure you're right, laddy.'

IV

'And then,' Cressida continues, grabbing Milo's arm, 'he tells me that he's made something for his son, something special so his son will always know how much his dad loves him and then – Car-door slamming! Engines starting! Car tyres screeching! And Griffin's gone!'

'But ... what? What did he make for me, Cressie?'

'Why, Beloved,' replies Cressida, leaning closer, 'he said he'd made you ... the Floating Island of Heart.'

— Ninety-five —

I

'The Floating …?' Milo jumps to his feet in excitement. 'But what …? I mean, what …? How …?'

'Calm down, Beloved, calm down.'

'But … *where* is it? Eh?'

'Why, laddy,' says the Cap, 'ye know how to find the Floating Heart, don't ye?'

'The … the … Phoenix of Secrets! We need the Phoenix!'

'Well, then,' says Cressida, clapping her hands together. 'Looks like we best find it! Cap – the Phoenix of Secrets if you please!'

And the Cap goes to the chest, rummages inside and produces the wooden Phoenix.

'But … I thought it was on the boat with you, Cap.'

'Nay, laddy. I wouldn't do that. Not when … we've got to *burn* it!'

II

'*Burn* it!' gasps Milo. 'But … oh, Cressie, we *can't*. It means so much to you. And if we don't *have* to burn it any more then –'

'But I *want* to burn it, Beloved. Sometimes a sacrifice has to be made. Sometimes we have to say goodbye to yesterday in order to say hello to tomorrow. So, yes, the Phoenix will be burnt. And out of its flames – like the Phoenix itself – a new future will be born. But first … let us get the precious thing out of the secret compartment.'

— 393 —

'But we never found the key.'

'Beloved, we never *lost* the key.'

'Wh-what d'you mean?'

Cressida puts the Phoenix in Milo's hands. 'Beloved, the key ... *is you!*'

III

'Me!' gasps Milo. 'But ... how, Cressie?'

'Put your hands on either side of the bird.'

'Like ... like this?'

'That's it ... Good! Now ... press gently.'

Milo does so and –

Priggg!

The chest of the Phoenix opens up.

'There!' Cressida exclaims. 'All you had to do was hold it the right way.' She takes something wrapped in tissue paper from inside the wooden bird. 'My precious thing!' she says, smiling. Then adds, 'Put the Phoenix of Secrets into the fire, Beloved!'

IV

'But ... oh, I don't get it!' insists Milo. 'What the Cap said was nothing but stories.'

'I told you,' interrupts Cressida, 'all stories have a truth. Sometimes even some of the *events* are true. Now ... burn it! NOW!'

And, with that, Milo drops the Phoenix on to the flames ...

— Ninety-six —

I

Smoke starts to rise from the bird.

Like a length of frayed rope, the smoke unwinds and heads towards the back of the cave, into murky shadows, where even the firelight cannot penetrate.

'Torches!' announces Cressida. 'If we're to follow the smoke we need –'

'Torches!' The Captain goes to the chest once again and removes four large sticks with cloth wrapped round one end.

Like big matches, innit!

II

The Captain gives a stick to each of them, then says, 'Light them.'

Cressida touches the cloth end of the stick to the fire and –

Vrooooosh!

It flares!

The others do the same –

III

Vroooosh!

Vroooosh!

Vroooosh!

IV

'They're from a production of Shakespeare's *The Winter's Tale*,' whispers the Cap to Milo. 'In it I gave the greatest performance as King Leontes–'

'Oh, do shut up!' snaps Dee.

'Just so,' agrees Cressida. 'We've got more important things to do than listen to your theatrical anecdotes.' She raises her torch above her head. 'Now of course, being as blind as a bat, I'm only holding this so you all get as much light as possible. Beloved? Can you see where the smoke is going.'

'Yeah! Into the dark, innit!'

'Then … lead the way.'

— Ninety-seven —

I

Milo steps forward, the smoke trailing above, leading him deeper and deeper into areas of the cave he never knew existed.

Behind him, Cressida, Dee and the Captain – their torches held aloft, tread carefully over the moss-covered rocks and wet sand.

Water's trickling down the rock, innit, and it's more and more echoey and the firelight is glinting and sparkling all over the place – Hang on! It's getting a bit narrower. Like a corridor …

'What's wrong, Beloved?'

'The smokes going through that narrow gap at the end.'

'Then follow, Beloved,' insists Cressida.

'Aye laddy, follow.'

'Pursue the smoke, Milo Kick.'

II

Smells really like the ocean, innit! Really fishy and sea and – oh, there's a rumbling sound. Like when I stick me head under the bath water.

'Be careful, Cressie! There's lots of puddles now.'

'Bless you, Beloved, but don't worry about me. Where's the smoke leading us?'

'Forward … into the dark.'

'Then … dark, here we come.'

Splash!

Splash!
Splash!

III

The rock around them is glistening with torchlight, the slime like emerald, patches of rock like burnished gold.

'It's magical here and no mistake,' says the Captain. 'Aye!'

'I do wish you'd stop that accent,' snaps Dee.

'I like it!' insists Milo.

Splash!
Splash!
Splash!

We're in a … well, it's like a mini-cave now –

IV

'Stop!' announces Cressida, squeezing Milo's shoulder tightly. 'It was here your dad came for those two days.' (*Oh, her voice is echoing all over the place, it's in me skull, in me skin.*) 'And the last time he spoke to me … he told me exactly what he did here.' (*Echoing, in me skull, in me skin, in me bones, innit.*) 'What he made … made for his son … his baby – There! You see, Milo! Imagine!'

'Picture the scene, laddy!'

'Griffin – your dad – is kneeling at the end of the corridor! He's making something out of stones and shells … You see, Beloved? You see? Your dad told me the very words he said while he made it … And if you listen to my voice … listen very hard … you will be there with him and hear his words … Listen … Listen and imagine …'

Yeah! Keep telling me, Cressie!

The firelight, the echoing, the smell of oceans and –

— Ninety-eight —

I

There's Dad!

He's kneeling in the sand – no! In a large puddle! And he's piling stones into the puddle! Moving the stones to make a shape. And –

He's talking!

II

'This is for you, Milo! I'm putting the stones very deep – so they'll always stay here! No one ever comes to this part of the cave. Theses stones will still be piled like this in a million years! And I'm sticking them together with seaweed and mud – Oh, it'll last for eternity, Milo!'

I stand beside him.

'I'm here, Dad.'

III

'And when you see this – Oh, Milo! You'll know that I love you. I'll always love you! But … oh, your dad can't stay here, Milo! Dad's worried he'll do something nasty! One day you will understand, Milo'

'I do, Dad.'

IV

'But love never goes away, Milo. No matter where I am I'll always have you with me. I'll have you in my heart. My love for you will go on and on and on. And I want you to grow up brave

and strong and know … oh, know that Dad is so proud of you.
You will believe that, won't you, Milo?'
    'Yeah, Dad.'

V

And then Dad stands up.
    There are tears in his eyes.
    I want him to hold me, to see me, but instead he says –
    'Goodbye, my beloved son.'
    – and runs out of the cave …

VI

Beloved!
    It was Dad who first called me Beloved!
    I'm Dad's Beloved!

VII

And then I look at what Dad's made.
    In the middle of the huge puddle is a shape. Like an island in
an ocean. And the shape is –
    'A heart!'

— Ninety-nine —

I

'Just so, Beloved,' says Cressida, holding her torch higher. 'There it is! I'm sure it's not as perfect as when your dad first made it, but –'

'Nah, nah! It is! Perfect.'

'Indeed, Cressida Bell! The heart is remarkably well-preserved.'

'It's a beauty, aye!'

'Beloved … stand in the Heart!'

II

Me – stepping forward.
  Splash.

III

Me – stepping on to stones and shells.
  Crunch.

IV

'I'm in Dad's Heart.'

V

'And now,' says Cressida, 'the very final piece of our Russian Doll of stories is revealed – Hold this, Dee!' She passes her torch to Dee, then begins unwrapping the thing – the most precious thing – she'd taken from the Phoenix. 'Remember me telling you that your dad stuck together some of the glass animals he broke?'

'Yeah! And he put wrong heads on wrong bodies and you said, "But it all seems to fit."'

'Just so, Beloved!' The precious thing is unwrapped now. 'Well, I want you to have it.'

'Me.'

'Yes, Beloved! Because –' and she puts the object in Milo's hand – 'your journey is finally over.'

VI

Milo looks and sees –
    A shark's head!
    A tiger's body!
    Swan's wings!
    Five octopus tentacles!
    An alicorn!
    All stuck together and sparkling.
    'Mighty Fizz Chilla,' he says.

Seventh Day

— One hundred —

I

'Beloved!'

'Milo Kick!'

'Laddy!'

'Coming!' Milo throws the last pair of socks into his sports bag, zips it up and heads for the door –

Wait!

II

Milo looks back into the room – at the four-poster bed, the window, the painting – and remembers how it once seemed so strange, so unwelcoming, how he'd shouted, thrown things, locked doors, insisted he needed no one. But now –

It's the most wonderful room in the world, innit.

'I'll be back,' says Milo.

'Aye, that you will, laddy!' The Cap strides up behind Milo and takes the bag from him. 'Let me take that for you.'

'I still can't get used to the way you look, Cap!' says Milo, wrapping his arms around the Captain's waist.

'This,' says the Cap, indicating his shirt, cravat, waistcoat and his long, grey hair in a ponytale, 'is style!'

'*That*,' chuckles Milo, pointing at the Cap's outfit, 'is pants!'

The Cap laughs and gives Milo a hug. 'Come on,' he says, 'let's get you downstairs before Dee blows her top.

She wanted to start the journey back to London five minutes ago and –'

Beep!

Beep!

'– that's her! In the truck already!'

III

'Oh, Beloved! There you are! All packed. Good! And – here! – I've made you some sandwiches for the trip. And … and … oh, I'm brimming up! I promised myself I wouldn't cry but – Oh, give your Cressie a big hug!'

Milo wraps his arms around Cressie.

Cressie wraps her arms around Milo.

And the Captain wraps his arms around them both.

'I'll visit soon!' says Milo. 'I'll bring Mum with me.'

'You *must*!' sobs Cressie. 'Tell your mum … Oh, tell her I'm a happy blind old thing. She mustn't blame herself for my condition. She mustn't feel guilty and keep away from Avalon Rise. Heaven knows I've told her whenever she's rung but … well, if she hears it from you she might believe me.'

'I'll tell her, Cressie, but why should Mum blame herself for your condition – Wait! Oh, Cressie, I've only just realized. How could I have been so stupid!'

'What, Beloved?

IV

'When me dad pushed ya … ya head – it struck the painting. And ya told me that what turned ya into a monumental mole was hitting ya head on something.'

'Beloved!' Cressie grabs Milo's arm and squeezes tight. 'No one is to blame. Accidents happen. And sometimes out of these accidents something wonderful is born. So … well, I lost my sight, but, believe me, I see life clearer than I ever did. And I want you to think of my home as your second home. Your room will always be waiting for you. I will always be waiting. Avalon Rise will always be waiting –'

'STOP FROTHING!'

V

Dee is standing by the front door, indicating her wristwatch. 'Milo Kick, we've got a nine-hour journey ahead of us. And I – as I'm sure you are aware – have to return here afterwards. That makes a total of –'

'Eighteen hours, innit!'

'Exactly! And we are now –' checks wristwatch – 'seven minutes late. So – MOVE IT!'

Dee strides out to the truck, revs the engine and –

Beep!

Beep!

Beep!

VI

'She's got a heart –' begins Cressida.

'– of gold,' finishes Milo, laughing. 'I know, I know.' He gives Cressida and the Cap another big hug. 'I dunno what else to say ... except ... except ...'

'Yes, Beloved?'

'Yes, laddy?'

'... I'll miss ya!'

VII

'Oh, Beloved! We'll miss you too. Won't we, Mr True – I mean Cap?'

'Indeed we will! Miss you more than the heavens miss starlight during the day and sunlight during the –'

BEEP!

BEEP!

BEEP!

VIII

'Oh, what a twiglet-legged terror that woman is!' whines Cressida, wiping tears from her eyes. 'She has no patience!' She kisses Milo's shaven head. 'Have you remembered to pack the glass creature your dad made.'

'Yeah. It's wrapped up safely in the middle of me bag.'

Ring!

Ring!

IX

'The phone!' Cressida dashes to the counter and picks up the receiver. 'Hello? Avalon Rise … Oh! Fliss … yes, yes, my dear … he's just leaving … Wait a moment …' She holds the phone out to Milo. 'It's your mum, Beloved.'

Milo grabs the phone and –

X

'MUM! IT'S ME! I'M COMING HOME!'